Shameless LOVE

KG Fletcher

By KG Fletcher

For Lynn.
My gorgeous, free-spirited, badass BFF.

Vinci Books

vinci-books.com

Published by Vinci Books Ltd in 2026

1

A CIP catalogue record for this book is available from the British Library.
Paperback ISBN: 9781036708177
The EU GPSR authorised representative is Logos Europe, 9 rue Nicolas Poussion, 17000 La Rochelle, France contact@logoseurope.eu

Chapter One

WALTER BENNETT

With the radio volume cranked, Walt drummed his fingers across the steering wheel and listened to a classic Garth Brooks tune on a local country station. His work truck picked up dust along the country roads of his hometown, Langston Falls, the truck bed loaded with his belongings, his intention to spend his first night in his new home.

Squinting in the bright sunshine, Walt noticed the trees along the roadside forfeiting the last of their leaves in the late autumn season. Thanksgiving had come and gone, and he wanted to be all moved in before the big family Christmas gathering. It was odd loading up his truck at Bennett Farms, the winery and Christmas tree farm the only home he'd ever known. Walt was the middle child of five kids, including his older brothers James and Ted, his younger brother Hank, and his only sister, Rebecca. He and James had shared the renovated carriage quarters near the main house on the land for many years, their daily work on the family farm something he was proud of. But having a new place to call his own at this stage in his life was thrilling,

1

the anticipation of moving finally filling him with excitement. Located several miles down the road, Walt had plans to transform the run-down Kirby property into something fitting for him.

Once the Kirby family moved out after a quick all-cash sale, Walt had brought his dad, Roy Bennett, to the house for a look-see. On the drive over, Roy used the word "shameless" to describe him. Did he feel guilty? Hell no, not anymore, especially after he learned Glen Kirby hightailed it out of town for good. The only thing Walt felt now was an undeniable satisfaction, his retaliation against a man who did his family wrong finally in his rearview mirror—and he had a right mind to rip that mirror off and never look back.

But shameless wasn't the word he'd use. Nope. There was only one word to describe what he'd pulled off: revenge. Call him what you want. Brazen. Spiteful. Uncharitable. Even hateful. He didn't care anymore. Because the sweet taste of vengeance was delicious, and he had no shame in allowing it to linger on his tongue.

As he and his dad pulled up to the ranch-style house, Walt's excitement was short-lived. Beer bottles and remnants of a huge bonfire littered the front yard. Bits of charred, broken furniture continued to smoke in the ashy pile, and Walt was taken aback when he noticed the sizeable spray-painted word, "killer" spelled out across the front door.

"You want me to call Sheriff Jenkins?" Roy asked, his face pinched with worry. The family patriarch was a fair man, but if you crossed one of his own, there'd be hell to pay.

"No, Dad. I don't want to have any more contact with Glen Kirby ever again. He had his last little hoorah. Good riddance."

"Well, let's take a look at the inside before you decide. If that son-of-a-bitch trashed the interior, you're gonna need to do something about it."

"Like what?" Their cowboy boots crunched across the barren front yard, Walt pausing to kick a broken beer bottle out of their path.

"I don't know. Press charges? File a restraining order? You had the locks changed after the local government put the new ownership on the books, right?"

"Of course, Dad. The recording happened on the day of funding when I handed over my life savings to Mrs. Kirby's real estate agent and lawyer."

They stomped up the worn wooden steps to the front door splattered with blood-red dribbled letters. Walt turned around and scanned the neglected front yard with his hands on his hips. He thought Glen Kirby must have been drunk out of his mind to pull off such a stunt. His dad was right. If things on the inside looked anything like they did on the outside, he'd have to give Sheriff Jenkins a call.

The Bennetts and Kirbys had turned into the fucking Hatfields and McCoys.

"Well, come on then. Let's make sure the inside is okay," Roy muttered.

Walt stuck his shiny key into the new lock and opened the front door to his first home. Pride bubbled up in his chest as he crossed the threshold, overcome with a territorial satisfaction he'd pulled this thing off. He promised Teddy he'd get rid of Glen Kirby outright. Stripping the man of his inheritance by taking over his family's house and land was the ultimate price Walt was willing to pay. Glen had no choice but to hightail it out of Langston Falls for good.

The home's interior was cold, the faint aroma of bleach hard not to notice. Leave it to sweet Mrs. Kirby to clean after the movers loaded up her life. She told Walt she was ready for a new chapter, off to live in Macon, Georgia, to be closer to her sister. After everything that had happened between their two families, Walt was genuinely happy for the woman, glad she could finally move on after the horror she'd been through losing her first son, Joe, and watching her other son, Glen, fall completely apart. Now, if Walt only knew where Glen had landed.

"There's no damage on the inside," Roy announced after scoping out the three empty bedrooms and two bathrooms. His boots clomped across the original hardwood floors as he took in everything. "And she left you the fridge. That's good. One less appliance you're gonna have to buy."

Walt nodded, his eyes tracing the large family room. A big picture window looked out across a small backyard before the fence line of the apple orchard started. A sly smile unfurled from his lips, knowing Glen Kirby would never see this pretty view again.

Roy palmed Walt's shoulder. "This place fits you, son. Congratulations."

Walt inhaled a deep breath, thankful for his father's blessing. "Thanks, Dad."

———

Walt parked his loaded pickup truck on the dirt driveway, eager to move what little possessions he had into his new home. It only took him a few trips to unpack everything. Slamming the lift-gate shut with satisfaction, he rested his hands on his denim-clad hips and surveyed his property with pride. He'd cleaned up the beer bottles and bonfire remnants and spent two hours scrubbing the red paint off the front door before repainting it a fresh forest green to match the shutters. Brittle leaves littered the drive, and trash he'd collected from Glen's last hurrah sat in a tidy pile by the roadside, ready to be picked up by the local garbage collector.

As Walt started up the front steps, ready to unpack and plant roots, he paused and listened. A chilly breeze rustled through the trees, and the loud caw of a single crow called out in the late afternoon. He gripped the back of his neck, his subconscious tickling his memory with something he'd forgotten in the truck cab.

Stomping back to the vehicle, he opened the door and reached across the floorboard, feeling around for the cool metal of his long-barreled shotgun. The weapon was locked and loaded, just in case. Resting the gun against his shoulder, he secured his truck and headed toward the house. Although his mood was buoyant, his senses stayed on high alert. This was his property now, and he wasn't about to allow a disgruntled guy like Glen leaving him shaking in his boots. Nope. Quite the opposite. If Glen still had a bone to pick with him or any of Walt's family, he'd be ready.

Deep in his thoughts, Walt considered a conversation he'd had with his brother, Ted, during their family Thanksgiving gathering when he'd told him about his home purchase.

"I did Mrs. Kirby a huge favor so she can keep her son, Glen, out of jail."

Ted scowled, his words catching in his throat. "Walt, you didn't…"

"Oh, yes, I did." Walt remembered the feeling of pure satisfaction, the Kirby homestead sale legitimate payback for his brother's astronomical medical bills. But it was more than that.

"You get what you give, Teddy. I warned Glen Kirby; you mess with the bull, you get the horns."

"Revenge, Walter? Really?"

"Karma's a bitch. Glen got what was coming to him." Walt had stood his ground, his demeanor smug, and his tone turned sinister.

Ted became noticeably rattled. "I can't think about this right now—how Glen reacted, how you managed to do this in such a short amount of time... What the hell, Walt? Are you trying to get me killed?"

Walt was taken aback. "What? No! I thought you'd be happy about this. Mrs. Kirby is the one who came to me. She wanted to sell her homestead to me."

Ted nodded like a bobblehead doll. "You do realize you've opened an entire new can of worms—or in this case, a can of whoop-ass."

Ted's words echoed in Walt's subconscious as he held the shotgun a little tighter. What if his brother was right and Walt unintentionally opened up a can of whoop-ass by buying the Kirby property out from under Glen? He was a fool rushing into the notion that Ted's life could somehow be perfect after all he'd been through, especially going into this next chapter with his fiancé, Robyn by his side. Had he ruined it for Teddy by buying the Kirby homestead outright? God, he didn't want to worry about the possibility something terrible might happen again—that someone like Glen Kirby could be waiting in the shadows, ready to strike —prepared to instigate a retaliation of his own. If an outsider came in and stole his family's land out from under them, Walt would go ballistic and do whatever it took to regain it. He realized Glen Kirby probably held the same fervor.

Ted had been through so much, serving five years

behind bars for a crime he didn't commit, and then dealing with the aftermath of Glen's rage. To finally see his big brother happy and healthy again was all Walt ever wanted. But now, his mind roiled with unmitigated fear. How could he have been so careless, subjecting his family to the potential of more danger?

But Walt had already made the deal, the ink on the mortgage papers dry and his belongings already moved inside. The old Kirby homestead, which included a vibrant apple orchard, was paid for with every last dime Walt had scrimped and saved. In turn, the proceeds from the sale were used by Glen Kirby's mom to pay off her son's court-ordered restitution. The proceeds from the sale immediately went to Walt's brother, Ted, to satisfy the ruling.

Glen was ordered to pay for the hospital bills incurred when Ted sustained severe injuries on the night of the Harvest Hoedown. The dollar amount was close to two-hundred and fifty thousand. Ted was incapacitated for over a week, in a coma from massive blunt trauma to his head and body by the hands of Glen Kirby and his bullies. The only way for Mrs. Kirby to keep her son out of jail was to pay Ted's hospital bills in full. And the only way to come up with the amount of money she needed was to sell her home and land, Glen's birthright. Walt had been waiting in the wings for the opportunity, ready to help the lady out— prepared to take Glen's inheritance right out from under him. Touché, cocksucker.

Ted's hospital bills were paid in full, thanks to the sale. And now Walt had a place to call his own. Ted would eventually come around and appreciate the gesture, wouldn't he? There was no other choice, and Walt was more than counting on it.

Later that evening, the can of soup Walt made for

dinner wasn't quite as tasty as the meals his sister, Becky, made back at the farm. She was a shining star in their family, her weekly YouTube cooking show blowing up her social media. Becky shared recipes she made for their family and the farmhands, her pretty smile and easy-going nature in the kitchen garnering tens of thousands of diehard fans. Her show was called *The Farmer's Daughter*, similar to *The Pioneer Woman*, featuring Ree Drummond on the Food Network. Walt wouldn't be surprised if Hollywood came calling someday soon, whisking his baby sister off to La-La Land.

Standing next to the sink, he sipped his soup from a cracked mug and looked out a small window into the dark night. He was thankful he'd installed outdoor light sensors and an interior alarm, not that he was afraid of anything or anyone. Still, he was prepared, and being alone for the first time in his life held a certain aura of caution, his family several miles away and his nearest neighbor beyond the apple orchard. He was used to the loud rhythm of family and dogs, sibling rivalry, and tourists. His work at the winery still mattered, and he would make the short commute each day, looking forward to seeing everyone. But at night, it was a different story. The odd quietness of his new world was definitely an adjustment.

The ping of his cell phone startled him out of his daze. Flipping the phone over, he grinned, realizing it was Becky calling to check up on him.

"Hey, Becks. How's it going?"

"Good. But I miss you!" she giggled.

Walt inhaled sharply, thankful for the loving reprieve. "You know I'm only a hop, skip, and a jump away. And you're welcome to come by and visit anytime. I'll even give you the grand tour."

"Walter, you only moved out today. And besides, I wanted to give you some time to put your stamp on things. You know, make the place your own."

Walt panned the kitchen area, which opened into the large family room. There wasn't a stick of furniture in sight. His neck grew hot; his voice traced with embarrassment. "Well, there isn't much to show you right now anyway. But give me a few weeks, and I'll throw a little party or something—"

"A house-warming party!" she screeched with glee. "Let me help you plan it. Please?"

Walt chuckled, the ache in his being foreign to him.

"Daddy can bring over some of the aged cabernet, you know, the good stuff, so we can christen your place properly. And I'll make those pimento cheese sandwiches and sugar cookies you love so much."

Walt's stomach growled at the mere mention of his sister's delicious food choices. Leave it to Becky to entice him with her cooking talents. Eyeing the cold soup in his mug, he set the container in the chipped farmhouse sink. "I'd love that, Becks."

"And maybe we can ask everyone to bring a bottle of liquor or a cocktail gadget, you know, a 'stock the bar' kind of gift for the new homeowner." Becky was on a roll, the event planner's side of her working on all cylinders.

"Whatever you want to do."

Becky was quiet for a beat. "What if… what if I came over now? I mean, I don't want to interrupt whatever you're doing, and I certainly don't want to be an annoying little sister. But silly me, I made one too many chicken pot pies thinking you'd be joining us for supper, like always."

Walt leaned against the kitchen counter. How was she so in tune with him? A peculiar knot formed in the pit of his stomach. At first, he thought it might be legitimate hunger from working too hard all day and skipping lunch. But then he thought it might be something more. Was it homesickness? He wasn't sure.

"I won't stay long. I'll bring over the pot pie, and you can give me the grand tour you mentioned."

Walt swallowed hard. He nodded before the words left his mouth. "As a matter of fact, I'd love a visitor right about now."

Chapter Two

WALT

Sitting cross-legged on a thick blanket unfurled across the middle of the empty family room floor, Becky seemed to eye Walt with curiosity. A big basket she'd brought was pushed out of the way to make room for a small charcuterie board she'd assembled. Leave it to his little sister to load him up with his favorite cheeses, meats, crackers, and grapes to get him through the night. The pot pie she saved for him was in the refrigerator, a meal for the next day.

Uncorking a bottle of Bennett Farms Merlot, she poured the wine into a stem-less glass and handed it off to him. "Cheers to your new home, Walt. It's lovely." She clinked her glass with his and took a small sip. "Now, you need some furniture and knick-knacks, and you're good to go."

"And dishes, pots and pans, towels, and more cleaning products." Walt sighed and scanned the blank walls. Two built-in bookshelves flanked the large stone fireplace. The shelves were the only thing left in the house that resembled any type of furniture, Walt's small assortment of hardbacks barely taking up space.

"I suppose I've got the rest of my life to fill this place up," he remarked.

"Which room do you want to start with first?" Her doe-eyes were bright with excitement as she looked at him, his sister's pretty features eerily resembling their late mother in the dim overhead light.

Walt rested his forearms on his knees. "I guess the bedroom, first. That's where I'll spend most of my time when I'm not working at the winery. I've got an air mattress set up for now, but a bigger bed with a real mattress is first on my list."

Becky nodded. "There's a ton of antique furniture stored at the farm, including some nice bed frames and headboards. You can get a new mattress in town, and I'm sure Daddy wouldn't mind if you took a look at some of the extra furniture and picked out whatever you want."

"You mean the old dusty crap we pulled out during the last barn renovation? The same stuff we stuck in one of the storage facilities on the outskirts of the winery? No, thank you."

"But Walter, some of those antiques belonged to our great grandparents. I know there's a gorgeous wardrobe, a table with matching chairs, a few dressers—"

"I'll think about it," he interrupted.

Becky laughed and plucked a grape from the board between them, popping it into her mouth. "Seriously, I'd love to help you spruce up this place. Otherwise, you'll sit on lawn chairs and look at pictures of dogs playing poker tacked up onto the paneled walls."

Walt chuckled. It felt good to have one on one time with his sister. Back at the farm, his family or the day workers were always around, and he never really got to spend much quality time with her. Too bad it took a move across town to make that happen.

"You're too busy cooking and recording your show or working on the next big farm event to help me out, Becks. Don't worry. I can do it myself. And I promise, no dogs playing poker."

Becky smiled. "Well, if you change your mind, you know where to find me."

Before Walt could respond, the floodlight on the back porch came on, the bright light seeping into the vacant family room and highlighting their picnic. Becky gasped, and Walt turned rigid.

"Becks, get into the bathroom and lock the door." His tone was serious as he slowly stood and reached for her hand, pulling her to her feet.

"Is someone out there?" she asked, her voice tinged with fear. She snuggled safely into his side as he walked her to the hallway.

"I don't know. I have a motion sensor on the flood light out there. I'm gonna check it out."

Becky stopped in her tracks. "I'm going with you."

"What? No, Becks. Get in the bathroom. I'll let you know when the coast is clear." He watched as his little sister firmly planted her feet and crossed her arms against her chest. The familiar pout she offered made him roll his eyes. "All right, but stay behind me, and have your phone out in case we need to call for help." Walt grabbed his shotgun off the mantle and started for the door.

"Please don't shoot anyone, Walt. Whatever you do, don't shoot," she whispered tersely.

Walt remained silent, edging his way along the wall toward the back door. Turning to eye his sister over his shoulder, he placed his index finger against his lips, and she nodded. Watchfully, he unlocked the deadbolt and slowly opened the door.

The night air was cold, the stars snuffed out by the clouds in the dark sky. His eyes traced the edges of the fence line, half expecting to see Glen Kirby jump out of the apple orchard and attack. Walt gripped the gun a little tighter and pointed the weapon in front of him, slowly panning the backyard with the barrel. The gnarled branches of the fruit trees in the night reminded him of the haunted forest in *The Wizard of Oz* and the air turned hushed and still. A flash of black caught his eye, and he was quick with a reaction, aiming the gun low to the ground toward the movement.

"What is it?" Becky whimpered, her grip on the back of his shirt intensifying.

"It's... it's probably an animal of some kind. A night creature."

"A night creature?"

A high-pitched mewl interrupted the quiet.

"It's a cat!" Becky exclaimed. She pushed her way around him, trotting confidently across the grassy backyard.

"Becky..." Walt's senses were on high alert as he watched his sister kneel near some bushes and coax the animal out.

"Here, kitty, kitty, kitty."

Was it a cat? Or was it a setup to get him outside? A flash of raven fur distracted him as a mature cat scampered out of the orchard and curled around Becky's legs, loudly meowing.

"Oh, Walter, look! Isn't she beautiful?" Becky scooped up the feline and rubbed her cheek against its head. "She's purring."

Walt frowned, wondering where the cat came from.

Coyotes and bears prowled Langston Falls, and this cat must've had more than nine lives to still be alive in this neck of the woods.

"Put it down, Becky. What if it's sick or has fleas?"

"No, she's purr-fect," Becky gushed.

Walt approached his sister and dared to pat the black cat on the head. The animal acted like it had died and gone to heaven with all the attention.

"I think she's hungry." Becky started for the back door, holding the cat against her chest.

"Wait a minute, don't take that thing inside my new house." He watched his sister go inside, cooing sweet nothings into the animal's ear.

"Dammit," Walt cursed, kicking at a tuft of grass. Gripping the shotgun by his thigh, he trekked back inside, intent on shutting this little feline party down.

"I'm so glad you have some skim milk. Just look at her, Walt. She's starving."

Walt took in the scene, the cat lapping up milk from a saucer on his kitchen counter. "Really, Becks? You couldn't have put it on the damn floor?"

Becky continued to stroke the animal. "She doesn't look lost. She looks like someone's pet. See? She's wearing a little blue-collar with tags. Oh, I bet her owners are worried sick." The cat made a noise in its throat mid-sip as if in agreement.

Walt was used to animals underfoot at Bennett Farms. He and his siblings grew up with several barn cats, dogs, chickens, goats, and horses. It wasn't unusual for a stray to show up; the animals always welcomed among the menagerie.

"Do the tags have a name or a phone number?" he asked.

"I don't know. Let me see." She fumbled with the collar around the animal's neck. "There's a rabies tag with this year on it. Oh! And yes, there's a phone number."

Walt grabbed his cell phone off the counter. "Read it to me." As Becky gave him the number, Walt typed it into his phone, a familiar name popping up, syncing with the number.

"Fuck me," he murmured.

"What is it?" Becky scowled. Walt held his phone out for her, the screen prominently displaying Mrs. Kirby's name and number. "Mrs. Kirby moved away and left her cat?"

Walt tossed his phone to the side and ran his fingers through his hair. "Looks that way."

"Who moves out of their house and leaves their pet behind?"

"I don't know, Becky. Someone trying to start over, maybe? Or maybe it's an outdoor cat, and she couldn't round it up for the move."

"Well, you can't leave her outside. She'll get eaten by the wolves."

"Coyotes, Becky. There aren't any wolves in these parts, just coyotes," he gently corrected. "Why can't you take it back to the farm with you? It can make friends with the other barn cats."

"No, Walt. This is her home. This is where she belongs. How would you like to get left behind?" She turned to look right at him, the worried expression and tone of her voice pulling at his heartstrings before she offered him a coy smile. "What if… what if *you* kept her? She can keep you company while you're out here all alone."

Walt shook his head and grabbed the cat by the scruff of the neck, intent on getting it off his kitchen counter. He stopped short of the floor, lifting the animal high above his head, the discovery making him laugh out loud.

"What?" Becky asked.

Setting the animal on the linoleum, he let go and watched as it immediately circled his ankles. "I'm afraid you're outnumbered again, Becks."

"What do you mean?"

"The cat. It's not a she."

"It's a he?" She huffed.

"I'm afraid so." He hesitated for a beat before he made a decision, the words leaving his mouth surprising the both of them.

"And I'm calling him... Garth."

Chapter Three

Christmas tree season at Bennett Farms only lasted three short weeks. It started right before Thanksgiving and ran through mid-December. All Bennett hands were on deck during this part of the year, the locals and tourists coming out in droves for the ultimate tree-picking experience.

Walt drove a tractor out to the tree fields, pulling a wagon loaded with folks. The hayride was a bonus feature for families looking for the ultimate Christmas tree experience. There were several areas of the farm where customers could choose a tree to cut and take home. For those crunched for time, fresh-cut trees from some of the other fields were available behind the big red barn, conveniently ready for purchase.

Bouncing on the uncomfortable seat of the tractor as he drove over the divots in the dirt road, Walt glanced over his shoulder. Several excited families were seated in the wagon, the wide-eyed expressions on some of the kids' faces making him grin. He loved this time of the year when the air nipped at his cheeks, and the townspeople and tourists seemed full of holiday cheer. When hot apple cider was readily available, and the sweet smell of hay infiltrated his senses.

Coming to a clearing near the edge of the Christmas tree field, he made a U-turn and brought the tractor to a complete stop. Hopping off the piece of heavy farm equipment, he trotted to the back of the wagon and unlatched the gate.

"All right, folks. Grab a measuring pole from right over there and find your Christmas tree to take home. The trees available to cut this season are marked with colored tags coordinating with the prices listed on the wagon's side."

Using a loud, authoritative voice, he slapped the worn wood with a gloved hand to gain their attention and showed them the color-coded price list. "You'll know exactly how much each tree is in the field, and the fee also includes securing your tree to your vehicle for the trip home. The measuring pole is extra helpful, so you can make sure you're choosing a tree that's just the right size."

A young father carrying a fidgety toddler on his hip waved his hand, garnering Walt's attention. "What if we find a tree without a colored tag, and we want that one?"

Walt shook his head. "Sorry, man. To keep our farm healthy for years to come, we're only allowing select trees to be cut. They're the ones marked with colored tags. If there's no colored tag in a tree, it cannot be cut this season." He remained professional as he offered assistance to an elderly lady coming down the rickety steps of the wagon.

"When you've found the perfect tree, and you're ready for it to be cut, wave your measuring pole in the air, and one of our chainsaw operators will come to you as soon as they can. They'll give you a ticket stub to present for payment and meet you back at the red barn. Y'all ready?" Eager adults and kids screeched a unanimous "yes."

"On your marks, get set—*go-ho-ho*!"

Children dashed into the evergreen field with anxious parents trying to keep up. Walt chuckled with his hands resting on his hips and watched the families scatter. It usually took folks a good thirty minutes to find the perfect Christmas tree, some of them posing for pictures before the big cut. This gave his brothers plenty of time to finish the last load, baling and tying trees to the tops of cars near the barn before they hightailed it back to the fields with their chainsaws ready for another round. They took turns managing the hayride to give each other a break from the grueling baler machines. The remnants of sticky sap and pine needles clung to their matching festive red and green flannels buttoned up over thermal shirts.

The loud thrum of an ATV grew louder as James and Hank raced up the hill, several chainsaws loaded and secured in the back end. Walt threw his hand up in a wave, ready to get this last group on their way before quitting time.

"Yo, Walt," Hank hollered, hopping off the all-terrain vehicle before James came to a complete stop.

"What's up?" Walt meandered toward him.

Hank's cheeks were chapped a rosy red, and his dark curls were windblown. His brother was counting down the days to the New Year when he and his band were scheduled to head to Nashville and record some of their original music. Hank's talent and tenacity were sure to make a splash in the world of country music. But for now, his youngest brother was still a hard-working Bennett, pitching in with all the grueling seasonal work.

Stripping off his work gloves, Hank pushed his hair out

of his eyes. "Becks needs you to stay for dinner tonight. She's got company and wants to introduce you."

"Who is it?" he asked.

James approached, carrying a chainsaw, his dark eyes filled with humor. "Two city-slickers from Atlanta. They're television producers, or something like that, from the Cook USA Network."

"Television producers from Atlanta?"

"Yep," Hank grinned. "Apparently, they found her cooking show on YouTube and wanted to meet her in person on the farm. Becks said they might want to do a screen test or something for their network. They arrived about an hour ago."

Walt rubbed the back of his neck, stunned by the news. "Wow. That's… that's great, right?"

James shrugged and tipped his chin toward several poles waving from above the Frazier firs in the field of trees. "We'll see. But first, we got some trees to cut and bale."

An hour later, Walt tied off the last Christmas tree of the day on top of a worn sedan, the news of Becky's guests all but forgotten. The little boy inside the vehicle waved at him with a mittened hand as the car sped off, Walt waving back. He often thought about these families, imagining them struggling to get the massive trees inside homes and apartments as eager children impatiently waited to decorate the branches with colored lights, ornaments, and home-made school projects. Back in the day, his mother made a celebration out of their tree trimming. The festive, loving memories of holiday music, hot chocolate with extra-large marshmallows, and family time were moments he'd never forget. He missed his mom and what she did for his family, the pure melancholy flashbacks often catching him off guard.

The sun had already set, and the cozy ambiance of the Edison-style string lights throughout the barn rafters spilled out across the loading area. Walt noticed his father, Roy, chatting with a man and a woman, both dressed up and looking out of place on the farm.

"During Christmas tree season, we also offer delicious homemade complementary treats such as hot cocoa, hot cider, and cookies," Roy explained to the couple.

The woman nodded. "All made by Becky?"

Roy smiled. "All made by my daughter, Becky, and her team, of course. She's the one who spearheaded this bonus during customers' choose-n-cut tree visits. It's been real popular this season." Glancing Walt's way, he motioned for him to join them. "You've already met Ted, James, and Hank. I'd like to introduce you to my middle son, Walter Bennett."

Walt approached the group and eyed the pair with curiosity. When the man shoved his hand out to shake, he immediately waved him off. "I'm afraid if you shake my hand, our skin might stick like glue with all the pine sap I've got all over me. How're you doin'? I'm Walt."

The man nodded, the hint of a northern accent noticeable in his chuckled reply. "Not a problem. I'm Albert Tompkins, VP of programming for the Cook USA Network, and this is Elyse Farrell, Supervising Producer of one of our popular cooking shows."

He turned toward the woman and their eyes met. He was taken aback by her exotic beauty up close. Her dark hair was slicked back into a knot at the nape of her neck, and her dark eyelashes framed the most beautiful blue eyes he'd ever encountered. Her flawless complexion was creamy, her lip-glossed smile demure. A thick scarf was wound around her neck, and her sleek winter coat covered her figure, dressed in black pants and high-heeled pointy boots. This woman was not appropriately dressed for a tour of the farm.

"Nice to meet you, Walter," Elyse greeted.

"Please, I'd prefer you called me Walt," he insisted.

"Walt it is," she smiled.

Roy started toward the main house, chatting continuously with the pair about the seasonal experience. Walt followed, walking in step with Elyse behind the two men. "Becky's ready for us to come in and eat. She's prepared the farmhands' favorite meal tonight, so you'll get a true taste of what she does."

"Sounds great," Albert said.

"I'm glad I could give you the tour while she finishes. Our winery operation here at Bennett Farms has a ton to offer. Of course, we encourage folks to pick out their Christmas tree *first* during the holiday season because it's a tried-and-true fact that wine makes your ceilings get taller."

Walt laughed, his father's little joke a staple over the years and one he'd heard many times.

"Is he always this charming?" Elyse asked, leaning closer.

"Always," he replied, catching a whiff of her expensive perfume. Even though tall lampposts illuminated the pathway to the house, Walt eyed Elyse warily. "Careful in those fancy shoes. The path can get a little uneven farther up."

As soon as the words left his mouth, Elyse stumbled. "*Oh!*" she squealed. But Walt was right there to catch her, holding her by the arm to keep her from falling to the ground.

Roy and Albert stopped and turned around, concerned by her outburst. "You okay, Miss Farrell?" Roy asked.

Elyse gripped Walt's bicep to steady herself, her blue eyes wide as she looked at him. Her lips parted in a sexy exhale. "I'm… fine."

Walt gallantly palmed her lower back and continued to hold her by the elbow as the group ascended a small flight of stairs leading to the back porch of the house. When she was safely on solid ground, he broke their connection.

Elyse's chest heaved, and she stood a little taller. "You're a real Southern gentleman. Thank you, Walt."

Walt mumbled quickly, "You're welcome," and watched with pleasure as Elyse entered the home. Running a hand through his hair, he shook his head with chagrin, knowing if his brothers caught wind of his chivalrous behavior involving the dark-haired beauty, they'd tease him mercilessly during dinner. Heat scorched the back of his neck, and he had to shift the growing bulge in his pants before he went inside.

Damn those pretty brunettes with blue eyes—he was a sucker for them every single time.

Chapter Four

ELYSE FARRELL

What was it about muscular, well-behaved men with good manners that left Elyse feeling lightheaded and giddy? Damn, just the thought of Walt Bennett palming her lower back mere inches from the waistband of her G-string had her coming undone.

Upon entering the home and greeting Becky and the Bennett boys again, she asked if there was anything she could do to help. Becky waved her off and pointed out her assigned seat. The table was laden with home-cooked food in various serving dishes. It was obvious Walt's sister prepared everything with love, the antique place settings and candles a lovely shabby chic touch to the meal. The aroma in the air was mouth-watering, and steam arose from the spread, ready to accommodate the large brood. Becky looked adorable in her frilly apron, the proud look on her face serving her dinner guests hard not to notice. One thing that first drew Elyse to Becky's YouTube channel was her pleasant disposition. The girl was the real deal, and Elyse knew she deserved a bigger audience.

Shifting in her seat, Elyse dared to watch Walt as he eased his muscled body into a seat directly across from her. Right away, she noticed he'd changed his shirt and combed his hair in record time. The burly Bennett brother seemed genuinely happy being surrounded by his family. His father, Roy, and his sister flanked either side of him. James, Hank, Ted, and her boss, Albert, filled the remaining seats, the conversation enjoyable, and the Italian-themed meal delicious. Becky had gone all out and prepared lasagna from scratch. Impressed, Elyse dug in and savored every single bite. She noticed Walt rip a piece of bread in half and dip it in the marinara sauce on his plate. When he popped the bread into his mouth, their eyes met for a millisecond before Elyse looked away. My God, even the way he chewed was sexy.

"So what the Cook USA Network is proposing is having Becky come to Atlanta and do a screen test for our popular competition show," Albert started.

Elyse reached for her wineglass and took a sip of Big Red, named after the red barn on the property. She was surprised by how delicious the full-bodied wine was, the beverage charged with notes of black cherry and hints of vanilla from the oak-aged barrels. Who knew a little country mountain town in Georgia had such a satisfying wine experience? As she enjoyed a rare glass of alcohol on a weeknight, she was glad to see her boss finally get down to business so she could stop fantasizing about the man sitting across from her.

"Can you explain what a screen test is?" Becky questioned.

Elyse cleared her throat. "I can. It's a mock taping of the show done with high-quality cameras and lighting in a studio."

"I guess that's better than filming on your phone, right, Becks?" Hank teased. Becky rolled her eyes as if used to the brotherly teasing.

Her oldest brother, Ted chimed in. "How long does filming a screen test take?"

Albert replied, "Well, we'd have everything lined up before Becky's arrival—the set, the camera angles, the menu. We'd love to play around with some ideas and see how your unique ability to charm your audience transfers onto the television screen."

"It all sounds amazing," Becky started, seemingly star-struck by the idea. "But I've never done anything with professionals before. And I've never been to Atlanta on my own either."

"Don't worry, Becky. We'll arrange everything for you. You won't have to worry about a thing," Elyse encouraged. "We can even hire you an assistant for the week to accompany you everywhere—"

"I'll accompany her," Walt interjected.

All eyes, including Elyse's, focused on Walt. He leaned back in his chair, swirling his glass of red wine in his hand. His confident swagger and undeniable love for his sister put Elyse at an immediate loss for words.

"Oh, Walt. Would you?" Becky asked. "I'd feel so much better having you with me in the city. You could be my bodyguard." She turned toward her father. "You could spare Walter for a week or so, right? Especially after the holidays during the winter months when things slow down. And having Walt with me would alleviate all your fatherly worries. Guys, don't you agree?" She looked poignantly at each one of her formidable brothers.

"I think it's a great idea having Walt accompany you," James said.

"Me too," Hank chimed in.

"I agree," Ted added.

Roy wadded up his napkin and set it on his empty plate, his chest rising in a deep intake of air. Turning in his seat to look at Walt sitting next to him, he palmed his son's shoulder. "I think it's the best idea you've had in a long time, Walt."

"Then it's settled," Albert grinned. "Elyse will secure the itinerary on the calendar and work out all the details for you and your brother's stay in Atlanta."

Becky squealed with delight. "Oh my goodness! I can't believe I'm going to do an actual screen test!"

Elyse eyed Walt again, the look of chagrin on his handsome face hard not to notice. His father and brothers looked at the situation from a protective angle, not wanting the only female Bennett in the family traveling alone to the big city. How sweet. But Elyse was looking at the situation from a different point of view. To have the opportunity to get to know Walter Bennett a little better was a heady, selfish consideration.

Walt's baritone voice startled her out of her daydream among the chatter around the table. "So, you'll show us a good time?"

"Excuse me?" Elyse palmed the fabric of her black turtleneck, wishing she could find some relief from the surge of heat trapped around her neck.

Walt stared back at her, one side of his mouth lifted in a sexy smirk. "In Atlanta? You'll show Becky and me a good time while we're there, right?"

Elyse licked her lips and sat up a little straighter, indicating to everyone at the table she was all business. "Absolutely."

But when Walt winked back at her, she wanted nothing but his pleasure.

"I'm pleased with how everything went," Albert said as he drove through the charming downtown area of Langston Falls. They were heading back to Atlanta, their little supper with the Bennett family a success in Elyse's book.

She eyed the heavily decorated lamp posts and storefronts as they neared the turn leading them to the interstate, the Christmas decorations fitting for the tiny mountain town. Her sigh was dreamy as she rested her chin in her hand, staring out the window, the wine from earlier giving her a pleasant buzz. "Yes. I can't wait to get started."

After a decadent dessert of homemade chocolate chip cookies crushed up in the cutest little mason jars and topped with a dollop of whipped cream and drizzled chocolate sauce, Elyse didn't think the night could get any sweeter—until Walt joined his father and sister outside, walking her and Albert to their car. As Roy and Becky said their goodbyes to Albert, Walt shoved his hands into the front pockets of his jeans, making his flannel-covered biceps bulge with manliness.

"I'm looking forward to seeing how all this works and what you might be able to do for my sister."

Elyse nodded. "I can assure you, she's in good hands. The network is going crazy over her brand. The first logical step is to have her do a screen test and possibly introduce her on our popular competition show. Who knows what might happen from there?"

"That's cool." He glanced at the others before taking a deliberate step toward her. "Well, I guess I'll be seeing you soon." He opened his arms wide, making Elyse hesitate. Chuckling, he lowered his arms and explained. "In Langston Falls, we usually hug goodbye."

"Oh," she nervously giggled. "Well, then. Goodbye."

Awkwardly, she opened her arms wide and stepped into his embrace. She memorized the feel of his hard muscles and the way his warm breath floated across the exposed skin of her blushing cheek. The man smelled like Christmas, the pine trees he worked with infiltrating his skin with holiday cheer. Oh, to be nestled in his arms during the most wonderful time of year…

"You good?" Albert was staring at her from within the confines of the dark car interior.

Blinking back at him, Elyse fumbled for a beat before she realized they were parked in front of her midtown apartment building, the Atlanta cityscape looming all around.

"Wow. I must've dozed off," she explained. Reaching for the handle, she opened the car door and carefully stepped out into the frigid night. "I'll see you tomorrow, Al. I can't wait to get the ball rolling with Becky."

Albert nodded from within the car parked at the curb. "Great work, Elyse. I have a good feeling about this girl."

Elyse nodded. She had a good feeling too. But it wasn't about a girl.

An idea had formed, and she was anxious to make it happen. Before she let Albert get away, she spoke with intention, hoping her words said out loud might manifest into reality. "Maybe we can convince the Bennett siblings to come right before New Year's Eve and play around with a holiday-themed menu? We could even invite them to the studio for the big staff party and introduce them to everyone."

"Great idea. We can wine and dine them before all the hard stuff," Albert replied.

His words were a running joke among the two of them, Elyse often coming up with little bonuses as they wooed potential talent to take on the grueling work of television production. The industry was hard, and any star treatment up front helped to soften the blow during the arduous process. If Becky Bennett was genuinely interested in taking her brand to the next level, she would have to jump through numerous hoops and drink from the mainstream entertainment firehouse. Having her brother by her side was a good call and a game-changer for Elyse—or so she hoped.

"Make it happen, Elyse. If anyone can convince *The Farmer's Daughter* and her brother to celebrate New Year's with the studio staff and special guests, it's you."

Elyse shrugged. "I'll do my best. Goodnight, Al."

"Goodnight, Elyse. See you tomorrow."

Elyse stepped off the elevator a few minutes later and entered her comfy abode. She shrugged off her coat and unwrapped the scarf around her neck, hanging it on the rack in the entryway. Continuing into her bedroom off the hall and into the en suite bathroom, she turned on the light and eyed herself in the large bathroom mirror. She ran her hand against her turtleneck, turning her head from side to side. Her angular cheeks were flushed, and her full lips glistened in the light. Smoothing the sides of her dark hair, she grinned, pleased there wasn't a single strand out of place.

Every part of her life was planned and arranged in such a way to satisfy her controlling nature. But every now and again, something or someone crossed her path, throwing her off course. Today, it was Walter Bennett. Even though she'd managed to remain professional and somewhat in control throughout most of the evening, every molecule in her being dared her to make a pass at the gorgeous Bennett brother. But there'd be time for that later.

Her black painted nails glinted as she untwisted the bun and hair tie from the nape of her neck. Shaking her hair loose, Elyse's dark strands tumbled over her shoulders in shiny, natural waves. For the first time all evening, she finally allowed herself to relax and contemplate her next bold move.

Moving forward, if she wanted to get to know Walter Bennett, she needed to plan things carefully. And if she played her cards just right, she might get to show Mr. Hottie a real good time.

Chapter Five

WALT

Christmas had come and gone on the farm in a flurry of family get-togethers which included good food and, of course, great wine. Walt enjoyed spending quality time with his father and siblings and was almost jealous his brothers Teddy and James had their girlfriends by their sides. Teddy had his fiancé, Robyn, and James invited Samantha into the mix. Sam, as everyone called her, was Ted's former parole officer and was now his brother's official girlfriend. There was much talk about Ted and Robyn's spring nuptials, Becky gifting the pair a promise to host a decadent couple's wedding shower in the New Year.

"Don't worry, Walt. I haven't forgotten about your housewarming party," she'd said after all the gifts under the massive Christmas tree were opened. "I still want to do a stock-the-bar theme for you."

Walt eyed the hoard of gifts he'd received from his family, the cookware, bamboo sheets, and bath towels practical in every sense of the word. His new home was coming along nicely since he'd added numerous pieces of furniture, including the large wardrobe and a sleigh-bed frame he'd found in the utility barn, thanks to his sister.

"There's no rush, Becks. Let's get through the holidays and your screen test in Atlanta first. You've already got a ton on your plate."

Becky offered a broad smile and wrapped her arm around Walt's waist. "It's exciting, right? I'm so glad you're going with me. I don't think I could've managed the trip alone."

"Of course, you could. You're Rebecca Bennett, Queen of Bennett Farms. It's a wonder you haven't been snatched up already."

Their father approached, the look on his face full of pride. "My little girl has certainly come into her own. We're all very proud of you, darlin'."

"Oh, Daddy," she blushed, switching her side hug to their father and leaning her head against his shoulder.

"Have you received your schedule from the Atlanta team yet?" Roy asked.

Becky nodded. "Yes. Elyse sent me the schedule a few days ago. The day we arrive, we'll check into our accommodations and then get a studio tour. The next day is New Year's Eve, so there's nothing on the schedule except get ready for the big party."

"What party?" he asked.

"The studio's New Year's Eve party, can you believe it?" Becky's voice turned up a notch. "Elyse wants us to come early for the festivities. The party is a bonus, and supposedly invitation only. She said some of the elites from the Atlanta film industry will be there, and we may even see Tyler Perry among the guests."

Roy looked surprised. "Wow."

When Walt learned Elyse wanted him and Becky in

Atlanta for the New Year's Eve party, he was dumbfounded. Surely there was more to it than a party? Maybe she was eager for her crew to meet Becky in a more relaxed atmosphere? Perhaps Elyse wanted his sister to post some party pics on her social media to get her fans in a frenzy? Walt had to admit, whatever the reason for the invite, he was excited too. For the life of him, he couldn't get the dark-haired beauty out of his mind.

Becky's face flushed with genuine excitement. "Dad, wait till I send you pictures of where we're staying near the studio. Apparently, they own a few of the cutest fully furnished condos with all the amenities, including a pool and gym."

"Well, I don't think you'll be doing much swimming this time of the year," Roy chuckled. "But I know a big studio party sure beats watching Dick Clark's Rockin' New Year's Eve on television. I'm glad you two will have a little fun together before you hit the ground running. And I won't have to worry so much knowing you have a chaperone," he admitted.

"You've got nothing to worry about, Dad. I'll take good care of Becks," Walt reassured.

Walt was never one to boast, but truth be told, he was excited to experience a VIP party in the big city. And the likelihood of actually indulging in a bona fide New Year's kiss with a certain exotic beauty was a thrilling possibility.

A few days later, as Walt zipped up his suitcase, he heard a horn honk from his graveled drive. Grinning, he knew it was his brother, Hank. He still had a few days before he left with his band to Nashville and volunteered to drop Becky off at his place so Walt could go over Garth's feeding instructions. Surveying the bedroom one last time, he grabbed a sheet of paper on which he'd written everything down and nodded. Garth hopped up on the bed and meowed. Stroking the animal's fur, he spoke with tenderness.

"Hank-ster is gonna take care of you, buddy. I'll be back before you know it."

With his heavy, wool-lined coat and cowboy hat on, Walt set the alarm, locked the front door, and threw a wave toward his siblings, who were getting out of the car. Hank helped Becky with her luggage and brought it to Walt's truck.

"You really gonna wear that hat in Atlanta?" Hank ribbed.

"Yeah. And you're one to tease," Walt countered. His brother looked like he'd just rolled out of bed, his wavy hair unruly and thick scruff on his face noticeable. "It's freezing this time of the year. Have you looked at the forecast? They're predicting snow on New Year's Eve," Walt informed them.

Becky squealed. "It sounds so romantic, doesn't it? Snow in Atlanta on New Year's Eve? I still can't believe we get to be a part of it." She lightly punched Walt in the shoulder.

Pressing his lips together to thwart off a grin, he remained composed, even though he felt as giddy as his little sister. "It's gonna be a ton of fun, but a lot of hard work too." Pulling the cat instructions from his coat pocket, he handed them to his brother. "The alarm code is there on top. The rest is easy. I left the food container on the kitchen counter. Just stop by once a day and fill his bowl. Oh, and make sure he's got fresh water."

Hank eyed the paper and nodded. As he folded it up and stuffed it in his jeans pocket, he said, "Got it." He held a hand over his forehead and turned toward Becky, shading his eyes from the bright morning sun. "You ready to knock 'em dead, Becks?"

"I'm ready to do my best. It's all anyone with an opportunity like this can do."

Walt was in awe of her confidence. Still, her pretty features and wholesomeness reminded him he was her protector during this exciting adventure.

"What if you totally kill it, and they offer you a mainstream television contract and want you to move to Atlanta? Would you?" Hank continued. Leave it to his youngest brother to get to the point, his honest questions leaving Becky mute.

They stood there and waited for her to reply. When she didn't say anything, Walt lovingly palmed her shoulder. "You okay? You're not having second thoughts about all this, are you?"

The space between Becky's eyebrows furrowed, indicating she must've been mulling over her response. "I don't think I could ever move out of Langston Falls. It's my home."

"And it will *always* be your home," Hank soothed. "Jesus, Becky. If you're not sure about the possibility of working in television, why are you even making this trip?" It was a fair question, and one Walt hoped his sister might answer.

She waited for a beat before she spoke, the self-assurance in her voice full of Bennett gumption. "If they see something in me and my brand they want to capitalize on, they'll have to compromise. We'll have to negotiate and devise a plan that satisfies both parties."

Hank glanced at Walt with wide eyes. "Shit. Our baby sister's gone and grown up on us." Walt chuckled as Becky stood tall, her chin thrust into the air.

"Get used to it, boys. I know exactly what I'm doing."

"You sure about that?" Hank bantered.

"Absolutely."

The ride to Atlanta was uneventful, and the highway traffic minimal as the countryside slowly morphed into the sprawling Southern metropolis. But as Walt carefully navigated his truck through the congested cityscape toward the airport on the south side of town, the traffic became unbearable. He honestly couldn't imagine living in the metropolitan area.

"Are we there yet?" Becky joked. The tone of her voice was laced with enthusiasm, gusto, and a hint of trepidation. Heck, he'd be nervous too if someone was interested in filming him and possibly changing the trajectory of his life.

"According to my GPS, we've only got a few more miles till we get there."

"Great! Elyse texted earlier, saying she'd meet us there. I'll let her know we're close."

Walt felt a peculiar tickle in his stomach, and his nerves amped up, knowing he was about to lay eyes on Elyse Farrell again. To be the recipient of her welcoming committee was a thrilling thought. Glancing at his face in the rearview mirror, he hoped it wasn't too obvious how excited he was. His face was shaved smooth since the last time he'd seen her, and he'd made a trip into Langston Falls for a quick haircut the day before. Yeah, he wasn't trying too hard.

"There she is, right over there!" Becky clapped with delight before pointing toward Elyse, who stood expectant on the driveway in front of a charming townhouse. All the homes in the area looked exactly alike, the small dormant yards with barren trees and perfectly trimmed boxwoods lined up in front of tiny porches.

Walt brought his pickup truck to a stop and turned off

the engine. Becky scrambled out of the cab like a teenager about to experience their first encounter with a celebrity, chatting animatedly while hugging Elyse. Taking his time, he stepped out of the truck and settled his hat onto his head. Coming around the side of the vehicle, he felt Elyse's gaze travel up and down his body, sending a shiver across his spine.

"Hey, cowboy." She smiled warmly.

His lips twitched into a genuine grin as he immediately took his hat off and held it to his chest. He was pulling out all the stops with his gentlemanly behavior. "Hey, Elyse. How are you?"

"I'm fine. How was the trip?"

"Uneventful." Putting the hat back on, he tucked his hands into his coat pockets, aware of the wild hammering of his heart.

The woman was gorgeous, standing before him like a badass professional in her trademark black coat and turtle-neck. She wore a different pair of shoes today, high-heels with red soles, and her hair was pulled back into a tight ponytail, the long strands curling ever-so-slightly near the middle of her shoulder blades. Her smile rivaled the noon-day sun, and he had the sudden urge to tug on that ponytail and lean her head back so he could ravage her neck.

"Let me show you around."

The three entered the condo, the interior lights ablaze, highlighting the space decorated in a soothing color palette of blues and grays. The place was immaculate, and Walt immediately noticed a large basket of goodies on the kitchen table.

"What's this?" Becky asked. Her expression held a perpetual smile.

Elyse waved her hand in the air with nonchalance. "It's a little welcome basket from the studio."

Becky tore into the cellophane, reminding Walt of Christmas morning back at the farm. "Oh, wow! Champagne, cheese and crackers, chocolate..." She turned to Walt with pleasure. "We can create a little charcuterie later tonight."

"We can," Walt nodded. He set his hat on the table near the basket. Turning toward Elyse, his next comment came out of nowhere. "Care to show me the bedroom?"

Becky's hands stilled, her fingers wrapped around the neck of the champagne bottle. She pressed her teeth into her lower lip, her eyes wide in response to Walt's cheeky comment. Holding his breath, he carefully considered his next sentence. Clearing his throat, he stood a little taller.

"I meant... can you point me in the direction of the bedrooms so I can bring the luggage in?"

There was a definitive twinkle in Elyse's blue eyes as she eyed him with pleasure, the smirk on her face indicating his little slip humored her. Her voice was smooth and professional, reminding Walt of a flight attendant. "There are two bedrooms upstairs with private bathrooms. Give your sister the one with the pale green walls. It's more feminine and to the left of the landing."

Walt nodded and started toward the front door. But Elyse's following comment made him pause.

"Your room is through the first door at the top of the stairs. The bed is large and the ambiance masculine—as if it was made just for you."

Chapter Six

ELYSE

God bless America.

Elyse watched Walt's backside disappear out the front door, his manly essence left in his wake. What was it about a real cowboy that made her insides turn to mush? Even the back of Walt's head was sexy, his recently trimmed neck noticeable from a fresh haircut. The man was a handsome devil, her mind going haywire being in such close proximity to him. And good Lord, what was the cologne he was wearing? She'd never smelled anything so yummy before in her entire life.

"Sorry about that," Becky lamented.

"About what?" Elyse feigned innocence, shifting in her stance.

"My brother. Sometimes he doesn't think before he says stuff. In fact, he usually doesn't think before he says or does anything at all." She giggled, placing the champagne bottle back in the goodie basket.

Elyse had the urge to pull her trademark turtleneck away from her neck to let out a puff of wanton steam.

Instead, she motioned for Becky to follow her toward the stairs. "Your brother is charming and extremely polite. In this day and age, he's a rarity. And it certainly helps he's so good-looking."

"Ew," Becky giggled.

"Well, I'm only telling you the truth. I swear both of you belong on a billboard advertising Ralph Lauren products. You know, high society meets red, white, and blue, home-grown America. I'm glad he's staying with you while you're in town."

"Me too."

Walt came through the front door with the bulky luggage in both his hands. "After you, ladies," he motioned with his head.

Elyse took the lead and started up the staircase, aware of the intentional swing she added to her hips. Although her moves were subtle, she hoped the handsome man took notice, her ultimate goal to receive a midnight kiss on New Year's Eve.

"Here we are." She opened the bedroom door farthest down the hall and gestured for Becky to enter.

"Oh, my," she said with a dreamy voice. "This is beautiful."

Becky stood in the center of the room, taking in the space that was hers for the next few days. The queen-size bed was perfectly made up with a crisp white duvet over pale green sheets, the delicate color matching the walls. A large dresser with an attached mirror was on the other side of the room, and there was even a crystal chandelier hanging from the middle of the ceiling, the intentional feminine touch classy and not over the top.

"It's perfect." Becky beamed.

Walt set his sister's luggage down with a thump and looked around. "This fits you, Becks."

She nodded. "Now, let's see yours."

The threesome strode down the hallway to the other bedroom. Elyse opened the door and revealed a king-size bed with a crimson duvet taking up an entire wall.

"Wow," he stuttered, stepping into the space. "The bed is huge."

Elyse licked her lips, her eyes flicking to the seam of Walt's pants and imagining something else that might be categorized as huge. "We want our guests to feel comfortable during their stay."

"I don't think being uncomfortable will be a problem at all. Thank you," Walt replied.

Their eyes locked, something searing and captivating passing between them. The man was sexy as sin, pinning her with his stare.

Becky seemed oblivious and skipped toward her bedroom. "I'm going to unpack."

The air was thick with possibility, the heat around Elyse's neck growing uncomfortable. "I should leave you to unpack as well. Do you have everything you need?" she asked, daring to bat her lashes at him in quick succession.

Walt ran a thick finger across his jaw. "Yeah. I think so. Thanks."

Elyse offered a quick nod. "You're welcome. I'll wait downstairs while you unpack. Take your time. We've got the entire afternoon to tour the studio." She turned to leave and give him privacy, taken aback when he grabbed her by the wrist. Her head snapped, her eyes traveling from his heated fingertips up his substantial arm to his face. His chiseled features up close left her breathless.

"Was there something else, Walt?"

His eyes were large brown saucers staring back at her as he squeezed her hand. The low rumble of his voice vibrated through her core. "This means a lot to my sister. Let me know if there's anything I can do to help her through the process. I'm here at your beck and call."

Elyse swallowed hard. Did Walter Bennett just offer himself as a cabana boy?

"I'll… uh. I'll definitely let you know." She glanced at their hands before boldly looking at his face again. "I'm a huge fan of beck-and-call guys."

Walt's nostrils flared, and Elyse was stunned when he raised her hand to his lips, placing a chaste kiss on her knuckles. The move was classic Southern American male. "I was hoping you might be."

Elyse swooned in her high heels.

Driving a black golf cart like a bat out of hell, Elyse traversed the massive studio grounds with her special guests on board.

"So, here's the back story. Georgia has quickly risen to become the top state in the country for the television and film industry."

"Why is that?" Walt asked from behind.

Eyeing his good looks from underneath his cowboy hat in the rearview mirror, she smiled. "The tax incentives are number one. Filmmakers can receive up to thirty percent in tax incentives filming here. There are thousands of locations to suit any production, such as large cities, mountains, forests, beaches, small towns… Christmas tree farms and wineries." She looked toward Becky and winked.

"I can't imagine a film crew in Langston Falls, let alone on Bennett Farms," Becky laughed.

"It could happen," Elyse replied. "Live Oak Studios has access to more than a thousand production suppliers and support companies. And don't forget, Atlanta-Hartsfield Jackson International Airport has hourly flights to cities around the world, conveniently located less than ten miles from here."

"What about the movie stars?" Becky asked. "Do they stay in the condos y'all own when they're in town filming?"

Elyse harrumphed. "Hardly. Atlanta is full of luxurious and plentiful accommodations for A-listers, along with high-end shopping and dining. Although, believe it or not, we've had a few stars request our humble abodes."

"Like who?" Becky asked with eagerness.

"I can't say. Confidentiality agreements," she explained, wrinkling her nose. The golf cart wobbled as she took a corner a little too fast.

"Easy, girl," Walt said, gripping the oh-my-god strap from the cart's ceiling with one hand while palming the top of his cowboy hat with the other.

"Sorry." Slowing the cart down, she continued with the tour talk. "Live Oak Studios can accommodate all types and sizes of productions, from small independent films, scripted television series, and shows like ours on the Cook USA Network."

"How many acres is the complex?" Walt asked.

"The in-town Atlanta studio complex is ever-expanding. There are nearly one hundred and fifty acres across two adjacent campuses."

Walt whistled. "Impressive."

"I know, right?" Elyse was a proud Cook USA Network employee. Since relocating from New York, they'd been filming their food shows at Live Oak Studios for over a year. Truth be told, she was glad to be out of the Big Apple, the southern climate and more easy-going nature of Atlanta folks a breath of fresh air. A charming gentleman like Walt was a bonus. As a Supervising Producer for one of the most popular shows in the food television industry, she was right where she was meant to be.

Pulling next to a large warehouse, she turned off the golf cart and swung her body around so she could talk directly to both Becky and her brother. "Are you ready to see where the magic happens?"

Becky's eyes grew large. "It's in there? Where I'll be cooking?"

"Yup. Consider Stage Three your new home for the next few days." She climbed out of the cart. "Twenty thousand square feet of space is dedicated to the Cook USA Network." Glancing at her watch, she nodded. "Al should be here in a few minutes. You'll be using the new *Sally's Southern Kitchen* set for your test. They start filming new episodes in mid-January. We thought it would be the perfect setup for you and a couple of other southern cooks we're testing this week."

Becky stopped in her tracks. "Did you just say *Sally's Southern Kitchen*?"

Elyse noticed Becky's worried countenance—or maybe it was stage fright? "Yes. We thought it would blend nicely with your brand, *The Farmer's Daughter*. Don't you agree?" She kept her tone upbeat. It wasn't unusual for the talent she found to end up with a bad case of nerves. But stress usually happened during filming. That it happened before Becky even saw the layout of the studio interior made her cringe.

"I'm... I'm a huge fan of Sally. I've been watching her for years," Becky stuttered.

Elyse looped her arm through Becky's and guided her through the studio door, patting her hand with reassurance. "Great! Then this is a good sign."

Walt brought up the rear as the threesome entered the building. The interior was warm, the bright stage lights on full throttle highlighting the kitchen set. A few crew members milled about doing various odd jobs as Becky let go of Elyse and practically floated toward the butcher block counter where Sally created her famous Southern cooking recipes.

Elyse and Walt lagged, watching Becky with pleasure. Crossing her arms at her chest, Elyse smirked. "Your sister's star-struck, and Miss Sally isn't even on the property."

Walt chuckled in agreement. "I've always loved Beck's childlike wonder. She's like this with everything."

"Everything?" Elyse turned and eyed Walt's profile, his handsome face highlighted by the stage lights. He'd taken his hat off and held it in his hand by his side.

"Yes. Everything. We could all learn a lesson or two by watching Becks." The look of brotherly love was apparent in his tone and expression.

The two of them silently continued to watch Becky familiarize herself with the set. The girl seemed mesmerized, gently touching the decorative props, and investigating the appliances and kitchen gadgets, her golden hair drenched in light. Elyse remembered what it felt like for her too, when she excitedly stepped onto her first sound stage as a low-level associate producer when she was first starting out in New York. Taking a deep breath, she reveled in the memory, her lungs filling with the reminiscent scent of fresh lumber, stale coffee, hot lights, and creative buzz. There was nothing else like it in the world. Her television career was something she was damn proud of.

Her body turned rigid the moment she felt Walt's finger lightly stroke her hand hanging by her side. Flicking her eyes to his, the sight of him looking at her was nearly too much to handle. She could almost feel him undressing her with his stare. His attractive face held a provocative smile, igniting an ember in her chest, causing warmth to spill and pool in her belly.

God bless America.

Without saying a word, she boldly hooked her pinky finger with his and stood a little closer to him, keeping their hands hidden between them.

"Do you feel it?" he mumbled.

"Mmhmm," she replied. She needed to focus on the present. Remain calm. Cool. Collected.

"Sparks," he exhaled.

"Chemistry," she whispered.

"A connection," they uttered in unison.

Stunned, she jerked her head and looked at him again, her pinky grip growing tighter. And it was then she knew her beck-and-call man was on board—ready to do whatever she asked when the right moment came along.

Chapter Seven

WALT

Dripping wet after a hot shower, Walt had barely tucked a towel around his midsection when he heard a frantic knocking on the bathroom door.

"Hold on," he hollered, adjusting the towel so it wouldn't fall off. He poked his head out, cracking the door open among a heavy cloud of steam. "What's up, Becky?"

His sister stood on the other side of the threshold, holding two dresses. She wore a pink robe, and her hair was in curlers. "I can't decide what to wear tonight." She seemed worried, and the space between her pretty brows indented as she scowled. "Tell me which one I should wear to the party."

Walt eyed the dresses and shrugged. "They both look good to me."

"Walter," she moaned. "I'm dead serious. *Help me.*"

Opening the door wide, Walt stepped out of the bathroom, heat vapors following him into the bedroom. He held the towel in place, careful not to lose it and embarrass her. Since the studio tour and a meeting with VP of Programming, Albert Tompkins and some of the crew the day before, Becky wasn't herself. She was fidgety and a bundle of nerves. Before coming to Atlanta, he'd made a promise— to be there for her every step of the way, even if it meant helping her with a crucial wardrobe decision.

Becky held up a blue and white dress with a high collar, the flower pattern reminding him of a tablecloth at a country picnic. "This one screams *The Farmer's Daughter*, but is that what I'm trying to convey tonight? Should I be a walking advertisement for my brand?"

She paused and held up the other dress, a long red velvet gown. "Or do I go with a holiday dress theme in the appropriate seasonal color and enjoy myself as a guest at my first A-list party in the big city?"

Walt scowled when he noticed the thigh-high slit of the red dress, the provocative fashion sure to lure a strange man's eye. "Where did you get the red one from?"

"Robyn let me borrow it. She told me tonight was a once-in-a-lifetime event and that I needed to make a grand entrance."

"Oh, you'll make an entrance in the red dress, all right," he mumbled.

"Pardon?" Becky asked.

Walt inhaled a deep breath, unsure if he should be pointing his little sister in the red gown direction. "I know for a fact Dad would kill me for allowing you to wear a dress like that in public." He pointed to the fiery color. "But you're a grown-ass woman who'll be hobnobbing with some of the big guns tonight. You need to stand out." Eyeing the flowery dress again, he wrinkled his nose. "You don't want to look like a Sunday school teacher on New Year's Eve. Live a little, Becks. I say, wear the red one."

Becky squealed with delight, energized by Walt's decision. "Thank you, Walt! I knew I could count on you!" She ran out of the room in a flurry of red, white, and blue, leaving Walt standing there holding a literal towel.

Chuckling, he eyed his black suit hanging in the open closet. It was still wrapped in the plastic film from the dry cleaners, his white shirt starched and his jacket and pants wrinkle-free. His black cowboy boots were spit-shined and ready, and he decided to forego a traditional bowtie and wear a bolo tie instead.

Wiping the steam off the bathroom mirror with a hand towel, he eyed his reflection and ran a hand down his smooth jaw. When was the last time he was this excited to attend a party? Bennett Farms held events every season; the party atmosphere on the family property fun and festive. But this was different. He felt—grown up. Mature. Confident in his own skin. He was a man on a mission, intent on wooing the beautiful Elyse all evening until the clock struck midnight when he could finally meld his mouth with hers.

The New Year's Eve kiss was the easy part. There'd be a crowd of people surrounding them, tipsy and oblivious to the traditional lip locks happening all around the room. There'd be champagne toasts and folks singing *Auld Lang Syne* at the top of their lungs—plenty of distractions to take advantage of a memorable kissing moment.

But there was one caveat to the equation he wasn't so sure he could get around—his sister, Becky. He didn't want his selfish craving for Elyse's luscious mouth to overshadow his sister's big evening. This was Becky's night, and he was her designated sidekick and guardian. Knowing his sister and her recent nerves, she'd be clinging to him all night long in a roomful of high-class strangers, uneasy in the sexy red gown as grown men gawked at her. He was no fool. Rebecca was a stunner, her innocence beguiling. Still, he hoped to God he could steal a few precious seconds in which to taste the object of his desire.

Standing tall, Walt slid the polished gemstone clasp of his bolo tie up the leather braided cord. Taking in his dressed-up image reflected in the wall-mounted mirror behind the bedroom door, he muttered, "Not bad." He was proud of his family roots, his strong jaw line, and Bennett nose formidable. He hoped his manners and good looks carried over into La-La Land, where he'd fit right in with the other male guests, many of whom Elyse mentioned were celebrities.

"You ready, Walt?" he heard Becky holler.

Adjusting his suit jacket one last time, he nodded with anticipation. Who knew what the evening ahead held?

"I'm coming."

Walt's truck idled near the security entrance of Live Oak Studios, the line of luxury cars in front of him impressive. Looking over at Becky in the passenger seat, he could tell she was antsy to get inside. Her arms and décolletage of her dress were bare; her hair pulled back from her face accentuating the softer side of the Bennett features. Her makeup enhanced her brown eyes, and her lips glossed a shimmering red. She was the epitome of a blonde bombshell.

"Are you excited?" he asked.

Becky nodded with eagerness. "Of course. I hope you won't have to park far away from the entrance. I didn't bring my coat because it didn't match my fancy dress."

"Don't worry. I'll drop you off so you won't have to walk far. But be careful in those high heels. Seriously, I don't see how you ladies walk in those things."

Becky giggled. "Be glad you don't have to. My feet are already killing me."

A security guard checked Walt's identification, comparing it with a clipboard in his hand. "Enjoy your night," he politely confirmed.

Elyse told him the party was being held at the largest studio on the lot, the same building where a recent Marvel movie was filmed. Two rotating-beam searchlights flanked the entrance foyer as party guests wearing formal gowns, and tuxedos stopped for photos. He was thankful he and his sister dressed the part.

"Look, Walt! There's even a red carpet!"

Becky's animation was contagious. Pulling up to the curb, a male greeter opened her door, offering his assistance.

"I'll see you inside, Becks. You look amazing. Knock 'em dead!"

Becky shot him a grateful glance over her bare shoulder before exiting the truck, her skin flushed and her smile genuine.

Another couple of security guards waved Walt into a parking space, the efficiency of the entire setup at Live Oak Studios impressive. The air was brisk as he exited the truck and adjusted his jacket, ready to lay eyes on his muse.

The interior of the studio was decked out to look like a nightclub. Slim cocktail tables with shiny black tablecloths peppered the space around a large dance floor where folks were already grooving to the sounds played by an energetic DJ in the corner. The colorful light show pulsed to the beat of the music, the loud tunes thunderous in Walt's ears. His heart synced to the rhythm as he searched the room for his sister. The sophisticated crowd sipped on various drinks, and he noticed several bar stations set up in the peripheral of the building. Intent on scoping out a cold beer after finding his sister, he finally spotted her from across the room and held his hand up in a wave to garner her attention.

Her youthful face glowed in the light as she chatted with Albert and another couple, acknowledging him with a quick nod. In her hand was a champagne glass, his sister appearing very cosmopolitan and chic in her red gown. She looked like she was having a good time, her earlier nervousness vanished. His shoulders relaxed, and he decided to belly up to the bar to get that beer.

"What would you like, sir?" the barman asked.

"Bottled IPA if you have one."

The bartender quickly pulled a long neck out of a beverage tub full of ice. He promptly popped off the cap using a church key with a flick of his wrist.

Walt started to take his wallet out of his jacket pocket before the bartender stopped him. "No tipping tonight, sir. Please, enjoy the party." He handed the bottle off to him.

"Thanks, man."

Walt took a long pull from the beer and surveyed the room again, making sure Becky was still in his sight. A few more folks joined their conversation, his sister holding court and reminding him of a queen. Chuckling, Walt decided to hunt for another Royal Highness.

It didn't take him long, his gaze landing on a side view of Elyse near a cluster of swanky couches and chairs. Her long black dress sparkled underneath the club lights, and her dark hair was down, spilling over her shoulders in sexy waves. It was hard not to stare, her exotic beauty making every cell in his body buzz with desire. When she turned around, all the breath left his lungs in a giant exhale. The cleavage of her dress plummeted to her belly button, the contours of her creamy breasts noticeable.

"God damn," he muttered, taking another hefty swig of beer.

She immediately noticed him and posed with one hand on her hip as if waiting for him. Lifting the bottle to his mouth, he downed the rest of his beer in two big chugs, hoping the liquid courage might tame his burning need. Setting the empty container near the bar, he stealthily started toward her, aware of a slight burgeoning between his legs. This woman was gorgeous, her figure statuesque in her sky-high heels and her eyes captivating with smoky, sultry shadow surrounding her blue irises.

"Happy New Year, Walt," she greeted.

"Happy New Year. You look… damn, girl."

"What?"

"I was gonna say, you look fucking amazing." Her engaging smile left him staggered as he leaned forward and kissed her supple cheek.

"Thank you. You don't look half bad yourself," she teased, fiddling with his bolo. "I love this tie. I haven't seen one of these in ages."

He stood perfectly still and allowed her to fuss over him, her black-painted fingernails matching her gown. It was hard not to stare at her daring dress, her subtle movements causing the fabric to gape around her fleshy mounds. He'd give his right nut to cup her breast and suckle her tit at that moment.

"Your dress is quite revealing. Kind of hard not to notice," he stated.

Her baby blues pinned him with a look he'd seen before: one part professional, one part vixen. The woman was a siren and knew precisely what she was doing.

"You like?"

She provocatively leaned forward with purpose, palming

his chest with both hands. Her breasts were dangerously close to spilling out of the shiny black fabric. He knew she was purposefully flirting with him. The need to touch her was a legitimate craving he needed to quench. Well, two could play this game. Walt intentionally stroked his finger down her warm skin, skimming the curves of her bosom. Her mouth opened in a hot exhale of breath.

"You're the most gorgeous woman I've ever seen, Elyse."

Her crimson lips curled up into a titillating smirk. "I like the way you notice me."

Chapter Eight

ELYSE

Before Walt could respond, Becky's voice cut through the music, Elyse quickly taking a step back from her hottie brother.

"Hey, Elyse. Happy New Year!"

"Happy New Year. Wow, you look gorgeous."

"Thanks. So do you. You look like a movie star."

Elyse shook her head. "You're too kind. The holiday gives us all a good reason to dress up and feel glamorous. The staff will later hand out tiaras and crowns for the big balloon drop."

Becky squealed like a little girl. "I don't know who your party planner is, but this is amazing. You've given me so many ideas for our events back at Bennett Farms."

"Becks, you need to relax and enjoy the party as a guest. Quit thinking about work," Walt chided.

"I know, I know. But it's hard not to think about all the possibilities when I'm surrounded by inspiration." She swung a pale arm enthusiastically into the air, making them laugh.

"Well, I agree with your brother. You need to put work on the back burner and enjoy tonight." Elyse eyed Becky's empty hands. "You look like you could use another drink too." The trio started toward the nearest bar. "Have you tried the Sterling wine? It was served at the Oscars."

"Ooh," Becky replied. "I'd love to try it and see how it compares to our family wine."

Elyse asked the bartender for a round of Sterling Reserve Napa Valley Chardonnay. She held hers in the air when they each had a glass in their hands. "Cheers."

"Cheers," Walt and Becky echoed in unison, clinking their wine glasses with hers.

She eyed Walt and noticed how he inhaled the aroma with his nose near the glass before taking a small sip. He seemed to swirl the wine around in his mouth, focused on the flavor as he swallowed.

"What do you think?" she asked, intrigued by his actions.

"I like it. This has classic Chardonnay tones of ripe apple, pineapple, and pear. There's also a notable acidity with an oaky spice of subtle caramel and vanilla bean." He took another lingering sip. "And I like the memorable finish. It's very nice. Great choice, Elyse."

With one eyebrow cocked, she leaned her free arm on the bar's edge. "Spoken like a true sommelier."

They drank more wine, nibbled on hors d'oeuvres off silver platters offered by polite servers, and talked for hours. Albert introduced the brother and sister duo to several people, including some Hollywood big-wigs and two other screen test candidates in town for filming. The siblings were both polite and genuine in their conversations. They were a breath of fresh country air in the usual stiff high-society circles Elyse often worked with and entertained.

When the wait staff started handing out flutes of champagne, she realized it was getting close to the midnight countdown. She stood up from the large sofa they'd been camped out on, handing off her flute to Walt.

"Here. I'll be right back."

"Where are you going?" he asked, his dark eyes raking over her figure.

"The ladies' room. Don't worry. I'll be back in time for the balloon drop." She picked up a festive plastic tiara from the side table and placed it on her head. The headband was adorned with black feathers and a "Happy New Year" cutout bejeweled with gold glitter. "How do I look?"

"Like a dream," he said with a grin.

"Hold that thought."

Clutching the edges of her dress, she hurried through the crowd toward the restrooms, eager to make it back to Walt for an anticipated midnight kiss. She'd been thinking about it all night, the hours of banter and laughter a kind of foreplay before the big moment she was sure to come.

After using the facilities, she washed and dried her hands, eyeing herself in the mirror. Her cheeks dotted with color as she adjusted the tiara on her head, the evocative smile unfurling from her lips ramped up with excitement. Back out on the studio floor, she was stunned when she noticed Walt and his sister were no longer sitting on the couch. Anxious, she scanned the room, her heart pounding as the DJ started the countdown from ten.

"Where are you?" she muttered, standing on her tiptoes.

"Three... two... one... *Happy New Year!*" the crowd hollered. The ceiling above the dance floor seemed to give way as hundreds of gold, and black balloons fell onto the guests below.

Elyse stepped back near the bathroom hallway, her focus

turned upward at the sight, disappointed she'd missed the night's crescendo. But then she felt a strong arm wrap around her middle and pull her close. Shutting her eyes, she sighed with relief, leaning back into Walt's hard physique.

"Happy New Year, Elyse." His hot breath tickled her ear.

Gripping his bicep, she turned around to face him. "Happy New Year."

His eyes smoldered as he stared back at her, mouth clenched, and nostrils flared. Bringing his hands up to her face, he cradled her cheeks with tenderness. And then he crushed his lips against hers, kissing her passionately. The air was heavy with thumping music and the smell of expensive perfume, thick with obsession and euphoria, nerves and elation. It was a sensory avalanche between the crowd's pitchy chorus of *Auld Lang Syne* and the roar of applause.

Their lips disengaged, and she threw her head back with her eyes pressed shut, Walt's nose and lips running a heated trail down her exposed neck.

"Oh, God. Yes," she mumbled, hooking her leg around his calf. She kissed him again, reveling in the pressure of his mouth against hers as balloons continued to rain down on the crowd.

Walt grabbed her by the hand and pulled her through the dim-lit hallway. Palming the ladies' room door, they were frantic to disappear into the empty room, closing themselves into an oversized stall. With the latch locked, Walt pinned her against the door and pulled back the fabric of her dress against her chest, exposing her breasts. His lips landed on a pebbled nipple, and he nipped and suckled fervently. Her fingers threaded into his hair, and she tugged with pleasure.

"I want to taste you," he whispered.

Before she could respond, he was on his knees, lifting her gown and disappearing between her thighs. She panted and palmed the door while spreading her stance, her calf muscles taut in her intentional "fuck me pumps." Overjoyed by the sensations and pure pleasure Walt was dialing up with his hands and mouth, heat flooded her core.

His lips hummed against her skin, his growl obvious. "You're not wearing any panties."

She giggled, glad she'd decided to go commando to the party. Her lack of undergarments was intentional, giving Walt full access.

His deft fingers flicked her swollen nub before she felt the tip of his tongue trace her wet folds straight up her center. Tensing for only a moment, she was overcome by the sheer erotica she experienced. He palmed her fleshy ass and grunted as he pulled her closer, his tongue teasing, and tasting. Her entire body turned rigid, and she had to bite her lower lip to keep from screaming as she reached the top of the mountain and free-fell into bliss.

Her chest rose and fell in deep cleansing breaths as she felt Walt gently smooth her gown back into place. When she opened her eyes, he was standing right in front of her, his dark hair thoroughly tousled and his lips glistening with her essence. His gaze held her captive, his brooding manhood the most seductive visualization she'd ever witnessed. As she reached out to stroke the tented area of his pants to return the favor, he grabbed her by the wrist and shook his head.

"I better get back out there before Becky gets worried," he muttered, licking his lips. He kissed her palm before he let go, turning his attention to fix the gaping fabric of her dress back over her bosom.

Elyse nodded, unable to respond with a reasonable sentence.

His sparkling smile challenged the giant disco ball in the center of the dance floor, his expression filled with glee. "You good?"

Elyse nodded again.

Cupping her cheek, he pressed his lips against her forehead in a tender kiss. "I'll see you out there."

"Okay," she finally managed, her thin voice unrecognizable.

Moving out of his way, she watched him exit the stall in a whoosh of testosterone, her feral mind reeling from what had just happened. He stopped in front of the mirror, ran his hands through his hair, and straightened his jacket. With a quick wink in her direction, he exited. Swallowing hard, Elyse locked herself in the stall and sat on the toilet seat, feeling utterly contented.

A midnight kiss was one thing—but a midnight orgasm? Holy shit! Walter Bennett was everything she imagined he could be—and more.

Several minutes later, Elyse finally pulled herself together and exited the ladies' room. She was wide-eyed and weak in the knees. Carefully, she made her way through the dancing, drunk crowd, scanning the space for Walt and his sister.

She needed to keep her wits, giving herself an inner pep-talk. "Just act natural. No one will know." Palming the empty space between her breasts, she spied the duo on one of the couches near the exit. Elyse was coy and tucked her hair over one ear as she approached. Immediately, her brow furrowed when she noticed Becky leaned against her brother as if asleep.

"Is she okay?" she asked. The loud music continued, the ramped-up crowd dancing and blowing party horns and whistles.

"Hey!" Becky blinked open her eyes and greeted her with recognition. "This is some par-tay."

Walt chuckled, palming his sister's back. "Becky's not a huge drinker. I think she might've overindulged a little bit tonight."

"Just a tad," Becky giggled, holding her hand up with her index finger and thumb showing space between them.

Elyse sat on the other side of Becky and gently moved a wayward strand of blonde hair away from her face. "Can I get you anything? A glass of water? Something to eat?"

"I have an idea—let's do Fireball shots!" Becky tried to stand but ended up falling back onto the sofa with a heavy thump. "Oooo… the room is spinning like the Tilt-A-Whirl…" She palmed her forehead.

Walt shook his head. "I need to get her home. But maybe I should wait until the crowd thins out. I may have to carry her out to the truck. She's going to be so embarrassed tomorrow."

"She doesn't have to be. It happens to all of us." Looking around, Elyse got an idea. "Come on, Walt. Let's help her up. There's an emergency exit right over there. I'll text my car service to pull around so she won't have to face anyone leaving through the front."

Walt wrapped Becky's arm over his shoulder and hoisted her into a sitting position as she moaned. "You have a car service?"

"Yes. I always do for events like this." Elyse positioned herself on the other side of Becky, and the two of them managed to help her to her feet.

Becky started bobbing her head to the pulsing bass line of the music. "I love this song," she slurred.

"Time to go home, Becks," Walt said.

"But I don't wanna go home. I wanna par-tayyyy!" She kicked at a wayward balloon in their path.

"Get the door," Walt instructed.

Elyse pushed it open, and they exited without incident into the chilly night. A few minutes later, a black town car pulled up next to them, the driver getting out and opening the back door.

"Come on, girl," Walt lovingly commanded, helping his sister get in. Once inside, he eyed Elyse with care. "I'll follow you back to the condo. My truck is parked right over there." He pointed toward the crowded lot.

"Okay. I'll see you in a few." Elyse jogged around to the other side of the car and got in. Palming the gaping front of her dress, she twisted in her seat and looked out the back window at Walt ambling toward his truck. Becky leaned against her shoulder and closed her eyes, mumbling the lyrics to Auld Lang Syne. As the car passed the rotating searchlights at the front of the building, a beam of intense light shifted across Elyse's face, the brightness highlighting her sexy smirk.

Elyse knew the second she laid eyes on Walter Bennett, she wanted him with every fiber of her being. The first night they met on the farm, the atmosphere changed on a dime, the air pulsing with electricity as if a thunderstorm rolled in. Bringing her fingers to her lips, the dizzy feeling of his midnight kiss and unexpected orgasm came over her again.

The hum reverberated through her body when she realized the wish she'd put out into the universe had manifested into reality.

Chapter Nine

WALT

"Easy does it, Becks," Walt coached. He gripped his sister sturdily and prayed she wouldn't bust it in her high heels as she clumsily walked up the front stoop.

"Do you need any help getting her inside?" The way Elyse stood there in the moonlight with her hair hanging over her shoulders and her pouty lips glistening from a recent swipe of gloss ramped up his idea.

"I'd love some help. And I'm not ready to say goodnight to you yet. How about you give your driver the rest of the night off, and I'll personally take you home in the morning?" His ulterior motive was to wipe the gloss right off her mouth in a seductive kiss before fondling her breasts and exploring every delectable curve underneath her designer gown.

"I can do that."

He swore he felt all the blood in his veins surge to his center; his walk turned bowlegged from his girth-y appendage spiking between his legs.

The town car drove off into the darkness, the actuality

of Elyse spending the entire night on the forefront of his mind. Once inside, Walt turned on a few lights with his free hand before he scooped his sister into his arms and carried her upstairs to her bedroom. More than once, his gaze landed on the gaping front of Elyse's dress, her tits tempting him to ravage her bosom later. But he'd have to be careful with his sister around. Even though Becky was thoroughly fucked up, he wouldn't put it past her to somehow catch him in the act.

"There we go, easy does it." He settled her on the edge of the bed. "I'll get your jammies out for you. Top drawer, right?" Walt made sure his sister was solidly seated on the edge of the bed before he opened the dresser drawer.

Becky dramatically threw her body backward onto the plush mattress. "What a night!"

By this time, Elyse was kneeling on the carpeted floor, unfastening Becky's shoes, and tossing them to the side. Walt offered her a grateful smile as he handed her the pajamas.

"You want me to help her get dressed?" she asked.

"If you don't mind. I mean, I can do it, but I'm sure she'd much rather have a female help her undress than her older brother."

Elyse's smile was slight as she nodded in agreement. She took the night clothes from his hands and said, "I got this."

"Great. And hey, if you want to change out of your gown into something more comfortable for the night, feel free to borrow one of my t-shirts and some sweats. They're in my bedroom in the dresser."

Elyse stood tall, her hair disheveled and sexy from the fantastic evening. "You sure you want me to stay the night?"

Before Walt could respond, Becky bolted upright on the bed, overhearing the conversation even in her intoxicated state. "Yes! A slumber party! We can make popcorn and watch a movie—"

"Okay, okay," Walt interrupted with a chuckle. "But first, you have to get out of your dress and into your pajamas." His eyes grew wide when his sister jerked her arms out of the red fabric, exposing her chest. He respectfully turned away.

"I'll be down in a few," Elyse laughed, ushering him toward the door.

Thankful for Elyse's help, Walt exited the bedroom and shut the two women inside. He waited for a beat before pressing his ear to the door, overhearing his sister going on and on about how much fun she had at the studio party and how glad she was they were friends. Grinning, he decided to leave the ladies to fend for themselves while he changed into something more comfortable.

Twenty minutes later, seated on the couch wearing sweatpants, a thermal shirt, and with a glass of bourbon in hand, he exhaled and waited patiently for Elyse to make her entrance. When she finally came around the corner, she presented herself wearing one of his oversized t-shirts. The tee looked like a nightshirt covering her sexy curves, the edges hitting the tops of her knees. Her legs were bare, and he was surprised she was barefooted, her toenails painted a bold red. A whiff of soap permeated the air, and he noticed she'd washed her face clean. Her hair was still a tousled mess, her sultry image reminding him of a Van Halen video.

"She's out for the night," Elyse informed him. "Mind if I join you?"

"Please," Walt replied, patting the empty space beside him. He'd set the bottle of bourbon and an extra glass on the coffee table, hoping she might indulge him.

Elyse sat, tucking her legs up under herself. That's when Walt remembered she'd gone commando all evening in her fancy dress. His face flushed with heat, wondering if she was still bare underneath the t-shirt.

"You, uh… got anything on under there?" His tone was low and even.

Elyse cocked an eyebrow and shifted on the seat, playing peek-a-boo with the edge of the fabric. Walt blinked a few times before he realized she was wearing a pair of his boxers—Christmas boxers, to be exact, with little red and green Santa silhouettes all over them. The same comical underwear his brother Hank-ster gave all the brothers in the family.

"Hope it's okay I snagged your undies for the night. I promise I won't mess them up."

Now, it was Walt's turn to cock his eyebrow. Mess them up?

"Darlin', I don't think they'll be on long enough to get messed up." Walt shook his head, pouring bourbon into a glass and handing it off to her. He was enjoying their flirtatious banter.

Elyse leaned back, comfortably unprovoked by his comment, and eyed him from across the couch. "Do you think Becky will remember any of this tomorrow?"

"No way. Becky's a lightweight. Always has been. I haven't seen her let loose like this since her high school graduation."

"Really?" Elyse laughed. The pleasant tone pinged the air.

"Really. But enough about my sister. I'd like to make a toast."

Walt held his glass into the air, happy she reciprocated with eagerness.

"Some things are meant to pair together—a good bottle of wine and a good cheese. A ripe strawberry dipped in dark chocolate." He paused. "But tonight, it's a shot of bourbon and a bodacious babe wearing my boxers."

Elyse eyed him with playfulness, her perfect brows arched from above her stunning eyes. He was more than ready to dive into the deep end of those cerulean pools.

"Cheers, Elyse," he said simply.

"Cheers."

The alcohol was smooth and warm sliding down his throat, his inhibitions nonexistent in his current state of pleasure. He knew he would make love to the beautiful Elyse Farrell at some point in the night, whether his sister was in the townhouse or not. Aroused by the thought, he figured, why not now?

Setting his rocks glass on the table, he stood and offered Elyse his hand. Her eyes flicked to his face as she placed her delicate hand in his. Standing in front of him, he watched her throw back her bourbon in one swallow before she handed him her empty glass. He set the glass down and stared at her glistening lips, no doubt lingering with the taste of sweet caramel.

"You're a goddamn dream," he whispered seductively.

Elyse smirked and shimmied closer to him, palming the front of his chest with her splayed hands. "You're just what the doctor ordered." There was fire in her eyes, the sureness in her tone causing him to growl with need. Scooping her into his arms, she squealed.

"You're gonna have to be quiet. Think you can do that?" He headed for the stairs, his sole purpose to get this woman naked in his bed.

"Mmmmm," she replied, nipping at his ear. Her

luscious tongue traced the edges of his lobe as he took the stairs two at a time.

The lamp on his bedside table was on, and he settled Elyse onto the mattress. Stripping himself of his sweats and shirt, he towered over her, leaning his thighs against the mattress, his dick straining between his legs.

He watched Elyse's mouth gape as she took in his length. And then he watched her pull his tee up and over her gorgeous body, exposing her ample breasts. She shifted to her hands and knees using cat-like moves, crawling toward him with purpose. Walt swallowed hard, the mere thought of her succulent mouth closed over his cock making him rock hard in an instant.

"Did you lock the door?" she softly purred.

Walt nodded like an idiot.

"Good." She ran her tongue across her lips before closing her mouth around him, the sensation emoting only primitive pleasure instantly.

"Fuck," he hissed. "That feels so good." His voice was raw with arousal.

Staring down at her dark head bobbing to a sensual rhythm humming beneath the surface, her blue eyes flicked up to his, and the sight of her gazing up at him while sucking his dick was almost too much to handle. His vision blurred, and he knew he was on the cusp of release.

"Stop... *Stop*, Elyse. I need to be inside you." Palming the sides of her head, he stepped back, his chest rising and falling in deep pants. The woman was an obedient little minx, following orders and laying back among the bevy of pillows, stripping herself of his comical boxers and casting them aside. She willingly offered herself to him in a wide spread of long legs.

Walt opened the top drawer of his dresser and retrieved

a condom from a newly purchased box. He'd anticipated a night with the lovely Ms. Farrell and came prepared. Sheathing his throbbing disposition, he crawled up and over her, leaning his forearms on either side of her head and teasing his tip against her wet folds.

Their mouths hovered inches apart, Walt's teeth bared in an exhale of hot breath. He was almost frantic to be inside her, ready to pump her hard and fast, pulled tight against his body. Clamping his hand over her mouth, her dark brows drew together.

"You can't make a sound, or Becks will hear us. Think you can keep quiet while we do this? While we fuck?" He didn't mean to sound so crass, but he'd never been this turned on before, desperate to pummel her lying beneath him.

Her head quickly bobbled in a nod from beneath his hand, her expression filled with a mixture of concern and desire, her eyes flaring with unmistakable heat and hunger.

Keeping his hand over her mouth, he eased himself into her deep heat. A strangled cry erupted from her mouth, and he shook his head, keeping his hand firmly clamped over her lips.

"Shhh," he pulsed slowly. The feeling of her pussy clenched around his throbbing manhood was nothing but pure bliss. Sweat dribbled down his cheeks as they focused on each other. "You're so beautiful," he huffed. Inhaling deeply, he was drunk on the scent of her skin and how she writhed beneath him as if egging him on.

Elyse pressed her eyes shut, her nails scraping down his lower back and over his muscular ass. Using all his strength, he thrust deeper, her squeals against his palm becoming urgent, indicating she was close. With her arms clinging to him, he pumped her hard and fast, grinding against her center.

"Oh, *fuck*, Elyse," he panted frantically. "I'm gonna come…" He lifted his hand from her mouth as his arms strained and flexed on either side of her head.

"I want you to." The erotic tone of her scratched whisper wasn't lost on him, her sultry words permitting him to let go.

He took a final deep breath, filling his lungs with the sweet scent of sex that defied description. And then his body stilled, the intensity of his orgasm knocking him senseless. Knowing his sister was passed out on the other side of the wall, he willed himself not to howl in sheer ecstasy.

His body shook in an uninhibited release of control—of self-consciousness—of everything.

Chapter Ten

ELYSE

"I'm gonna grab some water. Do you need anything?" Walt asked, pressing a kiss against Elyse's temple. He'd been softly stroking her hair back from her face, his actions emoting a relaxed stare, her droopy eyes pinned to the ceiling.

"I'm good," she whispered, finally blinking.

Walt sat up and fumbled for his sweats, shrugging them on. Elyse let her gaze drift lazily over his broad shoulders and strong back. He was a well-built guy and moved with a confident swagger that left her speechless. The smooth, hard muscles of his back flexed as he pushed himself off the bed and went into the en suite bathroom.

Elyse sighed against the bank of pillows behind her head. The passion she felt for Walt was intense, and she thought she couldn't handle it, like it might split her wide open. She'd never felt this way with any other man. They came together, both falling over the edge, obliterating every muscle and cell between them. And then he held her to his chest so closely she could feel his heart beating, his powerful arms wrapped around her with such tenderness and care. It was the exact opposite of when he had her pinned against the mattress with his hand clamped over her mouth like a kidnapper.

Funny. Being silenced and dominated by Walt was erotic and, dare she say—thrilling? Giving a man complete control and submission wasn't like her. She was usually the one in charge, calling all the shots in her career and in the bedroom.

A substantial silence settled over the townhome, a completeness leaving her immobile. Eventually, Walt returned to the bed, and she shifted her body so they spooned, pulling the sheet up to her chin. She liked the feel of his rough fingers stroking her belly; her figure pulled taut against his heat. Barely breathing, she listened for a moment, trying to remember every detail: The feel of his hands. The hair of his legs as he ever-so-slightly played footsie with her. The way his quiet snuffle expelled small puffs of air into her hair when he finally fell asleep.

She wasn't sure what they had brewing beneath the surface—or what she'd done to deserve this night, this sexy man. But she was completely satisfied.

Elyse must have fallen into a deep sleep because she startled awake, blinking against the bright morning sun streaming in through the windows. Unsure of where she was, she sat up, covering her bare bosom with the sheet. Walt was noticeably absent; the bedding crumpled where he'd been lying. The strong scent of coffee perked her interest, but then she remembered Becky and was concerned about how she might explain things if she wandered into the hallway and downstairs. There was also the problem with her wardrobe. There was no way she could hang out wearing her evening gown, the very thought of the night before and her daring commando disposition underneath the dress sending a tingling sensation straight to her basement.

Happy New Year, indeed.

Before she fell into a handsome cowboy daydream, Walt pushed the bedroom door open and entered, carrying a mug of coffee. He was shirtless, and his low-hanging sweat-pants revealed the deep V radiating from his hip flexors. When he noticed her upright in the bed, he pressed his index finger to his mouth, and she nodded.

"Good morning," he whispered, easing his rock-hard body onto the edge of the mattress.

"Good morning."

"I wasn't sure what you liked in your coffee or if you prefer something else. Coffee is all I have to offer, and there's a splash of vanilla creamer in this. Does that work for you?" He offered her the mug.

"Perfect," she smiled.

Their eyes met, something provocative and sexy passing between them. His hair was mussed, and scruff was starting to appear across his prominent jawline, his broodiness replaced with what appeared to be contentment. Running his finger lightly across her shoulder, she swooned.

"Becky's not feeling all that great this morning."

"As expected. Does she know I spent the night?" Elyse took a small sip of coffee and eyed him over the mug's rim.

"Yes. I told her you're here."

Elyse's eyes grew wide.

"Don't worry; I explained I needed your help getting her home last night and insisted you stay because it was late. I also told her I let you have my room while I slept downstairs on the couch. She believed me, but she's mortified you saw her drunk. I don't think she'll come out of her bedroom anytime soon. So…."

"So?" She kept her voice quiet, her body wide awake and ready for anything, as long as it was with Walt. "What did you have in mind, Cowboy?"

The smug expression on his face said it all. "I have a lot of things in mind I'd like to do to you." He cleared his throat. "I mean, with you."

Elyse shook her head, her lips high jacked into a wide grin, their flirtatious teasing something she enjoyed. "Well, it's New Year's Day. Did you and your sister have any plans?"

Walt nodded, taking the wind out of her sails. "Becky always makes a New Year's Day feast back at the farm. It's tradition: black-eyed peas and turnip greens, spoon bread, and pork tenderloin. She's already bought all the groceries, but I have no idea if she's still up to it, feeling like she does after last night. But I know my way around a kitchen. I was hoping maybe… you might want to spend the day here and help me cook?"

The way he was looking at her with those big brown puppy-dog eyes made Elyse light-headed. Being a Supervising Producer for a popular Cook USA Network show taught her well over the years. Although she wasn't a Master Chef, she knew her way around a studio kitchen. She also knew the best kind of pork was the tenderloin, and turnip greens were delicious when you added a big chunk of salt pork or bacon grease to the pot as they simmered. She wasn't sure what spoonbread was, but if she had to guess, it was some kind of southern cornbread dish.

"I'd love to help you, Walt. I had nothing on my schedule today. We're off because it's an official holiday."

His face lit up with an authentic country boy smile. "Fantastic."

"There is one thing."

"What's that?"

"I don't have any clothes."

Walt leaned forward and lifted the sheet from her chest, peering at her bosom. "Hmmm. No clothes? I guess you'll have to walk around butt-naked all day. I certainly won't mind."

Elyse giggled. "Walter."

His smile shone bright like the sun streaming in through the open blinds. He was a total comfort in his skin, all warmth and even-tempered. He stretched his arm toward her and lightly grazed his index finger across her cheek. "If I'm being totally honest, I'd like to see you naked again very soon." His gaze dropped to his tented sweatpants before he looked at her again.

Elyse felt her pulse quicken and watched Walt scoot closer. He captured her lips in a soft kiss. She wanted to touch him so badly, but her hands were tightly wound around her coffee mug, making sure it didn't spill.

"Did you enjoy last night?" His whisper was unrestrained.

"Yes."

Her one-syllable response made him pause. Using his index finger, he lightly traced her lips. "I didn't hurt you, did I? When I put my hand over your pretty mouth?"

Elyse felt her insides clench, the electricity between them powerful. If it weren't for his sister being in the townhouse, she'd ask him to do it to her all over again in a heartbeat.

"I'm fine. I... I liked what you did," she boldly confessed.

Pleasure flashed in his eyes, his nostrils flaring with virility. "As I said earlier, there are so many things I'd like to do with you, Elyse."

"Promise?"

They stared at each other, neither one of them relenting. The sexual tension in the room was so thick you could cut it with a champagne saber.

"*Walt?*" Becky's muffled voice came through the wall from her bedroom on the other side.

Walt dropped his gaze and hung his head, his shoulders lifting in a deep sigh. When he looked back up at Elyse, his smile was soft. "Let me go see what she wants, and I'll borrow some clothes for you while I'm in there."

"Are you sure it's okay?"

Walt stood tall, towering over her with his hands resting on his sides. Damn those deep hip flexors.

"Elyse, with you, the answer is always… yes."

Chapter Eleven

WALT

Elyse sat at the two-person kitchen table and continued breaking off large turnip green stems, placing them in a trash pile on a paper towel. The woman was comfy in her own skin, her hair tied back from her fresh make-up-free face, and her bare feet sticking out from under a pair of pink lounge pants she'd borrowed from Becky. His oversized t-shirt hung off one of her shoulders, and he had the sudden urge to nibble her creamy, exposed skin.

The pork tenderloin was pre-seasoned and already roasting in the oven. Because his sister was out of commission for the day, Walt opted for an easy batch of corn muffins from a box instead of the semi-complicated spoon-bread recipe. Elyse seemed solid, taking care of the turnip greens, the domestic scene they'd created comfortable and aromatic.

The two talked about nothing in particular, his curiosity about her back story piquing his interest. As easy as it was to get her to open up to him sexually during the night, things were a bit more difficult in broad daylight. Elyse was reserved yet pleasant, her vibe mysterious but full of confidence. Her demeanor baffled him into boring chitchat.

"I'm gonna check on Becky and see if she needs anything."

"Okay," she smiled, continuing her work on the greens.

Walt hesitated, staring at the gorgeous woman who seemed to fill his kitchen with sizzling heat. What was it about her that put him under her spell?

"Hurry back," she teased. Her breathy words put him in motion, his desire to get to know the beautiful Elyse throwing him off.

Jogging upstairs, he opened Becky's door. His hung-over sister lay across the bed, one hand draped dramatically over her eyes.

"How are you doing?" he asked.

"I'm never drinking again," she moaned.

Walt chuckled. "Yes, you will. You're part of a successful winery family. It's in your blood. By the way, Elyse is staying for dinner," he announced matter-of-factly.

"Great. Tell her I promise I'll come down later. And tell her again how sorry I am for my behavior last night. I hope I haven't blown my chances with the network."

He approached the bed and sat on the edge of the mattress. "You haven't blown anything. There were many tipsy people at the party last night. You weren't the only one."

"Ugh," Becky exhaled. "My head is killing me."

Passing off a water bottle and a container of aspirin from the bedside table, Walt gave her instructions. "Take two of these, drink all of this, and get some more rest. When you wake up, take a hot shower, and I guarantee you'll feel more like yourself. Don't worry. Elyse and I are making dinner. You don't have to do a thing."

Becky struggled to sit upright, the expression of horror comical across her tired features. Her blonde hair was a mess of tangles framing her face, her shoulders slumped with mortification. "You're really going to make my producer cook for me? God, Walter. Why don't you order take-out instead? She's our guest."

"Becks, chill-lax. I asked her to stay, and she asked what she could do to help. We already bought all the food, remember? Elyse works for a food show and knows her way around a kitchen. And besides, she had nowhere else to be today. It's a holiday, so the studio is closed. I promise you, she doesn't mind. She told me she was actually looking forward to it."

The deep indentation between Becky's brows softened. "Oh. Well, when you say it like that…"

"Get some rest." He patted her knee and started for the door.

"Walt?"

"Yeah?"

"If I forget to tell you later, you and Elyse made the most delicious meal I've had in ages."

Walt chuckled, blowing his sister a kiss. When he reentered the kitchen, he spotted Elyse standing in front of the sink rinsing off the greens. He rested his ankle on his bent knee after taking her vacated seat at the table.

"Tell me a little bit more about yourself, Elyse. Even though we've spent the last twenty-four hours together, I still don't know much about you."

Turning off the tap, she angled her body to look at him. "What do you want to know?"

"Well… where are you from originally?"

"Kansas City. I was born and raised in the Midwest but moved to New York right out of college to pursue my dreams in television. I'm the walking definition of uprooted and restless. The needle in my compass pointed anywhere but Kansas."

"Do you still have family there?"

She nodded, shaking the colander of washed greens in the sink like a pro. "I do. My dad has an HVAC business, and my mom is an elementary school teacher. They've been married for over thirty years and still live in the same house where I grew up. They're the epitome of the American dream."

Walt grinned, happy they were kindred spirits and experienced devoted parents who'd spent a lifetime together. He wished his mother was still alive to continue their epic love story.

"What about you?" she asked.

"Huh?" Walt perked up, realizing he'd been lost in thought, thinking about his late mother.

"What about your parents? I met your dad when Albert and I visited the farm. Are your parents still together, or did they get divorced like fifty percent of most folks I know?"

Walt shook his head. "My mom passed away a few years ago. My parents were married for over thirty years, just like your mom and dad."

"Oh." She wiped her hands on a towel and approached the table. Pulling out the seat across from him, she sat and laid a hand over his. "I'm so sorry, Walt. That must've been hard on all of you. Your family seems very close."

"We are." He stared at her hand covering his, the gesture sweet and thoughtful. Entwining his fingers with hers, he changed the subject. "Do you have any brothers or sisters?"

Elyse nodded. "One older sister, Ava. She's married to

Rick, and they have a young son. My nephew's name is Jagger."

"You mean like Mick Jagger from the Rolling Stones?"

"The one and only," she laughed, squeezing his hand. "Some of their friends set them up on a blind double date to a Stones concert. And the rest is history."

"Your family must be super proud of you and your career," he said. The intimacy of their conversation and how she stroked his hand with her thumb felt natural as if they'd known each other for a long time.

She lifted one shoulder in a half-shrug. "I guess so. My mom complains I'm never home, and my sister is desperate to have a little cousin for Jagger. They've never really seen me in action, only heard me talk or complain about the long hours and some of the difficult diva talent. But I'm the only Farrell in the family who's ever graduated from college, and I've been making it on my own ever since. So, I hope you're right. I hope they're proud."

Walt brought her hand to his mouth and kissed her knuckles. "I can't wait to see you in action. Albert introduced Becky and me to a few other candidates in town for screen tests at the party last night. You've been busy. I guess this isn't a done deal with Becky, huh?"

"Nope." She pulled back from his grasp, eyeing him from across the table. "But truth be told, Becky's my favorite. And I'm not saying that because I'm attracted to you."

"You're attracted to me?" His voice lilted with satisfaction.

She waved him off, not even responding to his obtuse question. "Walt, I'm the one who brought Becky to the network after discovering her YouTube channel. She's a natural. If she nails this screen test with the director, I think viewers will go gaga over her brand."

Pride bubbled up in Walt's chest, knowing Elyse was on to something. "I appreciate your honesty. Now let's circle back to that little part where you said you were attracted to me…"

She laughed. "First, I want to know more about you, Walt."

"What do you want to know? I'm an open book."

Elyse crossed her arms in front of her chest and smirked. "Are you always this charming and accommodating to the opposite sex?"

Walt ran a hand through his hair. "When I see something I like, I go after it. And then I let the natural ebb and flow of the universe take me where it wants. And right now, it's telling me to kiss you."

"Really? The universe is telling you to kiss me? Right now?"

"It is."

They were silent, the air crackling with certain desire.

"Mr. Bennett, I believe our planets are in alignment."

A crooked grin lifted one side of his mouth, and he arose from his seat, anxious to use the planetary energies wisely. "I love it when that happens."

Combing his fingers through the sides of her hair, he leaned low and kissed her with the skill of an adoring lover. When he pulled back, she looked up at him from her seated position, her dark pupils eclipsing the blue in her eyes.

"Have you always been an amazing kisser?" she asked in an exhale of longing.

Gripping the sides of her chair, his forearms flexed with strength, their faces mere inches apart. "I don't know how to answer your question, darlin'. I was just following your lead." He gave her a quick peck on the cheek and stood tall.

"Hmmm. I have one more question."

"Fire away." Walt sat back in his seat, basking in Elyse's favorable attention.

"I was wondering, how do you charm the ladies back in Langston Falls if you're still living and working at Bennett Farms? I mean, is it weird bringing dates home, or is your family open to it?"

"What makes you think I still live at home?"

"Don't you?"

It was Walt's turn to smirk. He leaned back, clasping his fingers together behind his head with cockiness. "I recently bought a house a few miles down the road from Bennett Farms. It's a fixer-upper on twenty acres with an apple orchard on the property."

"Really?" Her tone held surprise.

"Yeah. I, uh, was living in the carriage house at the farm with my brother James before…" He stopped.

"Before what?"

Walt brought his hands to his lap and struggled with his inner demons, his boastful attitude doused with uncertainty. Should he open up and tell Elyse about the Kirby family and the shameless way he acquired his new home? Or should he keep his cocky mouth shut and personify the confident cowboy façade he knew she was attracted to?

"I lived with my brother before I decided I wanted a place to call my own. I felt like it was time for me to put down my own roots."

Elyse nodded as if she understood. "Good for you, although I've never wanted to settle down. I've always had one foot out the door. Still, you and I are similar. We move to the beat of our own drums, and like you said, we let the natural ebb and flow of the universe take us where it wants. Nothing wrong with that."

Walt licked his lips, averting her gaze. He'd held one burning question close to his chest and decided now was the perfect time to casually bring it out into the open.

"When you, uh, scout for talent... do you do any kind of background check on folks? Look into their family history or anything like that? I mean, the big barbecue fella named Bubba I met last night at the party might have some skeletons in his closet. For all you know, he could be a wanted serial killer." His laugh was forced, and when he raised his gaze to meet hers, she appeared amused yet unruffled.

"We check references if anything." Stretching her arms across the table, she tented her fingers over his. "Why would you ask this? Are you concerned about Bubba, or is there something you need to tell me, Walt?"

His eyes narrowed, looking back at her. Did she already know? His brother Teddy would always be linked to the Kirby family's downfall; the media circus and headlines splashed all over the national news. For Elyse not to know what happened would be a fluke. But in the off chance she was clueless, he wasn't about to open that can of worms.

The white lie easily fell from his lips. "I've got nothing to hide, darlin'. Like I said, I'm an open book. There is, however, something else on my mind."

"I'm all ears."

"I don't mean this in a derogatory way, but I hope you and I..." He motioned between them. "I hope we're more than a one-night stand."

Her eyebrow cocked as she listened.

"I wish I could quit you, but the truth is, this thing between us feels too good. Something about you makes me think we could, I dunno, have some more fun together?" Good God, now he was babbling like his drunk sister. What was the matter with him? And why was his heart driving percussively in his chest like a jackhammer? Tilting his scruffy chin in the air, he threw a Hail Mary.

"Whatdoyasay? When this screen test stuff is all finished, why don't you take a break and come back to my place for an extended visit? I've got a king-sized sleigh bed I need to christen. You seem like you might be up for the challenge, especially after admitting you're attracted to me." He offered her his most dazzling, come-hither cowboy smile.

Her mouth fell open. And for the first time since coming to Atlanta, and without his hand intentionally covering her mouth to prevent her from screaming, Elyse Farrell had no reply.

Chapter Twelve

ELYSE

"Thanks for the great day," Elyse said.

Walt parked his truck in the guest spot outside her apartment building and turned his body to face her. "I'm the one who should be thanking you." Cupping her neck at the nape, he pulled her forward for a wet kiss, his tongue sweeping across the ridge of her mouth.

Elyse gripped his bicep, steadying herself. The way he was nipping, teasing, suckling, and moaning left her trembling with desire. It would be so easy to invite him upstairs —to strip him of his clothes and drink in his handsomeness in the safety of her own bedroom. Hell, she could scream in ecstasy all she wanted with no little sister to hear them. Flashbacks of their night together pushed at her seams, the memories threatening to overwhelm her—the rumble of his voice, the smell of his skin, the feel of him inside her. She pulled back from the lip lock, burrowing her nose into his neck, the taste of his kiss lingering on her lips.

"Walt, I'd invite you up, but—"

"But you have an early call."

"Yes. Five-thirty," she bemoaned.

"I understand." He lifted her face, holding her cheeks firmly between his hands. "Don't be a stranger tomorrow, promise?" His dark eyes held her captive, the need to kiss him again very real.

"I promise. But you should know I'll be swamped. Don't take it personally if I can't give you undivided attention like this." Pressing her lips to his again, heat flared in her belly. She growled in her throat.

"What?" He chuckled.

"I sure hope you take rain checks," she mumbled against his mouth, almost giving in to temptation.

"Abso-fucking-lutely."

———————

The next morning, Elyse fell into her natural rhythm as supervising producer. With three screen tests she was overseeing and coordinating on the docket, the studio was crowded with tech and production crew getting the space ready for filming. All three potential candidates for the cooking show competition were in hair and makeup, getting primped and ready, including Walt's sister, Becky Bennett.

Looking around the room, she wondered where Walt was, his absence making her fidgety under the stressful, time-sensitive conditions. Spending time with him over the holiday was exactly what she needed. The man was sex-on-a-stick, his deft hands, banging body, and scrumptious mouth leaving her pining until the wee hours of the morning.

Lifting a double-shot espresso latte to her lips, she willed the caffeine into her veins, scanning the room for the umpteenth time.

"Girl…"

Elyse turned and eyed her assistant, Geneva Roberts. "Hey!" Kissing both of her cheeks, she squeezed her arm with her free hand. "How was your New Years? I missed you at the party."

"I know. I missed you too. My flight didn't get in until way past eleven. By the time I got back to my place with my luggage, I knew it was too late to try and make it."

"Bummer."

"Was it fun? Did you have a good time? Or were you too busy working the floor, as usual, catering to your prospective clients?"

The pair started toward the Green Room, where an assortment of breakfast foods and drinks were spread out to accommodate the large team. Elyse watched Geneva fill a plate with fruit and a croissant, the grip on her coffee cup intensifying.

"Actually, I had a great time at the party," she said simply.

Geneva's hands stilled, her eyes going wide with the revelation. "The cowboy, right? He's the pretty blonde girl's older brother, the one you told me about when you visited their farm?

Elyse felt heat surge up her neck, her signature turtle-neck hiding the red and blotchy skin she was sure was forming underneath. She nodded, pulling her friend toward the corner of the room away from prying eyes and ears. "His name is Walt, and the blonde is his sister, Becky. She's the one from the YouTube videos I showed you."

"That's right." Geneva nibbled on a strawberry, her eyes fixated on Elyse. "Tell me everything."

Before Elyse could utter another titillating word, Walter Bennett interrupted them.

"Good morning," he greeted with boldness.

Elyse turned toward the sound of his voice, her gaze taking in the handsome Bennett brother. Her slow exhale was intentional, her inner sex goddess demanding she keep things on the downlow. "Good morning, Walt. I'd like to introduce you to my assistant, Geneva Roberts."

Geneva grinned from ear to ear, quickly thrusting her hand out and shaking his. "It's *very* nice to meet you, Walt."

"You too, Geneva." He eyed her plate. "Y'all have quite a spread going on in here. Everything looks delicious. Too bad I already had a protein shake for breakfast."

Geneva waved him off with the green stem of her half-eaten strawberry. "Just wait till you see what they put out for lunch and dinner. You won't be hungry for a week."

Elyse watched Walt with the prowess of a lioness, her senses ticking with a particular craving. She'd give up all the food in the world to have a taste of him at that moment. Clearing her throat, she tilted her chin in the air, reminding herself she had a job to do.

"I was just about to go into hair and makeup and check on Becky. Would you like to join me?"

A smile burgeoned across his handsome face. It was apparent he'd shaved that morning, his jawline smooth and masculine in the fluorescent lighting. Her fingers twitched to stroke his skin, her body craving his like an addict needing a hit.

"I'd love to."

As Walt started for the door, Geneva grabbed Elyse by the arm and mouthed "Oh. My. God." behind his back. A giggle erupted from her mouth, knowing her friend approved.

The medium-sized room designated for hair and makeup was brightly lit with round bulbs running the length of a massive wall of mirrors. Racks of clothing lined the other wall, and a slew of characters flitted about doing their jobs. Elyse eyed Becky in the far chair of the room and motioned for Walt to follow her.

"Here she is," she announced.

Becky looked back at them in the reflection of the mirror, her brown eyes holding big orbs of light. A dark-skinned woman wearing numerous jangling bracelets grinned at Elyse while holding a mascara wand.

"What do you think of our blonde bombshell?"

Elyse eyed Becky, unsure if a full red lip was the way to go. "I don't know, Shira. The lip color might be too bold, but we'll see how it looks on the sound stage. I like the lashes, though."

Becky blinked back at them, not saying a word. Elyse wondered if she was still feeling under the weather. Or was she out of sorts working with a glam squad for the first time?

"What do you think, Becky? I'm sure Shira explained that in television, makeup goes on a little heavier than you're probably used to." All three of them waited for Becky to respond.

Clearing her throat, Becky offered a conciliatory smile. "It's fun playing dress-up, and Shira here is extremely talented. You're right about the heavy makeup, though. It's a lot. I mean, you can't even see the birthmark on Bubba's cheek anymore." She motioned to the big guy two chairs over.

Elyse eyed Walt, who stood there with his arms folded against his broad chest. His expression was passive, the man clearly uninterested in makeup talk.

"Wait till I get her pretty hair out of these curlers and

styled. She's a beauty queen about to burst onto the scene."
Shira was animated, clearly enjoying her job.

"Well, we'll let you get back to it." Palming Becky's
shoulder, she squeezed. "I'll see you out there."

Becky nodded, the faraway look in her eyes hard not to
notice. As Elyse exited the room with Walt trailing behind,
she stopped in the hallway. "Something's off with your sister.
Did you notice it? Was she feeling okay this morning?"

"She's fine," Walt soothed. "She said she was nervous
on the way over here, that's all. Once the camera starts
rolling and she's working with her hands creating one of her
signature recipes, she'll be fine."

Elyse nodded, hoping what Walt said was true. But deep
down, she had a nagging feeling it wasn't something as
simple as nerves. Her cell phone buzzed in her pants pocket.
Pulling it out, she glanced at the screen, a lengthy text
stream staring back at her from Shira.

"I'm sorry, Walt. I need to respond to this. See you out
there?"

Walt nodded. "Sure."

Elyse watched him turn and head toward the sound
stage, his glorious backside causing her insides to flutter.
Eyeing her phone again, her shoulders slumped, rereading
the message.

Girlfriend refuses to put on the dress.
Says she's nervous about her tits.
Also hates the red lip.
I thought you said she was sweet?

Shira ended the text was an emoji figure with wide eyes
and a thin line for a mouth.

"Fuck," Elyse muttered under her breath.

As a television supervising producer, she understood

stage-fright was a legitimate factor, especially with newbie talent surrounded by a strange crew and a two-hundred and fifty-thousand-dollar camera pointed at your face for the first time. But Becky Bennett was sweet and a natural. Elyse had seen her in action numerous times on the hundreds of YouTube videos she filmed in her farm kitchen back home.

Albert and the director, Phil Lynch, insisted they glam Becky up to look like a bombshell. Their intention with the revealing cleavage of her dress, fluttering eyelashes, and red lips were to lure in more male viewers. But God forbid their chauvinist plan backfired, and Becky walked out before the director even hollered the word, "action." Elyse was not 100 percent on board with their vision, warning them they might be pushing the envelope. Flustered, she turned on her pointy heels and hightailed it back to hair and makeup.

If anyone was going to coerce Becky into at least trying this look out on camera, it would have to be her—Cook USA Network's only badass female supervising producer. She'd find a way. She had to.

Becky Bennett was her protégé and a star in the making.

Chapter Thirteen

WALT

Walt stayed tucked in the shadows of the studio beyond the giant cameras and crew, watching from the sidelines. He knew the minute they walked into the hair and makeup room that something was off with Becky, the vibe in the room disconcerting. Of course, she was nervous. Who wouldn't be? But he knew his sister could muster through this, her natural abilities in the kitchen taking over and revealing her massive talent.

Maybe after thinking things over, she realized this competition wasn't something she wanted to get mixed up with after all? But the potential opportunity after the contest wasn't something to snub; other contestants vying for the same thing—their own television show. But Becky never said she wanted her own show on a major network. She had her own thing going on her YouTube channel, and she was thriving and happy. Still, being invited to the city and given a chance to show off her talent in front of the big wigs was exciting. And if she hadn't agreed to the screen test, he would've never hooked up with Elyse.

Walt laughed at a joke Bubba told as the cameraman zeroed in on his chubby face, the twinkle in his eyes apparent. No food was being cooked today, the director talking each contestant through their marks in full makeup and costume. The good 'ole boy was funny, his Southern accent way over the top, and his overalls added to his overt redneck image. Too bad he sweat profusely, Shira and her makeup team having to make adjustments between takes.

Walt was fascinated looking over the cameraman's shoulder at the screen and seeing what the general public would see on their televisions at home. He was happy Elyse was always nearby, giving Bubba pep talks between the director's takes, her professionalism, and expertise noticeable. Watching her in action was pretty special.

When director, Phil Lynch, yelled, "Cut!" everyone scattered. Walt overheard him talking to Bubba.

"Great job, Bubba. How'd it feel?" Phil clapped a hand over the man's huge shoulder as they ambled out of the lighted scene.

"Felt good, Boss. A little hot under those lights, though. I felt like a QP with cheese hanging out in a warming bin at Mickey D's."

Phil laughed out loud. "Well, you probably won't even notice the hot lights when you're working with the food tomorrow."

"Thanks, Boss."

Elyse approached the two men with a smile. "Shira has another outfit for you to change into, Bubba. She'll also retouch your makeup, and we'll do another round after Becky. Sound good?"

"Sure thing."

Walt wasn't prepared when his sister made her grand entrance and walked out into the bright lights. Her blonde hair was pulled back from her face, Pamela Anderson style from the 90s, the messy curls held in a high ponytail leaving her bangs and some face-framing pieces out. Her makeup was flawless, the dark lashes and red lips accentuating her pretty features. Even her fingernails were painted to match her lips. Becky looked more like a Hee-Haw Honey caricature than a pretty farmer's daughter from Langston Falls.

But it was her dress that left him reeling with suspicion, the powder blue and white gingham pin-up style leaving little to the imagination. Good Lord, had his sister always been so… buxom?

"Fuck, yeah," the camera operator muttered, gaining Walt's attention.

At first, he wasn't sure what the guy was alluding to. But when he saw him blatantly zoom in on his sister's cleavage as she stood behind the butcher block counter listening to Phil give instructions, his blood boiled.

Walt gritted his teeth and watched as, one by one, the boom operator, stage manager, and a grip moseyed around the tiny screen to take a peek like a bunch of voyeurs on the downlow. The way these dipshits seemed to leer at his sister made him see red.

"See something you like?" His voice was deadpan as he calmly approached the group and slapped the cameraman on the back, making him flinch.

The boom operator dared to nod and point at the screen. "Check it out, man. I give this pretty little gal two thumbs up."

"You mean, two tits up," the cameraman said humorously. The men laughed.

Walt didn't think twice. Clenching his fist, he reared his arm back and struck the man across the jaw in a direct hit.

"*What the hell?*" the guy roared, falling on his ass.

The other stunned men scattered, getting out of Walt's way. Phil, Becky, and Elyse looked over with surprise, his sister bolting like a jackrabbit to his side.

"What are you doing, Walt? Did you just hit him?" She grabbed him by the bicep as he postured over the guy seated on the floor.

"What's going on?" Phil asked, waving over a security guard.

"Walt?" Elyse eyed him with caution.

Steam was coming out of Walt's flared nostrils, his knuckles turning white from clenching his fists in a death grip. "You son-of-a-bitch," he growled. "How dare you blatantly ogle my sister and coerce your sorry-ass friends to do the same?" He turned and glared at Phil. "What kind of shit-show are you running around here anyway?"

"I beg your pardon?" Phil gasped.

"Walt, what are you talking about?" Becky asked. Her ample chest rose and fell in deep breaths, the intentional cleavage of her dress causing Walt to see red again. He knew what these clowns were up to, and he'd be damned if they let them get away with it.

"Go put some clothes on, Becky. I'm not gonna stand around here and watch them film you and your... your assets."

"What?" Becky's face twisted with horror as she palmed the exposed area above her breasts.

"Come on, Becky. Let's try on the other outfit Shira laid out for you. It's a little less... revealing." Elyse calmly led her away from the group and out of the studio, but not before she gave Walt a penetrating look of unease.

Shaking his hand out, he noticed his knuckles starting to turn pink. The boom operator helped the cameraman to his feet, the guy palming his flaming red cheek. Yeah, Walt left a mark on the asshole, all right. The guy didn't dare say anything and intentionally backed up a few feet, his eyes wide with what looked like fear.

Phil ran a hand through his hair. "I'm not quite sure what to make of this. Deacon, are you okay? Do you need first aid?"

Walt harrumphed. The prick's name was Deacon? The oxymoron wasn't lost on him. The only deacons he knew of were self-controlled men of the church. What a joke. This asshole had no control; his shameless horndoggery focused on his sister's chest.

"I'm fine, Mr. Lynch. I don't want any trouble."

Phil spoke softly to the security guard, who nodded and stood tall, his beady eyes trained on Walt. The director shifted his focus and glared at him. "I'm going to have to ask you to leave."

Walt narrowed his eyes at the man. "As long as my sister is in this room with this dick-weed filming her, I'm not going anywhere," he seethed.

Phil seemed to size Walt up, his lips puckering to the side with a decision. "Well then, I guess your sister won't be finishing her screen test with the Cook USA Network."

"Man, don't do that."

"You leave me no choice. I can't have fist fights breaking out every time a man admires a pretty woman."

"Are you fucking kidding me right now?" Walt moved closer to Phil and pointed his finger in the man's face. "How dare you put my sister in this predicament, intentionally clothing her in some ridiculous, inappropriate costume? This is a fucking *food* network, not the *Playboy* channel!" he hollered.

"Sir?" the security guard warned.

Walt held up his hands. "I just have one more question, and that'll be it." Inhaling a deep breath, Walt took his time and squinted disapprovingly at Phil. "Tell me, Mr. Director, what exactly are you trying to sell here anyway? Because it ain't *pink grapefruits*."

Everyone in the studio was silent for a beat, the stage manager pressing his lips together to keep from laughing. Walt shook his head. He knew he wasn't going to get anywhere with these clowns.

"Ah, fuck off." He stormed out of the room, intent on finding his sister and getting them the hell out of there. He was taken aback when he saw Becky standing rigid in front of the lighted mirror, scrubbing the red lipstick off her face, her fury apparent.

"Please, Becky. Don't do this. I promise we can try again with another outfit you approve of," Elyse begged.

"Nope. I'm done—d u n, done!" She'd already changed into her jeans and a sweatshirt, the blue and white dress tossed onto the makeup chair in a pitiful heap.

Shira had her arms folded across her chest and rolled her eyes. "I warned you about the dress, Elyse. But no, you didn't want to listen to me."

"Shut up, Shira."

Shira threw her hands up and passed Walt on her way out of the room. "I don't blame your sister one bit. Good for you, looking after your family and taking the bull by the horns."

Walt nodded. The phrase she used was one from his own playbook.

"Walt, I'm going to the bathroom, and then we can go. I'll be right back," Becky touted with her head held high, leaving him and Elyse alone in the room.

The space between them was cavernous, and Elyse's expression appeared pained.

"I'm sorry, Walt. I warned Phil not to go this route with her—"

"You mean the country-girl slut-look?" he interrupted. "Because I think fans would have tuned in by the millions, don't you?" He didn't mean for his tone to be so patronizing.

Elyse's shoulders slumped in shame. "Believe it or not, I'm on your side. I had nothing to do with this decision. We have different looks for our screen test participants. Unfortunately, Phil was adamant with his vision, this one leaving Becky in the crossfire of the crew. But she is a beautiful girl with or without the revealing dress and makeup. She's a star in the making."

Walt crossed his arms against his puffed-out chest, mimicking Shira's earlier stance. "Don't give me that weak-ass bullshit, Elyse. You must have some say in all of this. I thought you told me you were some kind of bad-ass producer around here? Well, you're not acting like one."

All the color drained from her pretty face, Walt wishing he could take back the jabs he shamelessly hurled her way, his words wounding her spirit. What the fuck was wrong with him?

"I'm sorry. I have a short fuse when it comes to my family. I didn't mean it..." He moved toward her but stopped when she held up her hand.

"Yes, you did." Her baby blues were bright with unshed tears, and he watched her inhale a deep breath. Gone was the beautiful vixen he craved. In her place was a hardened professional television producer trying to make amends regarding his humiliated sister.

"Do you think you can talk Becky into a do-over? I

promise, I won't let any form of sexual misconduct from our team occur. I will certainly be Becky's number one advocate, and I assure you those who offended her earlier will be dealt with swift disciplinary action."

Elyse was back in business mode, her thick walls erected to keep his sorry ass at bay. The way she was looking at him with her piercing blue eyes left him reeling, the gnawing need to fold her into his arms leaving him shook. He knew he'd crossed a line, just like those pricks ogling his sister. And wasn't he just like them, using his cockiness to put her in her place? What a piece of shit.

"I can try." He meant it too. He'd take Becky back to the condo and sit down with her, going over the pros and cons of her television venture. But deep down, he already knew his sister was out—he could feel it in his bones.

"I appreciate your efforts, Mr. Bennett."

"Mr. Bennett?" His face contorted in a scowl. Why was she completely shutting him out like this?

Elyse offered him a final, tired smile before she bowed her head and walked toward the exit. Walt grabbed her by the wrist in a last-ditch truce effort. She paused, her bosom rising and falling in deep pants.

"This isn't the end, Elyse. Please don't let this be the end." His voice was hoarse with emotion, the thought of leaving on such short notice unsettling to his core.

Her nod was slight. "I look forward to hearing from your sister soon," she muttered.

Breaking their connection, she left him alone in the room as the heat from the bright makeup lights sizzled his waning anger. Closing his eyes, he deeply inhaled the unmistakable scent of Elyse's perfume left in her wake.

The woman was undoubtedly a little piece of heaven in his singular world. Nothing had ever felt better. Even though their encounter was brief, their passion was off the charts magical. Walt wasn't about to let her get away—he couldn't. He wanted more. He *needed* more.

The time they'd spent together felt like what he envisioned his forever might be—at least for a little while.

Chapter Fourteen

WALT

"You want another one?" the bartender asked, eyeing Walt's empty beer bottle.

"Yup."

Walt bellied up to the bar in the Langston Falls Pub on Main Street and waited for his brother, James, to join him. They'd completed winterizing the Christmas tree farm equipment, hanging up the last chainsaw earlier that blustery afternoon in the utility barn. They had a brief winter respite before the winery kicked into high gear in the spring. They'd spend the remaining seasonal cold days organizing and planning for the first crop, the vineyards mostly pruned, and the wine-making process one he always looked forward to.

Nodding at the bartender, who traded his empty bottle for a full one, Walt tipped the beer to his lips and took a long pull. Since coming home from Becky's screen test fiasco a week ago, he hadn't heard a peep out of Elyse. Well, except when the dark-haired beauty visited him in his dreams where his mind played back the moments they had together in full erotic Technicolor.

He'd never opened up to anyone like her before, and he chastised himself for remaining aloof since they'd parted ways. The mere thought of kissing her lips touched his soul with a fire burning bright and hot, and there wasn't a day that went by when he wasn't thinking about her. His fingers twitched around his phone as he contemplated for the one-hundredth time to make a call. But for some reason, he couldn't do it. He didn't mean to mess up what they had, but maybe he'd pushed her too far, his underlying temper embarrassing her in front of her peers.

The silence felt way too loud, yet something in the universe continually pulled his thoughts back to Elyse repeatedly. He longed to hear her voice—to feel her touch and the closeness of her body against his. But maybe he was second-guessing himself? Maybe what they had was nothing more than a one-night stand after all—a temporary trip to paradise or an evanescent flash under the sheets. The only thing he could do now was hold on to the hope she might one day find her way back into his arms. Until then, he tucked his heart somewhere good and safe, just in case she wanted it again.

"Hey," James greeted, pulling out a bar stool and sitting beside him. He motioned for the bartender to give him the same beer Walt was drinking.

"Hey yourself," he grunted. "What took you so long?"

James shrugged off his winter coat and laid it over the back of his swiveling stool. "Samantha called. She's planning on driving back from Atlanta after being in court today instead of tomorrow with the snow in the forecast."

Walt scowled. "What snow in the forecast?"

James snorted. "Seriously, Walter. What is wrong with you? Your head's been in the clouds since you got back from Atlanta." He motioned his beer bottle the bartender passed off toward the flat-screen television hanging in the corner next to the shelves of liquor on display. "Snow-mageddon is on the horizon, and you're probably not even prepared, are you?"

"What do you mean?"

"Have you been to the grocery store lately?"

Walt nodded. "Sure. I was there yesterday and stocked up for the weekend."

"Good. I have a feeling you'll be socked in for a day or two once this storm hits. The weatherman is predicting a few feet of snow in these parts." He took a large gulp. "Hey, if you want, pack a bag and stay at the farm for the weekend. At least you wouldn't be alone."

Walt eyed the TV screen with bewilderment. How'd he miss this? He knew why—and her name started with an E.

"Maybe," he mumbled.

"So, tell me about what went down in Atlanta. Becky's been tight-lipped ever since y'all came back. She told me she was disappointed the screen test wasn't what she thought it would be. You'd tell me if something happened, wouldn't you?"

Walt nodded. "I guess now's as good a time as any."

Filling his brother in on the whole wardrobe mishap involving several horny crew members, Walt watched James bristle with agitation. "Are you kidding me? You watched this unfold in real-time?"

"Yup."

"Well, what did you do? I hope you reported those guys to someone in charge. Sexual misconduct is totally frowned upon these days."

Walt chugged the rest of his beer before holding up the empty bottle to signal the bartender he was ready for another one. He needed liquid courage to confess to his brother what he'd done.

"Oh boy," James palmed his shoulder. "Walter, what did you do?"

Sighing, Walt swiveled his stool and looked his brother in the eye. "I did what any loyal Bennett brother would've done under the circumstances to protect their little sister's virtue. I punched the camera guy in the face."

"Shit, Walter! You didn't."

"I did. And don't worry, he didn't want to press any charges."

James slumped in his seat and twirled the beer bottle between his hands. "No wonder Becks hasn't said anything. You ruined it for her."

"I did not. Elyse asked her for a do-over. She even told Becky the guys involved would be disciplined. And you're right, sexual misconduct is frowned upon in the industry, no matter the situation."

"What about assault and battery? Is that frowned upon too?" James was eyeing him with an expression he knew well—one part disappointed, the other part exasperated.

"Chill out, man. Like I said, the guy didn't want to take legal action. It was one punch. Thankfully, I embarrassed the hell out of him in front of his peers and taught him a lesson." Walt waited for a beat, his next thought something he'd been mulling over since they came home from Atlanta.

"Our sister grew up slow and good on the farm, James. She's loved fiercely by me and everyone else in this family. Sometimes she acts like she can't wait to start a life on her own. But maybe, just maybe, she's not quite ready to leave. Have you ever considered that? Maybe she *never* wants to leave. Becks is innocent, pure, and sweet. I didn't ruin anything for her. She was already tuned out before she stepped onto that sound stage. I trust she knows what's good for her."

"Hmmm. You have a point. Becky's always acted like she loves what she does on the farm. And she's grown up enough to figure it out on her own, I guess."

"Exactly," Walt agreed. The two brothers sat silently, nursing their beers, and watching the weather channel.

"Speaking of what's good for you, when are you and Sam gonna move in together?" Walt finally asked, breaking the stillness. "Y'all are meant for each other. She's good for you, and I already feel like she's part of our family."

His brother harrumphed. "I know. I just… I just wish she'd find a different vocation."

Walt frowned. "You want her to quit her job? Why?"

James turned in his seat to face him. "It's complicated. You wouldn't understand."

"Try me."

James ran a hand through his hair and swallowed a mouthful of beer before responding. "As you know, Sam chose a very… precarious occupation."

"You mean dangerous, right?"

"Yeah, that too." Leaning his elbow on the bar top, he rubbed his chin. "I love her, Walt. I do. But I don't love what she does for a living being a parole officer to a bunch of low-life thugs."

"Teddy wasn't a thug, and she was his parole officer," Walt reminded.

"I know, I know. But how can I forget the run-in she had with Glen Kirby on the night of the Harvest Hoedown, huh? I watched that son of a bitch clock her good. It's something I can never un-see."

His brother had a point. "Well, have you talked to her about maybe, adjusting her career? Have you told her you're worried about her safety?"

"All the time. We've had numerous conversations about it." James finished his beer in two gulps. "This is ongoing and something I hate talking about. Do you mind if we change the subject?"

"Not at all."

"What about you? Did you kiss Elyse on New Year's Eve? I heard you made a bet with Hank you would."

Leave it to his little brother to spill the beans. All the air left Walt's lungs in a slow exhale, visions of Elyse on that magical night penetrating his mind with lust. The wry smile curling from his lips was a dead giveaway to his brother's question.

"I take your salacious grin as a yes," he chuckled, signaling the bartender for another round. "Are you going to see her again anytime soon?"

"I don't know." His voice was monotone, the unlikelihood of ever seeing Elyse a morbid thought. "But I'd like to."

James clinked his bottle with his. "It's about damn time you found a girl you're interested in instead of hanging out with the local bar whores. What are you waiting for? If you want to see her again, call her and make some plans. Go back to Atlanta for a long weekend, or better yet, invite her to Langston Falls. Hey, we could even go on a double-date if you want."

Walt nodded. "I'll think about it."

James smacked his lips. "You see, there's your problem. Thinking about it isn't going to bring you two together again."

His brother had a point, making Walt suddenly question

his every move since he'd been back home. Every night as he lay in bed, his finger hovered over Elyse's name, ready to text or call. He wanted to ask her for another chance. But for some odd reason, he couldn't do it, the fear of rejection leaving him paralyzed.

"Jimmy, would you think I'm crazy if I told you I've been obsessing over her since the Atlanta trip?"

"Wow, obsessing is a strong word, bro. The New Year's kiss y'all shared must've been something else. Sounds like a definite connection." James hit the nail on the head.

"I think it's more than that."

"Really?" James' eyes grew wide.

Walt nodded, keeping tight-lipped about another connection he and Elyse shared—their sexual connection. They were two Roman candles, too dangerous to hold. They were two hearts that couldn't be tamed. James would never understand, labeling them a classic one-night stand. But Walt knew better. His time with Elyse was more than sex—so much more.

"Call me foolish, Jimmy, but I think it goes beyond a connection. Even though it happened really fast, I honestly don't think she's someone I can live without." He was relieved to finally vocalize what he'd been feeling.

"Are you serious? You've fallen for her?"

Walt chewed on his bottom lip, realizing some kind of sentimental feeling punched him in his gut. Was this love he felt? The type of love he'd been searching for? Or maybe it wasn't love after all. Perhaps it was nothing more than a dream. Whatever it was, it had a hold on him and wasn't letting go.

"I can't stop thinking about her: every day, every night, every single second. She showed me something I want, something I can't live without."

"And what 'something' is that?" James hung on to his every word.

"A flicker. A glimpse of…" he sighed. "—forever."

Chapter Fifteen

ELYSE

The radio in Elyse's sports car crackled with static, the local station going in and out along the lonely country road. Barbwire on fence posts whizzed by as a few pretty snowflakes fell from the sky, her windshield wipers thumping an irregular rhythm.

Phil Lynch, the director of Cook USA's latest project, was the biggest fuck-up she'd ever met. Not only did he ruin Becky Bennett's chances with his blatant, chauvinistic choices for the girl, but he'd also gone directly to Albert and filed a complaint, asking him to remove Becky from the project altogether. Elyse turned livid, vocally challenging Phil in a heated argument until he stormed out of her office.

"Take a break, Elyse. A little PTO for once in your life could do you some good. This will all blow over, and we can reconvene after this first round of talent. I promise," Al had said. Leave it to Albert Tompkins, the VP of programming and her friend, to always have her back. He hadn't removed

Becky from the project. But he insisted Elyse disappear for a little while until Phil calmed down.

For the first few days, she worked from home on other work matters, wallowing in self-pity, wishing she could go back in time and change how she handled things, especially with Becky. Since the "me too" global movement, some powerful men lost their jobs in the entertainment industry, and widespread sexual harassment, assault, and other misconducts were revealed. Ultimately, the positive changes in the workplace made Elyse think about gender and power more thoroughly. Too bad she was the one on leave and not the other way around. But she understood Al's insistence she take a break, Phil Lynch was under contract and hard to replace on such short notice. It was easier for her to lay low than to shelve the entire project altogether.

"Fuck Phil," she muttered under her breath. Her knuckles turned white as she gripped the steering wheel, her unvented anger simmering below the surface. At least the time off gave her a chance to wrap her head around another Becky idea she had percolating. It also gave her time to fantasize about the girl's handsome brother.

Walt.

She wanted to talk to him about a proposition regarding his sister and could've easily called him to chat about it. But she changed her mind last minute, making arrangements with Becky for another visit to the farm. If Walt happened to be there, she could kill two birds with one stone, right? Water two plants with one hose. Get two giggles from one tickle. She smiled, remembering the idioms of her childhood, the crazy idea put into motion when she shared a lingering lunch with her assistant, Geneva, the day before. Her rebel-minded friend dared her to take a chance and just... go.

"Seriously, Elyse. When have you ever not gone with your gut? I've worked with you for years, and every time you've listened to your inner voice, you've come through with flying colors," Geneva said.

"Yes, but those were strictly *work* decisions," Elyse reminded her. "You know as well as I do, my intentions for going to Langston Falls to visit Becky Bennett are more than just business-related. I want to see Walt again."

"Work. Play. It's all a yin and yang thing, you following me?"

"I don't know…"

"What's the worst that could happen, huh? Drive up to Langston Falls, talk to Becky about your idea, surprise the hunky farmer with a deliberate lip-lock, and see what happens."

Elyse mulled over her friend's words. She made it sound so easy.

"But what if I show up and he's there and doesn't want anything to do with me? What then?"

Geneva leaned back in her café chair, the cheerful smile on her face genuine. "Believe me, he hasn't changed his mind. When he takes one look at you all glammed up, exuding independence and sexual power, he's not going to be able to keep his hands off you…"

Elyse slowed her car, squinting through the snow flurries at the signage up ahead—Welcome to Langston Falls. She inhaled deeply, realizing she was close. She could almost feel Walt in the vicinity. According to her GPS, she only had a few more miles before the turn-off to Bennett Farms.

Eyeing her reflection in the vanity mirror of her car, she smoothed a stray hair back from her face. She was wearing her customary turtleneck, intentional with her sky-high fuck-me boots. If Walter Bennett was on the farm property, she'd see to it he noticed her right away.

The black and yellow Bennett dogs galloped across the greenway as Elyse parked her car near the house. The snow flurries had stopped, the front lawn dusted with white powder.

"Hey, Elyse!" Becky waved from the front porch.

"Hey!" Elyse made her way to the house, greeting the big dogs who panted beside her.

"Come on inside. It's freezing out here." She held the door open for Elyse to go through first.

A few minutes later, with her hands circling a warm mug of homemade cocoa, Elyse and Becky sat by a cozy fire in the great room, ready to chat.

"I can't believe you came all this way. We could've talked on the phone."

"I know," Elyse replied. "But I thought it'd be better to meet face-to-face." She set her mug on a side table and clasped her hands in her lap. "On behalf of the Cook USA Network, I want to personally apologize for the unprofessional behavior of some of our crew."

Becky wrinkled her nose. "I'm over it. It's no big deal."

"But it is a big deal. Sexual misconduct in this day and age is serious. I don't want you to think this is the norm with our crew. It's not. What happened that day was unfortunate, and I promise it won't happen again."

"You came all this way to tell me that?"

Elyse sighed. "Yes. And to discuss something else. I have a proposition for you."

Becky's brow furrowed. "A proposition? I already told you, I'm not interested in participating in a network television cooking competition. I have my own thing at home, and I'm happy."

"I know you are, which makes this proposition all the more compelling. Won't you at least hear me out?"

Becky gave her the side-eye but didn't say anything, her slight nod giving Elyse the green light to explain her idea.

An hour later, Elyse was back on the road, claiming she needed to get a move on if she was going to outrun the wintery weather system moving in. But what Becky didn't know wouldn't hurt her, the detour on the back roads of Langston Falls taking her to Walt's house. When she suggested she apologize to Walt too, Becky explained he was already at home for the rest of the weekend.

Snow came down harder, and Elyse forged ahead, ready to satisfy her urge to lay eyes on him. How would he react when she showed up on his doorstep unannounced? Driving on the back roads turned difficult in her sports car, the surrounding area becoming a white-out of snow. She thought she had time, but the weather changed on a dime. Her vehicle skidded, and she overcompensated by turning the steering wheel in the opposite direction.

"Come on, come on," she muttered, gaining control. "Almost there." She leaned forward, focused on what little slice of pavement she could see in front of her, anxious to be out of this mess.

Her meeting with Becky had gone well, with the two promising to talk more in the coming days about Elyse's idea. The girl was definitely interested, which was a great sign. And now, here she was following through with another idea, surprising Walt. He was the one who practically begged her not to let their connection end, but why hadn't he reached out to at least say goodbye before he and Becky decided to go home? Maybe he'd been waiting for her to make the first move? And what a move she was making, traveling all this way in a freaking blizzard to see him.

Elyse felt the car slide again. "No, no, no... please, no!"

Easing up on the accelerator, she allowed the vehicle to come to a complete stop, aware she was on the shoulder of the road. Relieved she hadn't gone over the edge of the mountain, she leaned her forehead on the steering wheel, the wiper blades barely able to keep up with the avalanche of snow falling from the heavens. Eyeing her GPS app, she calculated the remaining distance to Walt's house.

"Zero point five. A half-mile. I can do this." Zipping up her long coat, she pulled her knit hat from the pocket and shoved it over her hair. With a long scarf wrapped around her neck, she slipped her hands into her leather gloves, thankful she'd remembered them at the last minute. Reaching behind the seat, she grabbed her oversized handbag and flicked on the hazard lights to alert any other dumb drivers out in these elements. When she opened the car door, a frigid blast of old man winter stopped her in her tracks.

Accumulating white powder edged the side of the road, her heeled boots disappearing beneath her. What was she thinking driving in these conditions, let alone walking? And what if she slipped and fell, injuring herself in the process, only to be found during the first thaw, dead and frozen solid?

"You can do this," she said, giving herself a little pep talk. "One foot in front of the other."

The wicked wind bit at her exposed skin above the scarf, and the tips of her eyelashes gathered ice crystals, causing her to blink rapidly. Her intentions were noble, but her execution was horrendous. Pausing on the roadside, she looked back at the blinking yellow lights of her car in the distance and wondered if maybe she should've waited out the storm from within the warm interior. But she was so close. And she wanted to see Walt and hear his voice, lay eyes on his handsome face, and bury her nose in the crevice of his neck.

The smell of a wood-burning fireplace hit her senses, and she knew she was getting nearer. Her body shivered with longing, her arms and legs numb in the conditions. She squealed with relief when the small ranch-style home with the green front door and shutters came into view. She counted down her literal footsteps until she arrived within a few yards of the threshold of her desire, the universe urging her forward. A few more steps, and she struggled to make it up the stairs to the front door without slipping, dropping her bag on the stoop.

With chattering teeth, she stripped off her gloves and knocked. Seconds passed, which felt like an eternity, her panting breath coming out in a thick fog. Desperate for warmth and to lay eyes on Walt, she fisted her hand to knock again and was met with a whoosh of warm air as the door opened wide.

"*Elyse?*"

She was shivering hard, her entire body matched her bobbling head. "I'm... here. Sur... prise," she stuttered, posing comically with her hands splayed next to her face.

Walt looked beyond her shoulder. "Where's your fucking car?"

"It's... back a half... mile. Down the road." She pointed.

Their eyes met, relief sweeping through her when he finally stopped frowning and smiled. "You crazy girl. Get your ass inside before you freeze to death." Gripping her by the hand and elbow, he ushered her into the warm home. Before he closed the door, he fetched her handbag and tossed it in the foyer.

"Come into the family room. I've already got a fire going."

Elyse followed him, anxious to feel the heat from the blaze. His living room was comfortable and cozy. A cup of coffee, still steaming from a recent pour, sat on a small table next to an open book in front of the overstuffed couch. A roaring fire crackled and popped, the warmth soothing her frozen features. Peeling off her scarf from around her neck, she kept her back to Walt as she thawed her face and digits with relief. A black cat curled around her wet ankles, meowing a greeting. Kneeling slowly, she ran her hands through the soft fur.

"What's your cat's name?" she asked.

"Garth."

Walt's slippers appeared next to the cat, her eyes making a trail up his imposing figure and landing on his eyes staring down at her. "What in the hell made you think it was safe to drive here through a snowstorm? Why didn't you call me?"

Standing, Elyse blinked back at him. "I was in the neighborhood finishing a meeting with your sister."

Walt scowled. "You met Becky at the farm? Why didn't you let me know?"

"I told you, I wanted this to be a surprise."

His expression softened as he reached out and pulled the knit hat from her head. Smoothing her hair back from her face, his eyes traced her features as if drinking her in. "You're not a dream? You're really here?"

She nodded, thrilled he was happy to see her. "You once said you wished you could quit me, but it felt too good. I feel the same way, Walt. I… I can't turn off whatever this thing is between us."

Walt licked his lips as if mulling over her heartfelt words. He palmed her cheek, pinning her with a sexy-as-sin stare. She inhaled his masculine scent and closed her eyes when he roughly pulled her snug into his solid warmth. Damn, he fit her so perfectly. Elyse hadn't felt right up until she was finally in his arms again. And now, everything in the cosmos was in perfect alignment.

Whatever their crazy connection was—sparks, chemistry, or even love, now was the time to figure it all out. Without any interruptions.

Chapter Sixteen

WALT

"Here, drink this." Walt handed Elyse a warm mug. Gone was her heavy coat and boots, her body bundled up in a thick quilt as she rested on the sofa in front of the fire.

"What is it?" Steam vapors arose from the liquid as she held it to her nose and sniffed.

"It's a hot toddy made with Jack Daniels, green tea, honey, and lemon juice. My mother used to make them when we got winter colds growing up."

Elyse sipped the liquid, her eyes going wide at the generous taste of whiskey. He might've added more than the recipe called for.

"Your mother fed you Jack Daniels as a kid?"

Walt chuckled. Sitting next to her, he pulled her socked feet into his lap. "Just a splash. I always felt like a bad-ass drinking these when I was ten." He grinned at the memory, feeling powerfully homesick for his mom.

Licking her lips, Elyse smiled back at him. "We once did a cocktail segment on *Sally's Southern Kitchen*. I learned a hot toddy was a natural remedy for easing all the aches and pains associated with the common cold. Better than Nyquil, right?"

"You got that right. If I made it too strong, you don't have to drink it."

"No, it's fine. Really." She took another sip, staring at him over the mug's rim. Walt rubbed her socked feet, inducing a satisfying moan from her lips.

"I like the sound of that," he said.

Her eyebrows arched from above blazing blue eyes. "Do you, now?"

He grinned, enjoying her flirty innuendos. "Tell me about your meeting with my sister."

She set the mug on the coffee table. "Well, she made it clear she wasn't interested in network television."

"Do you blame her?"

"No, I don't. But here's the thing, Walt. She's a natural, and the camera loves her. She enjoys what she does in her own kitchen on the farm, and I want to help her."

"Help her? How?"

"Becky already has a substantial following on her YouTube channel. I can mentor her on monetization, sponsors, affiliate links…"

"Wait a minute. There's money in YouTube videos?"

A sly smile curled across Elyse's lips. "Oh, yes. So much money."

"And she's interested?"

"She seemed to be. We're arranging another meeting soon. I have a ton of ideas for her."

Walt stopped rubbing her feet. "Why are you doing this?" It was a fair question, one he hoped she'd answer.

Shifting her legs off the sofa, she studied him from afar. "I have a unique ability for discovering talent. When I first saw your sister in action, I knew she was something special."

Walt smiled. "She is special."

"Are you okay with me helping her? Because I don't know. I may be around from time to time, checking in on my protégé."

"I certainly wouldn't mind seeing you again."

She considered him silently for a moment. "Tell me why you never called me, Walt? And why didn't you say goodbye in Atlanta?"

Heat rushed up the back of his neck as he averted her gaze. "I'm sorry. I'm not real good at any of this."

"Any of what?"

"Flings? Umm, hook-ups?"

Elyse scowled. "Is that all I am to you? A hook-up-fling?"

Walt ran his hand through his hair. "No… I didn't mean it like that. I don't know. Like I said, I'm not good at this."

Peeling the quilt off her body, Elyse stood and offered him her hand. Walt's breathing turned shallow, and he was tentative in his actions, easing himself off the couch.

With her hand in his, she looked up into his face with such confidence and gumption, he didn't have the where-withal to say anything, curious as to what she was up to.

"I think you know good and well this is more than a fling, Walt. If you need a label for it, think of it as…" she paused, her pretty features twisting in thought. "Think of it as… a love affair."

Walt dropped her hand and dared to hold her face, his heart ramping up with primal need when she used the word "love" with intense enthusiasm. "I do like that much better."

He pressed his lips to hers, the faint taste of whiskey hitting his senses as his tongue pried open the seam of her mouth. She moaned again, the low rumble an invitation to scoop her up and carry her over his shoulder caveman style to his bedroom.

"*Walter*!" She laughed, patting his back with both hands.

He strode through the hallway and into his bedroom, gently setting her on the edge of the mattress. That's when he got to work, stripping her of her socks and pants. Eyeing her on the bed, she was a vision wearing only her turtleneck and a G-string. He held up one finger.

"Hold that pose." He jogged out of the bedroom.

"Walt? Where are you going? What did you forget?" The tone of Elyse's voice held confusion.

"I'll be right back," he hollered over his shoulder. Opening a kitchen drawer, he smiled, finding what he was looking for, and hightailed it back to his bedroom.

"What did you forget?" she asked again.

Walt leaned against the closed bedroom door, triumphantly revealing the kitchen scissors in his hand.

Elyse scowled. "What are you planning to do with those?"

"Lay down against the pillows," he instructed, his voice low and dominant.

Biting her lip for a beat as if thinking it over, her pupils turned dark. She was sizing him up, unsure what his intentions were. When she finally submitted to his authoritative tone and laid back, he stealthily moved toward her, deliberately opening and closing the scissors, causing a snipping sound. Holding the tips of the shears at the bottom edge of her turtleneck, he paused, piercing her with a commanding look.

"No more turtlenecks, understand?"

"Seriously?" She leaned on her elbows, eyeing him warily. "This one cost me a pretty penny. You want to cut it off me when I'm perfectly capable of taking it off myself?"

Her expression was amused, the twinkle in her eye indicating she was turned on.

"That's exactly what I'm going to do. I don't like turtlenecks. In fact, I despise them."

She gasped at the first crunch of the scissors cutting through the expensive fabric, her tummy clenching as he revealed her flawless skin slowly and intentionally from underneath. He continued up and over her breasts, gripping the neck fabric tight for the last cut.

"Hold still."

Her nod was slight, her breath hitting his cheek in an erotic exhale as she stared at him. With her neck freed, he tossed the scissors to the side and helped her sit up, sliding her arms out of the fabric. She was quick with her bra, removing the lacy undergarment and flinging it across the room. Her hands immediately nosedived to his sweats. She struggled to get them untied, giggling in her efforts.

"Maybe I need to cut you out of these," she teased.

"My favorite sweats? No way." Walt jerked on the string, exhaling with relief as he shifted off the bed and stepped out of them, his raging boner finally freed from the cloth.

"I've dreamt about this every night this week," Elyse confessed, stroking him. "When you told me you had a king-sized sleigh bed that needed christening, I couldn't get the idea out of my head."

"You seemed up for the challenge, especially after admitting you're attracted to me."

Dark pupils replaced Elyse's baby blues. Staring up at him, she wrapped her hand around his shaft and tugged. "I haven't been this attracted to anyone in a *very* long time."

Taking over, he pushed her flat on the mattress, ravaging her bare chest, nipping and licking her cool skin. She was a goddess in his bed, the epitome of a man's desire. He wanted to explore every inch of her luscious curves and memorize how pleasure moved through her. Kissing the inside of her thigh, she squirmed, his fingers dangerously close to her center. They had the entire day and night if they wanted, the snow outside coming down thicker in blustery gales. If he had it his way, they'd be snowed in together for the next week.

Teasing her porcelain skin with his fingers, he rid her of the lacy G-string and lightly grazed her pubic area with his thumb. Elyse eyed him intensely, her mouth slack and her chest heaving with anticipation. He intended to discover everything, making love to her in a deep sea of blankets. They were bound to be in bed for a while.

Using his tongue, he traced her wet seam straight up her center, making her yelp. He pushed her thighs to the side and opened her stance wide. Her hands fisted in his hair as he feasted, lapping at her wet folds primed and ready for him.

"Oh, God," she moaned with pleasure.

Walt dug his fingers into her fleshy ass and pulled her forward with force. All his inhibitions were gone, his ravenous nature when it came to Elyse coming out full force. He was frantic for her to come, to let go and scream his name into the air. Kneeling next to the bed, he was rough and pulled her to the edge bringing her legs over his shoulders. He sucked her hard, and when her back arched and she whimpered, he knew she was about to come undone.

"Let go, baby," he mumbled against her soft mound.

"Oh, Walt," she sighed, giving in to the erotic bliss. He watched her shatter in front of him, mesmerized by the sight. Elyse in ecstasy was a vision he could get used to.

Desperate for his own release, Walt was quick and sheathed himself with a condom.

"You don't want me to return the favor?" she asked, her bosom rising and falling as she watched him.

Walt growled. "I need to be inside you first. There'll be plenty of time for that later."

Crawling up and over her body, he pinned her wrists above her head and plundered her glistening apex, stealing the breath right out of her. His grunts were loud, the primal need to dominate obliterating any tenderness in his actions.

"Shit, you feel so good." His voice was raw with stimulation, his kisses demanding. He marveled at the sight of her lying beneath him, drunk on the scent of her skin. The feel of her tight pussy with the weight of his hips between her thighs was heaven on earth.

When he let go of her hands, she immediately ran her fingers down his back and over his muscular ass, pulling him in deeper. Their kisses were passionate, his moves gaining speed. Sweat poured from his brow as he pushed himself harder.

"I'm gonna come…" he wheezed frantically.

"Yes." Her reply was a breathless whisper as she writhed beneath him.

His body turned rigid, the hot white light behind his eyes blinding him in ecstasy. The rope of muscles in his neck and arms flexed and tensed, his orgasm obliterating every molecule into smithereens. Collapsing next to her, he shivered in the aftermath.

"You're unbelievable," he announced in a gasp of air. He reached for a tissue on the bedside table and removed the condom.

"So are you." Elyse snuggled into the crevice of his neck, placing tender kisses along his jawline.

Walt closed his eyes and relished the moment as his body slowly came down from the intense high. A substantial quiet settled over the bedroom, a wholeness.

Eventually, he shifted her body out of his arms and lay on his side, facing her. Pulling the blankets up to her face, he tucked a strand of hair that had fallen across her cheek over her ear. She didn't even flinch, out cold from their intense lovemaking. He stared at her, trying to remember every detail—the sweep of her dark lashes. The splatter of freckles across her nose. The way she clutched her hands in a praying position near her mouth while she slept.

Walt traced her cheek with the tips of his fingers, enamored by her soft skin. Her lips parted, and she exhaled slowly. He took a deep breath, her scent flooding his senses. God, she was so beautiful, and her aroma was pure ecstasy. Laying this close, the faint scent of citrusy shampoo, perfume, and sex filled his nostrils.

This woman who came to visit was unraveling him, slowly but surely. He could feel it happening. She gently removed his hardened exterior piece by piece, like unzipping a pair of jeans that fit too tightly. He could breathe when she was near, and being in her presence opened him up, leaving him defenseless and bare. No one else had ever managed that before.

Walt eyed the window and could make out the resplendent snow falling outside, the cocoon they created in his king-sized sleigh bed a shelter from the storm. And for the first time ever in his new home, he felt—safe and sound.

Chapter Seventeen

ELYSE

"What time is it?" Elyse yawned. She sat up in Walt's bed and blinked awake, keeping the sheet covering her bosom.

"It's almost suppertime. But it feels later with the sun setting so early these days."

"Huh," she exhaled. The wind howled outside in the dark, the seams of the window humming like a human in the gusts. "Still snowing?"

"Mmmhmmm." He was grinning at her, his head leaned lazily against one arm on a pillow. "I think you're stuck here for a while."

Elyse bit her bottom lip and realized he was right; she wasn't leaving anytime soon. Leaning forward, she ran her fingernails across the ridges of his bare abs, his solid body giving off heat. "Are you okay with me staying over?"

Walt was tender in his actions, slipping her hair behind her ears and cupping her face. "What do you think?"

His full lips pressed against hers, rendering her speechless. Walter Bennett was a man grateful for his family, a hot toddy, a home to call his own, and the chance to throw caution to the wind when it came to her. They were a lot alike, and she welcomed the joy in her spirit.

"What are you thinking?" he murmured, his lips skating across her temple.

Leaned back against a bevy of pillows, she clasped the edge of the sheet near her chin. "I was thinking I like to put my wishes out in the world so I can manifest them."

"Did you wish for me, Elyse?"

She didn't know whether it was the desire in his voice or the way his dark eyes held hers captive. Whatever it was, she knew good and well her wish had come true. "Maybe." Her eyebrow hitched with flirtation. "You don't think I'm a stalker now, do you?" she giggled.

"No. I like a girl who takes the bull by the horns."

She nodded. "For the record, I'm one of those independent girl types. I hope you're okay with that."

"What do you mean?"

"I don't waste time. If I want to be with a man, I don't dillydally—I make it happen."

A low growl emitted from Walt's mouth. "Do you have any idea how much that turns me on?"

"Really?"

"Hell, yeah. Normally, if a girl stalks me, it's a turn-off."

"Uh-oh."

"But you are my exception."

Walt continued to stare at her, the sexy growl of his voice causing heat to pool in her belly. Instinctively, she knew she had to have him again. Only this time, she wanted to be in charge.

"What are you doing?" Walt opened his arms wide as Elyse shifted to where she straddled him.

"I'm taking the bull by the horns," she said simply.

"And now you're gonna ride me?" His calloused hands held her tiny waist in a sturdy grip, humored by her actions.

"That's my plan." She wrapped her fingers around his engorged penis and massaged. "You're not afraid of a woman being in charge, are you?"

Walt's eyelids were heavy with lust, his mouth in an "O" shape as she intentionally fondled him. "Hell, no." He reached for a condom conveniently placed on the night-stand, his bicep flexing magnificently. "I'm all yours, darlin'. Feel free to go to town." He handed it off to her.

Ripping the package open with her teeth, she was slow in her movements, rolling the condom on his hard cock. Rising on bent knees, she positioned her gapping center over him and slowly eased on top of him.

"*Elyse.*" Her name fell from his full lips in a reverent hiss of longing before she surged forward and kissed him hard and long and deep, their tongues thrusting with want. He threaded his fingers through her hair and tugged at the roots as she raised and lowered herself, sliding up and down his shaft.

Staring into his handsome face, the indescribable feeling of being alive came over her again, and she let the hum reverberate throughout her body. Seeing him laying beneath her, heat began to burn in her center. His eyes and mouth. His shoulders and chest. Those biceps and strong hands gripping her ass like he owned her.

"Oh, God, Walt," she panted. "You feel so good…"

Before he could reply, his cell phone rang, the tone piercing the moment like a pinprick to a balloon, letting all the air out. They both tensed, Walt, stopping her mid-thrust. He grabbed the phone and answered it.

"Yeah?" His voice was gruff, still raw with desire.

Elyse tilted her head back and crossed her arms in front of her chest, his dick still throbbing inside her.

"No, Dad, I'm good. I promise." He chuckled at what his father said next, reassuring him he could ride out the storm—ride being an understatement.

"I still have power. I'll check in with you tomorrow, I promise." Another beat, and he said goodbye. "Love you too, Dad."

Tossing the phone onto the side table, he eyed Elyse with a sly grin donning his face.

"Is everything okay?" she dared to ask.

"Oh, yeah. Everything is perfect." Grabbing her by the hips, he was quick in his actions and flipped her onto her back.

"Hey, wait a minute! I wanted to be the one in control," she laughed. He suckled her neck, and she tensed. "Seriously, Walt. No more hickeys! You destroyed my turtleneck, so I have nothing to cover them up."

He pulled back from her, his teeth bared in a wicked smile and his hair thoroughly tousled. "So that's why you wear them, to hide the evidence." He wiggled his eyebrows before diving back into the crevice of her neck, suckling and kissing her skin, the love bites intentional and sending her into a titter of more giggles. When he thrust his dick into her thick core, she was transported back into a world of pure ecstasy, intoxicated by Walt's skill as a lover.

"Come for me, baby," he whispered wantonly near the shell of her ear.

And that's all it took before she free-fell into oblivion—plunging heart first into unchartered territory.

The firelight gave off a romantic glow in the family room, the patchwork quilt they lounged on covering the wood floor arranged with various snacks and the remnants of cabernet in a dark bottle. Sure enough, the power had gone out mid-evening, Walt's home shrouded in darkness. He was quick to get the fire going again, and he even found a box of old candles he'd saved from the previous owner, lighting several of them around the room.

Popping a cashew into her mouth, Elyse looked around, mesmerized by her romantic, rustic surroundings. Her goal in the afternoon was to stop by Walt's on her way back to Atlanta, hoping for an apology and maybe even a kiss. Hours later, with her apex sore and sated, she relaxed in her lover's presence, anticipating more incredible sex and deep conversations.

Walt refilled her short glass, his thermal shirt hugging the sturdy planes of his chest. "Did you get enough to eat?"

Elyse nodded, eyeing the picnic in front of them. He'd gathered an assortment of food items ranging from nuts and cheese to dry cereal and peanut butter. Garth looked on from his sofa perch. His paws were crossed, and he blinked slowly as if bored by the frolicking humans.

Elyse rolled up the sleeves of her borrowed button-down shirt and offered Walt a grateful smile. "I was starving. This really hit the spot."

"I'd planned on making spaghetti tonight, but my stove is electric."

"It's okay," she reassured. "I love everything you have out. I'm a snack lover at heart."

"You're some kind of lover, all right." Walt paused and looked toward the dark kitchen, one hand resting on the jeans covering his bent knee. "If the power doesn't come back on by morning, I can go out to the shed and get the generator I bought. It's still in the box, but it won't take me very long to get it set up to where we could at least use the stove."

Elyse demurely angled her head and batted her lashes.

"What?" he grinned.

"You really are sweet, you know that? Taking your dad's call, making sure I'm... fed."

He chuckled, picked up his wine glass, and took a quick sip. "I like to take care of people, especially those close to me."

Elyse mimicked him and sipped from her glass. "Earlier this afternoon, I was definitely close to you, Walt. As close as two people can get."

She startled when he crawled toward her on his hands and knees. Fire flickered in his dark eyes, his penetrating stare causing her to hold her breath. "What are you doing, Walt?"

He took the glass out of her hands and set it near the foot of the sofa. With his gaze fixated on hers, he lightly edged his index finger across the collar of her borrowed shirt. She was sure the fabric hid several intentional hickeys.

"Walter?" her voice groveled. Was it normal to feel heat surge between your legs because of one seductive stare?

"I want to be close to you again," his low voice rumbled.

Grabbing the shirt, he jerked the lapels causing the buttons to explode in a scurry of plastic skipping across the blanket and hardwood floors. Garth pounced on a button, swiping it playfully with his paw down the long hallway.

With her bare chest revealed in the warm glow of fire-light, Elyse thought she had never felt so sexually unrestrained. Maybe it was the weather imprisoning them together. Or perhaps it was the romantic gesture of a fire-side picnic? Whatever it was, Elyse willingly let go, caving to Walt and his mastery of seduction.

She'd allow him to be as close as he wanted for as long as he'd have her.

Chapter Eighteen

WALT

Walt held Elyse the entire night, both of them naked under a fort of blankets in front of the fire. Before they fell asleep, they took breaks from sex to nibble on snacks, drink wine, and talk. The woman was pretty shameless when it came to lovemaking. She was vocal, flirty, and not bashful about letting him know what she liked and how she liked it. She told him when she needed him to slow down or speed up, and when she wanted it harder or less intense. He would've never guessed Elyse was this way by looking at her. She seemed all put-together in her black turtlenecks, sky-high heels, independent nature, and demands. Walt liked this other side of her. He liked knowing her secrets.

Stoking the fire with the early morning light coming in through the windows, Walt paused and looked out at the winter wonderland. The gnarled branches of the apple trees were outlined in white, the meadow a pristine blanket of accumulated snow. His backyard didn't look real, the ice crystals glinting as the sun arose on the horizon.

After throwing a few logs onto the fire, the wood hissed

among lingering hot coals, flames coming to life almost immediately. The room was colder than usual since the power was out, and he hurried to get back under the blankets with Elyse.

"Good morning," Elyse hummed, snuggling her heat into his naked side.

"Good morning."

They were quiet for a moment, studying their fingers laced together in the watercolor light. Garth mewled, hopping on top of them and head-butting Walt with his forehead.

"Hey, fella. Good morning to you too," he said, stroking the animal's fur.

Elyse giggled and sat up. Garth purred and kneaded his paws on her blanketed lap. She was taken aback when he turned and held his rear end near her face.

"Don't worry," Walt chuckled. "That's a sign of affection."

"His butt in my face is a sign of affection?" she laughed.

Walt scratched the base of Garth's tail, inducing an arched back and another meow. "He's flirting with you because he thinks you're pretty."

"Garth thinks I'm pretty?" She looked at him with a "you gotta be kidding me" expression.

"Of course he does. Just look at him, all tomcat and full of swag." He chuckled and watched Elyse scratch underneath Garth's chin. "He's also hungry and thinks you might cave and feed him."

"I can feed him." Flinging the blanket off her naked body, she stood and shivered, crossing her arms against her chest. "Good Lord, it got cold in here overnight."

Walt stood and draped a blanket over her shoulders.

Their eyes met, something sweet and loving passing between them. "I'll keep you warm."

She eyed him provocatively. "Hold that thought. Where do you keep the kitty food?" She padded barefooted toward the kitchen, clutching the blanket around her. Garth followed happily at her heels.

"First cabinet on the left near the fridge in a Tupperware container." Relaxed, he shifted and stared at the substantial flames in the fireplace.

"One scoop or two?"

"One."

The immediate sound of dry cat food hitting a metal dish was heard, Elyse's high-pitched voice sweet as she cared for his cat. "There you go, Garth-y. Bon appétit."

Walt laughed quietly, humored by her cute side.

"What?" she asked, looking down at him with the blanket held tight across her body. Her hair was a wild mess, her cheeks dotted with color. When he focused on the hickey on her neck, she seemed to track with his gaze and palmed her throat. "I told you not to do that."

Walt stood buck naked and slyly came toward her. Tracing the passion mark with his finger, she seemed to hold her breath.

"Does it hurt?"

"No," she whispered. She grabbed his index finger and playfully bit down on his flesh. "But I'm gonna need my makeup to cover it up."

"Why? The roads are probably closed. No one will come by until all this weather passes and the plow trucks come through."

"I'd still like to get my bag from my car." She opened the blanket wide, allowing him to join her in the warm folds.

"You packed a bag?" He nipped at her earlobe as she wrapped her arms around his middle, her warmth pressed against his.

"I did. Too presumptuous of me?"

Holding her face in his hands, he reveled in the intense ice blue of her eyes. "You were thinking ahead, prepared to stay with me. I love that."

Elyse licked her lips and stared at him up close. Between the roaring fire, the heat from her bosom, and the scent of sex on her skin, he was in sensory paradise.

"I'll get dressed and brave the elements to get it for you."

She rewarded him with a seductive smile. "Are you sure?"

"Absolutely." He tenderly kissed her.

"Good, because I need to take my pill."

"Your pill?" His brow furrowed, concerned she had to take medication.

Using her fingernail, she traced his lips slowly. "My birth control pill."

When their eyes met, he inhaled a deep, invigorating breath, his manly chest inflating like his dick. "Does this mean..."

"—yes," she interrupted. "Unless you have some kind of underlying condition."

"Nope. I'm clean, I swear."

"Me too." The blue of her eyes reminded him of gas flames, searing and intense.

He kissed her cheek, excited to feel her—*all* of her again. "I won't be long."

Walt dashed into his room, digging through his drawers for his wooly socks and long underwear. Dressed in his warmest clothes, he pulled on the waterproof work boots he wore on the farm and laced them up.

"I feel like I should come with you."

Walt looked up to see Elyse leaned against the doorway with the blanket snug around her. He shook his head.

"No. You stay here where it's warm by the fire. I won't be long. Can you get me your car keys?"

She looked around the decimated room, their discarded clothing from the night before tossed here and there among the rumpled bedding. "Where did I put my handbag when I arrived?"

Walt snapped his fingers. "It's in the foyer. Come on." He grabbed her by the hand and walked briskly to the front of the house. Sure enough, her designer bag was near the front door, where he'd dropped it.

Elyse bent low and produced her car keys, dropping them into the palm of his hand. "Don't you need a hat? It's freezing out there," she fretted.

Plucking his black leather cowboy hat off the hall tree, he placed it on his head. "I'll be right back. Don't go anywhere."

"I won't," she giggled.

Trudging through the drift of snow on his front porch, Walt forged ahead. When he got to the top of his drive, he noticed the street had already been plowed, which was a good sign. His hot breath produced a cloud of fog as he continued down the road, a sly smile burgeoning on his face when he thought about Elyse waiting for him. Damn, the girl was sexy, fun, and everything he ever dreamed of in a woman. Could he dare to think she might want to pursue something more with him?

But they came from two different worlds. She was a freaking television producer. And what was he? A farmhand? A redneck sommelier? It could never work—or could it?

Walt eyed Elyse's car up the road, the hazard lights dark. "Damn," he muttered, knowing her battery must've died. Good thing he had some jumper cables in his truck. He'd get it started later in no time. Stomping the snow off his boots near the back of the vehicle, he fished out her car keys and popped the trunk. Sure enough, a small roller bag was sitting in the immaculate space, the signature Gucci design hard not to notice.

Pulling the bag behind him, he looked around his surroundings, praying no one might pass him on the roadside. There wasn't a soul in sight, the air still and crisp, the rolling hills and meadows a blanket of unscathed pure white with the North Georgia Mountains in the background.

"I'm a Gucci cowboy," he laughed. If any of his brothers saw him now, he'd never hear the end of it.

Chapter Nineteen

ELYSE

There wasn't much to do while Walt was gone except sit and wait. A hot shower would've been nice, but no power meant no hot water. Snuggling into the fabric of the wool blanket wrapped around her naked body, Elyse stared into the fire. The bright flames were mesmerizing, the heat lulling her into a relaxed state. Garth hopped up on the far end of the hearth and licked his paws, satisfied from his kitty meal.

The only sounds in the room were of the fire and a low purring from the cat. Glancing out the window, Elyse noticed gray snow clouds in the sky and marveled at the earth below covered in white. More winter weather looked like it was on its way. Her current setting and circumstances in her romantic igloo in the country were surreal, to say the least, her life at the studio tucked in the furthest recesses of her mind. Walt was everything she imagined he could be and more; their snowed-in situation like something out of a romantic movie.

Her eyelids drooped, and her body relaxed as the small

room warmed up. The ache between her legs hurt so good, the pain and pleasure something she wanted to explore again. Sex with Walter Bennett was the best she'd ever had, the man a regular Romeo sweeping her off her high-heeled feet. But as much as he wooed her with his romantic skill under the covers, he was also powerfully commanding, dominating her into submission. What was up with that? She'd never willingly allowed a man to rule over her, and her need for Walt shocked her. Oh, how she wished she could stop time and stay wrapped up in him, savoring every moment and making it last.

While trying to stay awake for Walt's return, Elyse stood with the blanket wrapped around her and ambled toward the bookshelf flanking the fireplace. Her eyes roamed the trinkets, books, and mementos arranged on the shelves giving her a glimpse into Walt's bachelor life. Picking up a framed photo, she smiled, knowing it was his entire family from several years ago, posed outdoors in front of the red barn at Bennett Farms. She recognized each youthful face, Roy, Ted, James, Walt, Hank, and Becky, joyful in their expressions. But there was one face she didn't recognize, the woman standing in the middle among the brood with her arms around Roy and Walt.

"Mrs. Bennett," Elyse whispered.

The woman had the same smile as Walt, her happiness apparent being surrounded by her loved ones in the snapshot. She remembered Walt telling her his mom had passed away. A shot of empathy pulsed to her heart as she put the picture back in place, thoughts of her own mother coming to mind. It had been a long time since she'd returned home to Kansas City for a family visit. Maybe it was time? She had to admit she missed her sister, Ava, and her funny husband. And the thought of her nephew, Jagger, made her pause. She thought he must be close to three years old by now. Is that how long it'd been since she'd seen her family? Three years? She decided right then and there she needed to do better. And booking a flight and taking some more personal time off to see her family might be good for her. Her mother's smile lingered in her memory, knowing she'd be ecstatic.

Perusing the books on the shelf, Elyse determined Walt was a thriller and science fiction fan. He also liked biographies, especially when it came to American presidents. A couple of old sports trophies gathered dust next to a few shiny plaques and distinctions from the wine world. Elyse ran her fingers across a diamond-shaped sparkling glass award. She was impressed, especially knowing wine competition judges were generally very disciplined and followed strict guidelines when tasting wines and awarding medals. That the Bennett family winery was acknowledged with competitive awards was amazing, and she wondered what Walt contributed to the win.

The relative quiet was interrupted by the front door opening and closing. Elyse turned around with a beaming smile, half expecting to see Walt come strolling in. Garth darted toward the hallway leading to the bedroom and disappeared.

"That didn't take you long. Did you find my car buried in the snow?"

She waited for a beat for him to reply. When he didn't, she furrowed her brow, clutching the blanket tighter around her body.

"Walt?"

The sound of boots on the floorboards grew louder, and when a strange man came into view, Elyse gasped.

"Where is he?" the large, bearded man gruffly asked.

His heavy camouflage coat matched his pants, and his boots were substantial and covered in remnants of snow. The man looked like he'd just arrived from a hunting trip.

"I'm sorry, you are...?"

The man swayed in his stance, his hairy face fixed in an exaggerated frown. His beady eyes roamed her figure from head to toe, making Elyse self-conscious.

"I'm... a friend of the family," he finally uttered. Grabbing the knit hat from his head with his thick fingers, he shoved it into his coat pocket and revealed a mess of overgrown hair. The man looked like a beast.

Elyse felt the tiny hairs of her arms prickle with a warning. This man wasn't a friend of the family. He would've knocked before entering or at least apologized for the deliberate intrusion if he was.

"Do you always make it a habit of coming in without knocking?" she dared to ask.

"Just tell me where he is. Where's Walt?"

Elyse dug deep and tried to remain calm. That's when she eyed the dark-stained mantle and noticed a shotgun slid all the way back to the stone edge of the fireplace. If she hadn't been standing this close, she would've never noticed it before.

"He's, uh... indisposed. I'll go, uh... tell him you're here." She started for the hallway, gripping the blanket tightly around her naked body.

"I'll be waiting." His tone was sinister, which made her jog a little faster.

Behind the closed and locked door of the freezing bedroom, Elyse looked frantically around for her pants and a shirt. She knew Walt would be back any minute but wanted to warn him about their unexpected visitor. If the man knew him by name, surely everything was okay, right?

Maybe he was, in fact, hunting in the area and wanted to stop by and say hello? Or perhaps he was just checking in on his friend since the weather turned dire?

Fully dressed and with socks covering her feet, she flung the sheets and blankets back, searching for her cell phone. Eyeing her handbag sitting on a chair, she dug deep, her heart pounding in her chest. Garth hopped up onto the chair and meowed. A knock on the door made her freeze her actions, the cat scampering under the bed.

"I'll be right there," she hollered. Her voice was two octaves higher than usual, the fear in her tone noticeable. "There it is," she whispered tersely. Pressing the phone screen, her cold fingers bumbled out a text message to Walt.

A strange man is in the house. He says he's a friend, but I'm scared.

She pressed send and immediately knew she was screwed when his phone pinged from the bedside table.

"*Shit*," she whispered. Pacing for a few seconds, she struggled to develop a game plan. Pulling up her big girl panties with courage, she took a deep breath and opened the door.

"Hi," she greeted the man on the other side. She walked right passed him with her held high, acting as if nothing was amiss. She was intentionally casual in her movements, her words careful in conversation.

"Walt stepped out for a few minutes. Since you're a friend of his, why don't you wait for him in the family room where it's warm by the fire. How are the roads out there anyway? Would you like something to drink?"

She was now in the kitchen, the man eyeing her with unease and remaining quiet. Grabbing a bottle of whiskey from the counter, she showed it to the stranger. "How does a shot of whiskey sound?" Her smile was forced.

The man eyed the bottle and opened his mouth, about to say something, but was immediately distracted and looked beyond her out the kitchen window over the sink. Jerking her head to see what he was looking at, she was horrified to see Walt trudging his way toward the house with her designer roller bag making tracks in the snow behind him, oblivious to what was happening inside.

Elyse wanted to scream his name at the top of her lungs in a warning but was stopped short when the man grabbed her around the waist and clamped his callous hand over her mouth. She lost her grip on the bottle of whiskey, and it crashed to the floor.

"You say one word, and this'll get ugly. Do you understand?" His hot breath skated over her ear, his menacing words sending a chill up her spine as he held a gun near her face so she'd see it. She nodded aggressively, submitting to the man's evil request.

"I want you to stand by the fireplace. Not a word, ya hear? Go on." He pushed her with force, and she stumbled, her body numb with terror. Her socked foot hit a puddle of whiskey and a shard of glass from the broken bottle. She grimaced, squeaking in pain, knowing she'd been cut.

She walked toward the flames in slow motion, the hellfire dancing in her wide, petrified eyes. Turning around, she stood there with her hands obediently clasped in front of her with her head held high. The sound of the front door opened and made her jump, Walt's innocent voice booming with life.

"Hey, I'm back," he hollered. "Did my dad come by? There are boot footprints through the front yard and all over the stoop."

Elyse knew he was taking off his cowboy hat and coat, unaware of the surprise lumberjack visitor awaiting him inside. Her eyes flicked to the kitchen, where the strange man hid in the dark shadows. She wondered if he could hear her heart slamming against her ribs.

"Elyse? Did you hear me? Who stopped by?" Walt appeared and stopped in his tracks when he noticed her, a look of disappointment marring his handsome features. "Why'd you get dressed? I was hoping to find you naked and waiting for me in front of the fire." His lip twitched in a sly smile.

Every part of Elyse shook uncontrollably, and it wasn't from the cold. When she didn't answer, he parked her roller bag and put his hands on his hips.

"What's wrong?"

Out of her peripheral vision, Elyse saw the stranger move. On instinct, she yelled, "*Run!*"

Walt startled as the man jumped out and aggressively pointed the gun in his face. Raising his hands high into the air, he bristled. "*Glen?*"

He waved the gun toward Elyse. "Get over there and stand next to her."

"Glen? What are you doing here? What do you want?"

"*Shut up!* Do as I say and get over there."

Elyse held her hand out, her fingers splayed and shaking, anxious for Walt to take her hand and follow orders. "Please, Walt. Come here."

Walt walked toward her, unhurried and keeping his focus on Glen. His jaw was clenched, and his broody eyes squinted at the man. Grasping her hand, Elyse limped into his arms and clung to him with fear. Walt's gaze shot to her blood-soaked sock, and he kneeled to take a look.

"Are you hurt? *Did you hurt her?*" he roared, jerking his head and glaring at Glen.

"*No*, Walt! He didn't hurt me, I swear. I… I dropped the

whiskey bottle and accidentally stepped on a piece of glass. I'm fine, Walt. Really." She talked fast, fearing Walt might retaliate and lunge at Glen if he thought the man had deliberately wounded her. The thought of the gun going off in the melee was terrifying.

"Right, Glen?" Elyse continued. "We met, and I offered you a drink, and then, silly me, the bottle slipped from my fingers and crashed to the floor." She was trying to diffuse the situation.

Walt slowly arose and firmly positioned himself as a shield, protecting her from Glen and his weapon. Holding out his hand, he spoke in an even tone. "Give me the gun, Glen. You look like shit, and you're obviously on something. Come on, we can hash this out fairly, but first, you need to give me the gun."

"Fuck you, Walt. I'm not giving you anything. You're the one who needs to be doing all the giving around here."

The two were in a standoff of sorts, Elyse confused. "What are you talking about, Glen? What is it you want?" she asked.

His laugh was sinister as he ran a hand down his scruffy, unkept beard. "I want back what's mine."

"I don't understand." She squeezed Walt's bicep from behind him, anxious for an explanation. When Walt didn't reply, Glen sauntered closer, lowering the gun to his side.

"This house and land belong to me. It's been in my family for over fifty years."

Walt remained rigid in his stance, his chest rising and falling in slow, even breaths. Noticeable sweat beaded across Glen's forehead, and there were dark circles under his eyes. Walt was right. Glen was obviously high on something.

Elyse frowned. "But... this is Walt's house. He lives here

now. He told me he recently bought the place and moved in. He even has a cat."

Glen threw up his arms in exasperation, the gun swinging erratically in his hand. "Are you kidding me? You kept my fucking cat?"

Walt backed Elyse up to the bookshelf keeping his body protectively in front of her. She glanced at the shotgun on the mantle, so close she could see the trigger. She wondered if it was loaded.

Glen's eyes were slits, narrowing at the pair, his voice turned down a notch as he threatened them. "You stole everything right out from under me." He cocked the gun and pointed it at Walt's chest.

"It's time I took back what's mine."

Chapter Twenty

WALT

Walt knew his shotgun was within arm's reach as he sheltered Elyse with his body next to the fireplace. But was there enough time to grab it before Glen pulled the trigger?

"Okay, it's yours. You can have it back, Glen. All of it."

Glen's forehead wrinkled in confusion, his swaying stance relaxing for a millisecond. "What?"

That's when Walt took action, shoving Elyse to the ground and grabbing the butt of his shotgun off the mantle. Glen's gun went off, barely missing Walt's shoulder, striking the diamond-shaped wine award on the bookshelf in an explosion of shattered glass.

Walt closed one eye and aimed the gun at Glen's head, his focus intense and his adrenaline pumping. Glen mimicked his stance, aiming his handgun at Walt as Elyse coward in the corner.

"Put the gun down, Glen," he instructed through gritted teeth. "You don't want to do this. I don't want to do this."

Sweat poured from Glen's brow, and his breathing turned erratic. His hand shook, trying to steady his aim, and then he did something Walt didn't see coming. He switched his focus and the gun toward Elyse on the floor.

"Okay, okay, Glen! You win!" Walt turned frantic, setting the shotgun on the floor. Holding his hands in the air, he was thankful Glen's attention diverted back to him.

Glen swiped his free hand across his sweaty brow, his face turning red. He looked—odd, his face twisting in a spasm. When his breathing turned labored, he palmed his chest. Walt knew something was drastically wrong.

"Glen?" Walt kept his hands in the air, astonished at what was happening right in front of them. Glen's eyes rolled into his head, and he fell backward with a thud. The gun escaped the clutch of his hand and skidded safely across the hardwood floor.

Walt looked over at Elyse, who dared to lift her head from under the shelter of her arms, the look on her face indicating she was terrified. Rushing to her side, he pulled her into his embrace and rocked her on the floor.

"Are you okay?" he whispered, peppering her cheek with tiny kisses.

"Yes." She was breathless, her entire body trembling in the aftermath. "What just happened?"

"I'm not sure."

"Did he pass out? Is he okay?"

"I don't know."

The two stared at Glen for a beat before Walt cautiously crawled toward the wayward handgun and snatched it up. Tucking it into his back pocket, he grabbed the shotgun and shoved it under the couch. Standing, he approached Glen and used the toe of his boot to gently probe him in the side, the large man's shallow breathing concerning.

Elyse stood next to Walt and clung to his arm. "He doesn't look so good. Do you know if he uses drugs? Or maybe all this excitement gave him a heart attack?" When she looked up at him, her eyes were wide and dark, the look of pure terror etched across her features.

"I wouldn't doubt it."

Walt knelt next to Glen and unzipped his coat. The man was out cold, his skin turning a blueish gray color.

"Help me sit him up so we can get this North Face off him. Maybe he passed out from the heat of the fire in the room."

Elyse nodded and came around to the other side of Glen, the two of them working quickly to get the heavy winter coat off him. As Walt propped Glen against a bank of pillows next to the couch, he heard Elyse gasp. Turning to look at her, he noticed the coat in one of her hands and drug paraphernalia in the other. She must've found them in his pockets.

"Fuck," Walt cursed under his breath. His focus shifted to Glen, and he gently patted his bearded cheeks. "Glen? Glen, buddy, you all right? Tell me you're all right."

Elyse rushed out of the room in a flash, Walt figuring she was in search of her cell phone to call 9-1-1. But when she returned, she held a strange contraption in her hand. He frowned.

"What is that?"

"It's Naloxone in an auto-injector." She knelt next to Glen's legs and stripped a red safety guard from the rectangular gadget.

"Are you shittin' me?" He was in awe watching her press the black end firmly against Glen's camouflaged thigh.

Out of breath, Elyse tried to explain. "I've never had to personally use one of these before, but I've seen one of the directors at the studio use one on an actor who was having an overdose in the makeup room." A click and hiss sound was heard as she held it steady. "The needle injects medicine that can stop an overdose. The studio passed these out to all staff, just in case." She continued to count to five. "One, two, three, four, five... there." She sat back on her knees, her chest rising and falling in deep breaths. "Can you roll him over on his side? We need to call for help."

As she started to stand, Walt gripped her by the wrist, pulling her back down. "How did you know?"

Elyse motioned with her head toward the discarded plastic bag she'd found in Glen's coat pocket, along with a lighter and a pack of rolling papers. "I think the white powder in the baggie is heroin. If it's not, the medicine I injected into his thigh won't hurt him. But if it is, I may have just saved your friend's life."

Friend? Glen wasn't his friend; he was the enemy. They looked at each other, the enormity of their situation alarming.

"I'll call the authorities so I can explain the quickest way out here in the middle of nowhere. Are you good to stay here for a minute while I get my phone from the bedroom?"

Elyse nodded. "I'll keep a close eye on him and make sure he keeps breathing. Hurry!"

Walt trotted into his bedroom and spotted his phone on the bedside table. When he held it up to make the call, he immediately noticed an earlier text from Elyse.

A strange man is in the house. He says he's a friend, but I'm scared.

His shoulders sagged, knowing she'd been frightened, his protective nature urging him on. With phone in hand, he returned to the living area and took in the scene. Right away, he noticed snow falling again outside the window. Elyse had tucked a blanket around Glen and sat stoically by his side, patting his shoulder with tenderness. Even after all of Glen's past threats to his family, severely injuring Teddy, trespassing, and firing a gun in his house nearly hitting him in the last fifteen minutes, Walt wasn't an evil man. He knew deep down Glen Kirby was a troubled soul, and right now, he needed some serious help. If Walt could give that to him, perhaps they'd finally be able to call a truce.

"Did you call the police?" Elyse looked up at him, her voice calm and composed.

"Not yet." Punching in the numbers, he waited for a ringtone. His phone remained silent, and he pulled it from his ear to check his battery power and bars of service. Being out in the middle of nowhere had its drawbacks, one of them being sketchy cell phone service, especially during bad weather.

"I'm not getting any service," he announced. "Where's your phone? Maybe you'll have better luck."

"Let me get it."

As Elyse disappeared, Walt paced in front of the large picture window looking out over his backyard and apple orchard. It was snowing heavily again, the falling frozen precipitation swirling in blustery gales. There was no way he could chance transporting Glen to the hospital in this mess without four-wheel drive.

Elyse returned with her phone in her hands, scowling at the screen. "I don't have any service either." She studied him silently for a minute. "Walt, what are we going to do?"

He reached for her hand, her immediate touch a lifeline in their precarious circumstances. With her fingers curled around his, he brought her hand up to his mouth and kissed her knuckles. "We sit and wait... or..."

"—or what?" Her voice was laced with hope.

"Or I go outside and investigate. Did you hear the

sound of a motor or an engine before Glen waltzed in unannounced?"

Elyse pressed her top teeth into her lower lip and shook her head. "No. I didn't hear anything, just his footsteps."

"Hmmm." Walt looked around for Glen's discarded coat and snatched it up. Feeling around in the pockets, his fingers landed on a set of keys. Fishing them out, he held them up for Elyse to see. "Aha! He must've parked his truck or an ATV vehicle close by. I'll go outside and see if I can find his tracks in the snow."

Walt shrugged on Glen's coat and started for the front door.

"Walt, wait!" Elyse pleaded. "It's a blizzard out there. What if you get turned around and can't find your way back?"

Walt cocked his head and smiled, touched by her concern. "I promise, I won't go beyond the road. Knowing Glen, he was trying to be sneaky and probably parked in a wooded area nearby. I'll be careful."

They walked to the foyer, where Elyse slowly wrapped a thick scarf around his neck. She started to say something but quickly stopped.

"What?" he asked, shoving his fingers into waterproof gloves.

Her blue-flame eyes traced his features, her face so pretty and intense it hurt. "Is it true what Glen said earlier? Did you steal this house and land from his family?"

Walt shook his head, disappointed she thought so little of him. "No, Elyse. I bought it from his mother, fair and square."

"Then why does he think you stole it?"

Walt rested his gloved hands on her shoulders. "It's a

long, complicated story I'll tell you later. Right now, I need to find Glen's vehicle so we can get him the help he needs."

"If you're not back in fifteen minutes, I'm coming outside to find you."

Walt chuckled, amused by her bravery. "I bet you will." Pulling Glen's handgun from his back pocket, he offered it to her. "Keep this on your person at all times. If Glen wakes up while I'm gone and goes berserk, you may need it to threaten him."

Elyse nodded, taking the weapon from his hands.

"Have you ever shot a gun before?" he asked.

"No. But I'm not afraid to."

Chapter Twenty-One

ELYSE

Elyse added another log to the fire and watched the sparks shoot up into the flue. The cold metal of the gun pressed against her hip as she shifted to look at Glen, who was still passed out on the floor. Crossing her arms, she watched his chest rise and fall in slow, labored breaths, thankful he hadn't overdosed.

After tending to a superficial cut on her foot, she borrowed Walt's slippers and found a broom and dustpan in the kitchen pantry. She was glad she had something to do while Walt was away. The shards of glass from the whiskey bottle and destroyed winery award cleaned up in no time. As she was about to put the broom back in place, she heard Glen moan from the other room. Peeking her head around the corner, she was wide-eyed and watched him struggle to sit up.

"Glen? Maybe you should lay back down." She was next to him in a flash, the feel of the gun on her hip giving her courage.

"Wha... what the hell happened?" He held his palm against his head, his voice scratched and breathy.

Elyse helped him into a sitting position, adjusting the pillow behind his back. "You had... an episode. You passed out."

"I don't feel so good," he groaned. "You got any water or something to drink?"

"Sure." She quickly got him a glass of water from the kitchen tap. "Here you go. Take it nice and slow."

Glen slurped a few swallows before he eyed her with confusion. "Who are you, and why are you being so nice to me?"

Nodding, Elyse left the cup on the floor and kept her distance. "I'm Elyse Farrell. I'm Walt's... friend." She wasn't about to tell him they were lovers.

At the mention of Walt's name, Glen's demeanor changed as if he remembered why he had trespassed. He growled, "Where is he?" The exertion of his comment made him sway, and his eyes drooped before he closed them.

"Try to stay awake, Glen. You need medical help. Walt went outside to find your vehicle. God, I hope it has four-wheeled drive."

"My truck is parked down the road."

Elyse licked her lips, hoping against hope Walt could find it in the snowstorm. "Was it drugs in the plastic bag in your coat?"

Glen's bloodshot eyes blinked open, and his face twisted with confusion. "What?"

"The baggie we found in your coat pocket. You do drugs, don't you?" She'd seen that kind of paraphernalia before, especially being around Hollywood actors.

Glen struggled in an attempt to stand. "You don't know

shit about me." His large body was too much to navigate, and he ended up slumping on the floor again in defeat.

"You're lucky I had Naloxone with me. I'm pretty sure you were overdosing."

He looked at her, the shock on his face apparent.

"Don't worry, I won't report you to the authorities. Not unless you try to shoot me again."

Glen turned frantic and palmed his camo pants before looking around the area. "Where is it?"

"Where is what? The drugs?"

He pinned her with a look of aggravation. "My gun," he seethed.

Elyse crossed her arms again, pursing her lips to the side. "Don't worry. It's in a safe place, big guy."

Glen grunted as he tried to get comfortable, the physical effort since waking up obviously taking a toll on him.

"You should rest," she offered.

He responded with a slow nod, his eyes closing in submission. Elyse knew he'd passed out again when his head rolled back, and his entire body went limp.

The sound of a vehicle honking outside threw her adrenaline into overtime, knowing Walt had found Glen's truck. Sprinting to the front door, she opened it in a burst of blowing snow, the dangerous wind zapping the warmth from her body in an instant. Walt ran from the idling truck, the wipers going full speed and the headlights barely making a dent in the reduced visibility.

"Hurry!" she hollered, waving him in.

Stomping snow from his boots in the foyer, Walt looked like a real-life abominable snowman. He was covered in icy flakes, his cheeks red and chapped from the elements. Peeling off his gloves, he blew a hot breath across his fingers. "It's a blizzard out there, Elyse. I don't know if we can make it into town."

Elyse shivered and watched him, concerned they might have to take care of Glen on their own. "What about Bennett Farms?"

"What about it?"

"Do you think we could make it to the farm? Your family could help us…"

"—and the farm has more than one generator." Walt clenched his jaw, thinking it over. "Glen's truck has four-wheel drive, so I think it's possible."

Elyse nodded. "We need help, Walt. Glen needs help."

"You're right." Walt stripped off Glen's coat and traded it with his own hanging on a hall tree. "Let me get Garth in his carrier and grab a few things. You do the same, and then we'll bundle Glen up and get going."

Elyse took off for the bedroom. She was quick, gathering a few items and shoving them into her purse. Sitting on the bed, she flung Walt's slippers off and pulled on her sturdy boots. She hurried out of the room with her purse over one shoulder and grabbed her roller bag on the way to the front door. Buttoning up her coat, Walt met her in the foyer carrying the handle of the kitty carrier. Garth meowed unhappily from inside.

"I'll get these in the back seat. Stay inside until it's time to get Glen."

"Okay."

The blast of snow when he opened the door was like a white confetti cannon going off. It took Walt two tortuous trips to load everything in the back, including her roller bag. Stomping his feet again on the wet foyer floor, he grabbed Glen's coat.

"Let's do this."

Glen was still slumped on the floor, the earlier raging fire nothing but hot embers sizzling in the aftermath. They managed to wake him up and got his coat zipped over his large frame and his knit hat on his head. Settling his arms over each of their shoulders, they struggled to get him on his feet. But once he was up, he didn't fight, and they slowly made their way to the front door.

"Come on, Glen, you got this," Walt encouraged.

Elyse was amazed by Walt's changed behavior. Gone was the intense, protective man ready to take a bullet for her. If she didn't know any better, she'd swear the two men were old friends by the way he was helping Glen. Once outside, the bitter wind bit at her cheeks, the ground beneath them slippery with ice and deep drifts of snow. It took every ounce of strength she had to help Walt transport Glen the few yards to the truck. Her exposed hair from under her hat blew haphazardly around her face, whipping and stinging her skin.

"*Almost there!*" Walt yelled into the wind.

Glen's hand shook as he held onto the door frame and shifted his large body into the front passenger seat of the cab. Once the door was closed, Elyse hopped into the back jump seat among their bags and other miscellaneous junk Glen had accumulated, including several empty liquor bottles. Her chest heaved as she leaned back against the seat, thankful for the warm interior. Garth mewled loudly, the cat obviously under duress. Glen remained quiet, his eyes closed and his breathing heavy.

Walt slammed the driver's side door shut and put the truck in gear. "Here goes nothing."

The truck tires spun underneath them for a few agonizing seconds until the truck lurched forward, the four-wheel-drive taking over. The scene in front of them was a complete whiteout.

"I don't know, Walt. This doesn't look so good."

"Don't worry, I can make the drive to Bennett Farms in my sleep. We're home free if I can just get this baby back on the plowed main road."

Elyse kept her mouth shut, unconvinced the drive was possible. The windshield wipers barely kept up with the accumulating snow on the glass, Walt cursing under his breath. The truck speed was scarcely five miles an hour. At this rate, the vehicle would be covered in a mound of snow, leaving them buried on the road.

Looking out the back window, Elyse couldn't make out Walt's house any longer. When Glen's body shifted during a turn and slumped against the truck door, she leaned forward to make sure he was still breathing.

"Come on, Glen, don't die on me, buddy!" Walt shouted, shaking his arm. His voice was panicked, and he sped up a few ticks.

"He's still breathing, but it's labored," she told him. Tears pricked the edges of her eyes, and she sniffled. "I'm scared, Walt."

Walt shot her a concerned look over his shoulder. "Don't wimp out on me, gorgeous. We're gonna make it, I swear."

Elyse nodded, sure they were lost in the storm. But then a miraculous thing happened, the giant steel sign spelling Bennett Farms came into view. She squealed with relief. "We're here!"

Walt's laugh was short-lived. "I don't think I can get up and over the hill to the main house."

"What do you mean?"

"It's steep, and if the truck slides, it'll go into the gully." He put the truck in park and turned to look right at her. "I'm gonna hoof it home, get my brothers on the ATVs, and come back for you, okay? You stay here with Glen. I'll leave the heat on in the truck. We're almost there. This is almost over."

Elyse gripped his arm resting on the seatback. Their eyes locked, something transformative passing between them.

"I love you," he suddenly whispered.

"What?" She struggled to hear his voice over the thumping wipers, the howling wind, and her thundering heart.

"I said, I love you, Elyse." Walt pushed her wayward hair back from her cheek.

"I... I love you too."

Chapter Twenty-Two

WALT

Walt had never uttered those three words to a woman besides his mother and sister in his entire life. Elyse's reply propelled him forward through the blizzard with newfound energy and determination.

I love you too.

Hot blood coursed through his veins, his strength and virility urging him through the snow drifts and whiteout conditions. The faint scent of burning wood through the wind made him smile; the image of his family cozily gathered around the hearth a welcome thought. Ice crystals hung off his eyelashes, and his jeans were frozen to his thighs, the needle-like pain compelling him toward safety.

When the first hazy images of the farmhouse came into view, Walt stopped to catch his breath, his chest heaving with exertion. Only a few more yards, and he'd be home.

The dogs barked a welcome when he threw open the front door, his hands numb and stiff in his gloves, barely able to grip the knob. Roy, Becky, James, Samantha, Teddy, and Robyn immediately entered the grand foyer with confused expressions.

"Walter?" Roy questioned, tentatively coming closer to him.

Walt took his cowboy hat off his head and stripped the scarf from across his mouth, revealing himself to his family, the relieved tone of his voice noticeable. "Yes! I need help, Dad, please!"

His family went into action, surrounding him with multiple questions. Walt was inundated, the barrage coming at him like snowballs in a fight.

"I need... the ATVs gassed up," he heaved. "We've got to get Glen Kirby and Elyse out of the truck at the bottom of the hill."

"*Glen Kirby?*" Teddy questioned. "What in the hell is going on, Walt?"

Flustered, he pushed through his crowding family and made a beeline to the kitchen's back door looking out over the red barn.

"Now wait a minute, son. Tell us what happened? How'd you get here through this blizzard?" Roy grabbed Walt by the shoulder, stopping him in his tracks.

Walt licked his chapped lips and tried to keep the anxious thrumming of his heart in check. He knew they were only trying to get to the bottom of the story, but time was of the essence. "Glen Kirby stopped by my house today. He threatened me with a gun."

"*What?*" Samantha gasped.

Walt held up his hand. "Don't worry, Elyse has the gun now. He dropped it when he almost overdosed..."

"—Walter, you're not making any sense," James interrupted. The entire family started talking all at once.

"*Shut up!*" Walt yelled, his angry outburst silencing them

all. Slamming his hat on his head, he pointed at the back door, inhaling a deep breath as his senses prickled with urgency. "I need those ATVs. Elyse, Glen, and *my cat* are in a truck at the bottom of the hill. If we don't get to them soon and bring them back here, the truck will run out of gas, and they might freeze to death. Does everybody understand?"

Teddy approached him and palmed his shoulder with reassurance. "We understand. Take a deep breath and calm down, Walter. We just need a minute to put on some warm clothing."

James agreed. "Yeah. And the ATVs are already gassed and ready to go."

Walt swallowed with relief, his adrenaline waning as a surge of brotherly love filled his senses. "Thank you."

Sam eyed him inquisitively as his brothers and father left the family huddle to dress in winter gear. "Do you need me to call the authorities?"

Walt didn't hesitate and shook his head. "No. But depending on how Glen's doing, we may need an ambulance."

Sam's brow furrowed. "How bad is he?"

"He's bad, Sam. Real bad. Thank God Elyse had that weird medicine... you know, the kind that reverses an over-dose?" For the life of him, he couldn't remember the name.

"Naloxone?" she asked in disbelief.

"That's the one. She carries it in her purse for work, you know, in case someone goes down on the set."

Becky and Robyn approached the two, curious as they overheard their conversation. "Elyse has been with you this entire time?" Becky asked.

Walt averted her bewildered gaze and pulled on his gloves. "Uh, yeah. She stopped by after she visited you and was about to head back to Atlanta when the storm struck. I advised her to wait it out at my place." His half-lie seemed to appease his sister.

Before anyone could ask another question, the guys clomped into the kitchen in head-to-toe winter gear.

"Let's do this," James announced.

Samantha kissed his cheek and adjusted the knit hat on his head. "Be careful out there."

"I will."

"You be careful too," Robyn instructed Teddy.

Walt watched as the two hugged affectionately, desperate to lay eyes on Elyse again.

Becky gripped their father's bundled arm. "Daddy, please take it slow out there. In fact, why don't you stay and keep us girls company? Let your boys handle this one."

Roy chuckled. "I'll be fine, darlin'. I'm just going along for the ride."

A few minutes later, Walt and his brothers revved the ATV throttles, each manning a vehicle in the vacant barn. Roy sat next to Walt and gripped the steel bar in front of him. Walt made it clear he only wanted James to help with Glen. They all agreed it would be better if Teddy kept his distance from the man who almost killed him in a fight. With the wave of his hand, they were off into the blinding winter storm like the cavalry on a combat mission.

The brothers formed a single file line, Walt cautiously leading the way over the accumulated snow on the steep hill in front of the farmhouse. His earlier footprints were already covered up, the angry blizzard whipping and tossing the frozen precipitation around them. Using the all-terrain vehicles, it only took them a few minutes before they arrived at Glen's pickup, one side of the truck already covered in a huge snowdrift. Walt waved his hand in the air and pointed, his brothers responding with high-pitched honks from their vehicles.

"I'll bet Elyse'll be happy to see you again," Roy shouted over the storm.

Walt's heart thumped rapidly as he offered his dad a quick nod. Happy was an understatement. Ecstatic was more like it.

Walt slowed his vehicle down as he closed in on the truck and was elated when Elyse opened the back door and jumped out with the kitty carrier in her hand. Cutting off the engine, he moved as fast as he could through the thick barrage of snow. When she lunged into his arms, his world felt complete.

"I knew you'd make it," she mumbled against the cold shell of his ear.

He pressed his lips in a quick kiss to her head and held her cheeks in his gloved hands. "Are you okay? Is Glen okay?"

Elyse nodded vigorously. "We're both fine. It's your cat you should be worried about." She held up the carrier and laughed, the sound a welcome ping to his ears. "Garth won't stop meowing and hissing."

Walt chuckled; relieved they were all in one piece. Staring into her gorgeous baby blues, she knowingly winked at him.

"Hold that thought." Taking her by the hand, he led her over to Roy.

"Hey, darlin'. Heck of a blizzard we're having today." Roy grinned and patted the space next to him. His cowboy hat was prominent on his head and dusted with snowflakes, and he'd shifted into the driver's seat, ready to take her back to the house.

Walt helped Elyse into the ATV and adjusted the carrier in her lap. "Hold on, it's a bumpy ride."

"Okay."

He squeezed her shoulder before slapping the hood of the vehicle. "Take good care of her, Dad."

"I will. Y'all be careful too."

"Will do." Walt watched as the ATV jerked forward, Elyse and his father disappearing into the whiteout. Turning his attention to his brothers, they got to work getting Glen out of the truck.

"Easy does it," James encouraged.

Glen was one hell of a large man, his dead weight not helping matters. He was groggy and mumbling incoherently to deaf ears. Teddy ended up having to help too, the three of them finally getting Glen into an ATV without incident. James manned the wheel, and once Glen was safely buckled in, the vehicle took off in a spray of white powder. By this time, Walt was frozen, his body shaking and shivering from being outside in the freezing elements for far too long.

Ted grabbed Elyse's roller bag from the back seat and slammed the door. "Come on, Walt. You need to get inside and warm up."

"G… good idea." He swiped his own bag from the other side of the truck and climbed into the passenger seat of the ATV, hunkered down and ready to face the harsh wind.

"I'm worried, Walt," Teddy announced over the vehicle's throttle. "I mean, bringing Glen Kirby into our home?"

"What was I supposed to do? Leave him to freeze to death or overdose at my house?"

"No, of course not."

Walt knew Teddy was nervous. After everything his big

brother had been through because of the Kirby family, who wouldn't be? He'd spent five years in the Georgia State Penitentiary, one year in a halfway house, parole, and endured a fight that almost killed him. It was a lot to handle. And here he was, bringing his brother's archenemy into their home on purpose. But they really had no choice.

"I p... promise, I'll be the one to keep an eye on him. He's not going to hurt you ever again."

Ted's face was covered with a thick winter mask, his expression obscured. But his eyes were focused, squinting in the elements as he powered the vehicle up the steep hill. Walt knew his brother worried about a plan for the night. His instinct to protect everyone he loved was one of the things Walt loved most about Teddy. The man sacrificed years of his life so others could live theirs. Walt could give up one night of sleep to protect his brother.

The sight of the Bennett family farmhouse was nothing short of a welcome mirage in the atmospheric conditions. Walt exhaled a loud, cloudy breath as they circled the house and pulled into the red barn. His brothers were already waiting for him inside.

"How do you want to do this?" James asked. He stood next to the ATV where Glen sat, his snow-covered shoulders slumped and his figure massive compared to his brother's.

Looking at Teddy and James, he wished Hank was there with them, his youngest brother scrappy and strong. But Hank was still in Nashville, recording original music. Thank God he didn't have to deal with all of this.

"I say we pull right up to the front porch with him. It'll be easier than getting him up those back stairs to the house we can't even see due to the snow."

The brothers looked out over the bulging area where the

stairs were somewhere underneath and nodded in agreement. Climbing aboard the vehicles again, they drove to the
front of the house and got as close as possible to the front
porch. Roy and Elyse came outside and waited for them.
Walt watched her shiver in the cold.

"Get inside," he scolded.

"No. I can help with our bags." She trotted to the back
end of the ATV and grabbed their belongings. As she
hurried up the three porch stairs, she slipped. But Walt was
right there to catch her.

"I've got you," he mumbled, helping her regain her
balance. His brothers must have noticed because they were
grinning from ear to ear.

Her blue eyes were bright, her cheeks flushed from the
elements. Or maybe she was embarrassed? "You're still a
real Southern gentleman, you know that?"

One side of Walt's mouth jacked up into a sly smirk.
"I'm your beck and call guy, always."

Chapter Twenty-Three

ELYSE

Elyse leaned against the kitchen island and watched in awe as Samantha calmly spoke with Glen. James stood protectively nearby, eyeing the enemy with his arms crossed against his chest. Glen seemed nonplussed, sitting in an overstuffed armchair in front of the blazing fire with a plaid blanket across his legs. More than once, Sam patted his thick arm, urging him to sip the hot tea Becky had made for him. Elyse sipped from her own mug, her frozen limbs finally thawing out after what they'd been through.

"Hey," Walt said, palming the small of her back. His touch induced a flush of heat across her skin.

"Hey." She turned and eyed his handsome face, his masculine features sharp and chiseled in the light. "Did you get Garth settled?"

"Yes. He's sequestered in the bathroom of our guest room. I don't want him roaming around out here with the big dogs. He'd eat them alive."

Elyse eyed the two unassuming Labradors sleeping

soundly on their beds near the fire and frowned. "The dogs would eat him, or he'd eat the dogs?"

Walt chuckled. "I'm afraid Garth would turn feral and go nuts around them. I didn't want to take a chance." He noticed Sam and Glen talking. "Is he doing any better?"

"I think so. He seems comfortable enough."

"You think he'll behave tonight?"

"Now that, I don't know." Making sure no one was looking, she pulled Glen's gun from her pocket and nudged Walt's leg. He nodded immediately, taking the firearm from her hands, and shoving it into the back of his jeans.

"I'll make sure Samantha knows about this when she'd done talking to Glen." He looked around. "Where's everybody else?"

Elyse set her mug on the counter, thankful the gun was out of her possession. "Ted and Robyn went upstairs. Your dad is in his office making a few phone calls."

"Is he calling Sheriff Jenkins?"

"I think so. Sam wants Glen out of here once the storm dies down. I think your dad is making arrangements to get him transported to a nearby hospital."

"Makes sense. I'm gonna see if my dad needs any help. You good for a minute?"

"Sure." Walt kissed her cheek, and she watched him walk away, his denim backside causing her eyebrow to hitch with want.

Becky reappeared and stood beside her, her stance mimicking her brother James with her arms folded across her bosom. Her intense glare focused on Glen, her voice low and even-tempered. "I can't believe that man is in our house." She paused. "I hate to say it, but he doesn't deserve to have my family taking care of him."

Elyse frowned. "Becky, please tell me. What exactly did Glen do to your family?"

Her mouth gaped in apparent shock, and her brown eyes grew large as she turned to face her. "Are you kidding me? Walt didn't tell you?"

Elyse shook her head. "There wasn't time. Everything happened so fast—Glen barging in unannounced and the gun going off."

"—Wait, *what?*" she interrupted, trying to keep her voice down. She pulled Elyse by the hand into the deserted hallway and whispered snappishly. "Y'all didn't tell us the gun went off. Oh, my God, Elyse. You could've been killed! My brother could've been killed." Her big brown eyes filled with tears.

Elyse grabbed both of Becky's hands and held on as she tried to convey nothing catastrophic had happened. "But we weren't killed. Glen was in a rage because of the drugs, which must've put him over the edge. And then he passed out right in front of us. Walt secured the gun. *Nobody* was hurt," she reiterated.

"Don't you think you should tell Sam about all of this? Glen Kirby is a dangerous man."

Elyse winced at the word "dangerous." "Walt's planning on telling her everything from start to finish once she's done talking to Glen. It's all good."

Becky sighed and offered a quick nod as if relieved. "Where are my manners? Do you need to change clothes? Are you tired? You can stay in my bedroom if you'd like. I'll stay in Hank's while he's out of town."

Elyse pressed her top teeth into her lower lip, unsure how to explain her sleeping arrangements for the night.

"What?" Becky asked. Her pretty brow furrowed with confusion.

"I'm, uh, staying with your brother tonight."

Becky blinked several times. "Walter?"

"Mmhmm," Elyse nodded, trying to gauge her reaction.

"Wait a minute. You and… *my brother* are an item?"

"Umm, yeah. Is that okay?"

"I mean, of course, it's okay," she giggled. "But… Walt? How did I not know this? Really?"

"Really," she nodded, her smile slight. "We, uh, hit it off on New Year's Eve. You were a little out of it that night."

"Ugh, don't remind me," Becky said, slapping her hand against her forehead. "Does the rest of the family know?"

Elyse shrugged. "I don't know what he's told your dad or your brothers. Maybe?"

"Well, I'll be." Becky rested her hands on her hips and smiled. "Way to go, Walt!"

The two laughed before Becky opened her arms for a hug. "I'm so happy for y'all. Now it makes sense," she mumbled into her ear.

"What makes sense?" Elyse asked, pulling back from her.

"Your trip to Langston Falls. Silly me. You didn't come here to talk about my career. You came here to see Walt."

Elyse was sure her cheeks were the color of a ripe tomato, thankful for the dimness in the hallway. "That's not true, Becky. I am interested in helping with your career. Absolutely."

"So, Walt is a little bonus for you then?"

Elyse coughed at the word *little*. "I guess you could say that. Walt is a… bonus."

"Well, I think this is cause for a celebration. You want a glass of Bennett Farms wine?"

"Sure."

As they started for the kitchen, Elyse grabbed Becky by the hand. "Wait."

"What?"

"You didn't tell me what Glen did to your family."

Becky's happy face morphed into a despondent expression. "I think it'd be best if Walt was the one to tell you all about it."

"Is it bad?"

Becky looked at the floor, her shoulders rising in a deep sigh. When she looked back at Elyse, there were more shimmers of tears in her eyes. "The worst. I don't think any of us will be getting any sleep with that monster in our home tonight."

A cold shiver ran the length of Elyse's spine.

"You know, maybe it'd be better if we took a rain check on the wine, okay? I'll make some more tea so we can keep our wits about us tonight."

Becky mustered a final smile before leaving Elyse alone in the hall. Numerous questions swirled through her head, her thoughts going crazy, wondering what awful thing Glen Kirby did to the Bennett family. For him to be inside their home was an anomaly, that was for sure. But what the hell had he done to distance himself from this lovely family? They'd been nothing but kind and accommodating to her.

And Walt. Handsome, protective, sexy, Walt. They had a connection—but was it a true love connection?

He'd uttered "I love you" in the heat of the crisis, both of them overwhelmed by what they were experiencing. There wasn't time to ask him why he loved her or how he knew. Love was a game-changer in her mind; those three little words lodged in her heart like a cupid's arrow.

The only thing Elyse knew for sure was that Walt

bought the Kirby's homestead, and Glen wanted it back with a vengeance. She needed answers before she handed her heart over completely to Walter Bennett.

And there was only one way to get to the bottom of the story. They needed to have an honest, uninterrupted conversation.

Chapter Twenty-Four

WALT

Walt softly tapped on the solid oak door to his father's office. "Come on in," he heard him say.

Roy Bennett sat behind his mammoth desk littered with file folders and an assortment of framed family photos from over the years. The paneled walls held floor-to-ceiling bookshelves making the space cozy like a library, the aromatic smell of well-worn books and leather prominent. Parking himself in a crackled buckskin-covered chair across from his father, Walt carefully slid Glen's gun across the desk toward him. Roy's deep sigh was audible, his usual friendly expression clouded with dismay.

"Thank God you and Elyse are okay," he said. He took the gun and secured it in the top drawer of his desk, locking it up with a key. "Sheriff Jenkins wants to know if you want to press charges."

"You talked to him? What did you tell him?"

"I told him Glen showed up at your place high on drugs with a gun and threatened you and Elyse. He's sending a squad car over once the weather lets up and the roads are plowed again."

Walt nodded.

His dad interlocked his fingers and rested his arms on his desk. "So, what do you want to do moving forward?"

Walt sighed, unsure how to explain what he was feeling. "I'm not sure, Dad."

"You're not sure?" The space between his brows deepened. "Son, y'all could've been killed back there. That son-of-a-bitch threatened your life. This has got to stop. And it needs to stop now. You have enough cause to get him locked up for a while. Isn't that what you've always wanted?"

"I ... I don't know anymore. I'm not sure jail time is the answer."

Roy harrumphed, perplexed by Walt's admission. "You'd rather Glen get off scot-free and roam around this town looking for another opportunity to hurt you? To hurt one of your siblings?"

"No, of course not." Walt watched his father's jaw clench, indicating he was in papa bear protection mode.

"Sheriff Jenkins wants Samantha to put Glen in handcuffs for the night. Even he knows what's at stake here."

"He's not gonna do anything tonight, Dad. The man is messed up and can hardly stand on his own two feet—and he's unarmed. You locked up his gun."

Roy arose from his seat and ambled toward the window. The view normally looked out over the vineyards rising from the fields. But now, it was nothing but a whiteout, the blizzard obscuring the winery land. With one hand on his hip and the other rubbing the back of his neck, he spoke, the pride in his voice evident.

"You're a good man coming to his aid, son," his low voice rumbled. "After everything he's put our family through, I'm proud of you for letting bygones be bygones in the heat of the moment and helping a fellow human out."

Walt sat rigid in his seat, knowing his dad had more to say, his wise fatherly advice something he coveted. When Roy turned around, the exaggerated frown on his face pinched his features.

"But you and I both know damn well this is never going to end unless we take a stand."

"What do you suggest, Dad? I'm all ears."

"I feel like you have enough cause to throw the book at him. I want him to go to jail. I want his ass locked up for a long time, so he can experience what your brother Teddy went through."

Normally, Walt would've thrust a fist into the air and agreed with a whoop of joy. He had all the ammunition he needed for Glen to serve some substantial jail time. It was the ultimate tit-for-tat for what he'd put his brother through. His father once called Walt shameless, his brazen revenge plot of buying up the Kirby property surprising everyone in town. He was a lone pirate taking over the house and land that rightfully belonged to Glen and his ancestors. Plundering the man's inheritance was one of the most satisfying things he'd ever done in his life.

But somewhere along the way, something changed. The sweet taste of vengeance had turned bitter in Walt's mouth, and he wasn't sure why.

Walt stood and approached his father, curling his hand over his shoulder. "Can we sleep on it?"

Roy scowled and studied Walt's face as if confused by his hesitation. It took him several seconds before he uttered a reply. "I don't think any of us will be getting much sleep tonight."

James and Walt managed to get Glen situated in a bed for the night in another guest room, away from the others. They decided to take turns and guard the door for a few hours at a time. Samantha suggested three-hour shifts, James volunteering to go first. Glen was still groggy and pretty much out of it; sleep the only thing he was able to do without much of a fuss.

"I'll see you in three then," Walt said to James, slapping him on the arm.

James nodded. "Get some rest. You look like shit."

"Well, it's been a helluva day."

"I'll say."

Walt walked through the quiet house, his family sequestered in their rooms for the night behind locked doors. The snow had finally stopped, and the air held a quiet, cold stillness. Shuffling up the stairs, he was dog tired, ready to lay horizontal next to Elyse.

"Is he settled for the night?" she asked as he entered the bedroom.

"Yes. He passed out almost immediately."

"Come here." She stretched her arm toward him, her fingers splayed and ready to entwine with his. Garth was curled up at the end of the bed in a black swish of fur, paying him no attention.

Sitting on the edge of the mattress, Walt noticed Elyse wearing one of his t-shirts, her dark hair brushed out and hanging over her shoulders. God, she was magnificent, her undeniable beauty causing his heart to clutch in his chest. The lower half of her body was already under the covers, and she scooted over to make room for him, the sheets warm from her body heat. He remained sitting on the edge, knowing he owed her an explanation.

"What's wrong?" The space between her perfect brows pinched with worry.

Walt swallowed and shook his head. "I'm... unsettled."

"Of course you're unsettled. I am too. It's because of Glen."

Walt felt deflated knowing he was responsible for her anxiety. "It's not just Glen. It's... you too."

"Me? What did I do?" She seemed taken aback.

His eyes traced her face, memorizing her deep baby blues staring back at him and how her shiny hair fell over one shoulder. He wanted to feel her tresses trailing softly across his chest as she straddled him, kissing and writhing her way down to his center. She was sexy as sin, immobilizing him with her stare.

"You made me fall in love with you, Elyse."

She averted her gaze, her dark eyelashes fluttering and the apples of her cheeks blushing with a pinkish hue.

"Look at me," he requested. When she looked at him, he felt his entire world shift.

"I said I love you, and I meant it. I've never felt this way about anyone before. I feel like..." He paused, trying to convey his feelings without sounding like an ass. Words escaped him, his explanation bumbled and juvenile.

"I feel like you shouldn't hesitate to say the words 'I love you' out loud when you sense it. I don't think you have to wait for a special occasion to say it either. If you're feeling it, you just... put it out there and say it." He was babbling like an idiot; sure she was confused.

Holding her hand, he leaned lower to catch her eye. "I'm unsettled because I don't know what's next for us. I want to be with you all the time. I want to protect you and love on you and get to know everything about you. But... but you live in Atlanta, and I live..." He looked around the room as a realization hit him in the gut. "I live *here*."

Elyse lifted her gaze to him again. "I know we have a connection, Walt." She paused.

"But?"

Her focus was laser-sharp, her demeanor calm yet intimidating. All she needed was her signature turtleneck and sky-high heels, and this lady boss could eat him for lunch.

"But before I can give you my whole heart, I need to understand why you bought the Kirby house and land. Was it revenge? Is that why you did it? Did it make you feel good taking something away from him? Please, explain to me what he did to your family so I can try and make sense of everything that's happened."

Walt arose from the bed and shucked off his boots. Peeling his sweater up and over his head, he threw it onto a nearby chair. As he unbuttoned his jeans, he finally looked over at her, mulling over his candid confession. Stepping out of his denim, he threw the pants toward the same chair and sat on the edge of the bed again. Wearing his boxers and undershirt, he shimmied under the covers next to her and sighed. "I guess I should start at the very beginning, huh?"

"If you don't mind," she said, shifting to her side to face him.

Walt nodded. "But first, I do have a confession to make."

"Oh?"

"You were right. I did buy the Kirby house and land as revenge. My father was not at all happy with me. He even called me, shameless."

She tensed, her reaction to his admission expected.

"But hear me out." He waited until she relaxed, her nod giving him the go-ahead to try to clarify.

"My temper can go from zero to death row in a heartbeat; just ask my brothers. In the past, I've always believed that karma's a bitch, and you get what you give. You mess with the bull; you get the horns." He rattled off some of his favorite sayings, the words harsh and unforgiving.

"I thought I was doing my family and everyone in this town a favor by buying out Glen and forcing him to leave and start over. For a while, I thought it was possible to turn the Kirby homestead into something of my own—you know? Plant roots and settle down. But the truth of the matter is—it's *never* felt like home to me. Not once. And this latest incident with Glen has made me realize something else."

"What?"

"It's *always* going to be the Kirby homestead. And this…" He waved his hand in the air. "… will *always* be Bennett Farms. Are you following me?"

"I think so."

Walt rested his head against a pillow and stared at the plaster ceiling. "For the first time in my life, I feel sorry for Glen. I feel sorry—for everything."

Shifting to where he was nose to nose with her, he was shocked by his own admission. "I don't want revenge anymore, Elyse. After what we went through today, I want to help him." He rolled his eyes. "God, I can't believe I just said that out loud. Have I gone fucking insane?"

"No," Elyse replied. "No, you're not insane." She changed positions and rested her head on his chest.

Wrapping his arm around her, he sighed with fatigue. "I don't want to fight anymore."

"Then don't."

Was it really that simple? Walt wasn't sure. Holding Elyse in his arms, he told her the entire back story from start to finish. How six years ago, his brother Teddy and his fiancé Robyn were, unfortunately, part of a prank that turned deadly, and how Glen's only brother, Joe, was killed. Walt told her how Ted took the fall and sacrificed his life so Robyn could live hers.

He told Elyse about the night of the Harvest Hoedown when Glen confronted Ted while he was out on parole, instigating a fight that put his brother in a coma. He told her about how Ted was the one punished again for a parole violation and sentenced to another two weeks in jail.

Elyse was silent, listening to him purge his anger and guilt, reliving those awful years in a sort of therapeutic admission. His purchase of the Kirby homestead was justifiable, helping Mrs. Kirby pay restitution for her son's punishment when he injured Ted. They needed the money to pay for Ted's hospital bills as required by the court so Glen wouldn't have to serve time in jail. And Walt was right there, ready to collect.

But what should've been water under the bridge was anything but, both families' roots in the town of Langston Falls running thick and deep. Walt realized he'd been blinded by his fury, never truly seeing Glen for who he was: a man drowning in sorrow from the loss of his only brother. A man ripped from his homestead and livelihood; a man desperate and crying out for help through drugs and his bullish actions against him and his family, and Elyse. Seeing Glen hit rock bottom in real-time, Walt didn't want to be the one who ultimately pushed him over the edge. There had to be another way.

"Say something," he pleaded.

"Hmmm," she hummed. "It sounds like the universe is trying to send you a message."

Walt frowned. "What do you think the universe is trying to tell me?" His question held desperation.

She lifted her head and rested her chin in her hand. Looking into his eyes, the words out of her lush mouth filled him with gratitude, her observation spot on.

"It's time to drop your shield and stop fighting. It's time for you to embrace your big heart and shine."

Chapter Twenty-Five

WALT

Walt left Elyse sound asleep in their warm bed and tiptoed through the quiet hallway toward the guest room on the other side of the house—the same guest room where his nemesis lay unconscious in a drug-induced sleep. James sat on a chair outside the room, his face droopy with fatigue.

"How'd it go?" Walt asked.

James' sigh was heavy after three long hours of guard duty. "Fine." The chair creaked as he wearily stood. "Haven't heard one peep out of him all night."

Walt nodded. "Good. I've got it from here. Get some sleep, bro." He reached for the antique glass doorknob, ready to enter the bedroom, but his brother grabbed him by the arm, stopping him in his tracks.

"Why are you going in there?"

"I want to talk to him."

"Don't do that." Walt shook his head. "You don't need to get Glen riled up in the middle of the night. At least wait until Sam wakes up so she can supervise."

"But I have some things I need to say to him. Don't

worry, I'll be quiet." Walt didn't wait for his brother's permission and boldly left him standing in the hallway with his mouth agape as he entered the room. Now was not the time or the place to get into an argument with Jimmy, especially with everyone else in the house fast asleep. Walt knew what he was doing.

A bedside lamp cast soft light across the bulging figure of Glen Kirby lying in the queen-sized bed. His face was turned away from the light, his chest rising and falling in deep, even breaths. The usually intimidating Kirby brother looked peaceful in slumber, the stern frown and broody expression replaced with a softer, serene version of the man.

Walt and Glen had been friends a long time ago, growing up together and attending the same schools. They'd fished together near the falls, played ball together, Glen and his brother Joe fast friends with all the Bennett boys. But things changed when Joe was killed; their family friendship history forever altered. And now, it was about to go through a metamorphosis.

Licking his lips, Walt slid a nearby chair closer to the mattress and sat. It was now or never, his courage to broach the subject of a truce on the forefront of his mind.

Glen snuffled and jerked awake as if sensing Walt's presence in the room.

"It's just me, Glen. It's Walt."

Glen struggled to sit up and rubbed an eye with his fist. Blinking against the light in the room, he concentrated his narrowed gaze on Walt's face. But Walt didn't falter. Instead, he offered a slight nod and a smile.

"Do you remember where you are?"

Glen looked about the room, taking in the muted surroundings. A substantial antique wardrobe was positioned directly in front of the sleigh bed with framed artist renditions of the red barn in various stages over the last hundred years flanking either side. Glen's eyes darted toward the darkened window before he shook his head.

"You're at Bennett Farms."

The man grunted and leaned back against a pillow in defeat. "Great."

"Do you remember how you got here?"

Glen slowly angled his head to where he looked right at Walt, his tired expression filled with surrender. The man had literally hit rock bottom. "I... I don't remember shit." His voice was scratchy and hoarse.

Walt nodded. "You came back to your house during a snowstorm."

"My house?"

"Yes. I was there with my girlfriend, Elyse. You threatened us with a gun."

Glen's face paled, and his bearded jaw hung open as if he remembered.

"It is your house, Glen. I'm living there temporarily until we can make arrangements to get you moved back in."

Glen blinked at him, and his forehead wrinkled with confusion. "What the fuck are you talking about?"

Walt mustered the strength he needed to come clean and repent. "I shouldn't have bought your house and land, Glen. It rightfully belongs to you and your mother. It's your inheritance. What I did was wrong and... and I'm so sorry."

Glen continued to stare at him as if he had two heads.

"I know you're tired and coming down from whatever drugs are in your system. And furthermore, I know you're confused, and you don't know which way to turn." Walt reached for his arm and squeezed. "But I'm here to help you now. You need help, Glen."

His expression softened as he stared at Walt's hand gripping his arm, his dark eyes brimming with tears. "Why?" he croaked. "Why do you want to help me after everything I've done to you and your family?"

Walt swallowed his emotions. It was a fair question. "Because now I understand. I don't blame you for your actions anymore. I understand your motivation." He knew he was treading on thin ice, his next words spoken calmly—evenly.

"You miss Joe—you miss your only brother."

"Yes." His voice was a strangled whisper as he tried to keep it together. He pressed his eyes shut, causing a stream of tears to trickle down his hairy, ashen face.

"And you miss your home. I'm so fucking sorry for taking that away from you. I'm sorry for everything that's happened between our two families."

Glen jerked his arm free and swiped at his face, his features contorted with pain. "Joe was everything to me."

"I know, Glen. I know." Walt swiped a tissue from a box on the bedside table and handed it off to Glen. "My brothers and sister are everything to me too."

Glen scrubbed the tissue under his nose, openly weeping. "And when you bought our house and land, I couldn't take it anymore…"

Walt moved closer. "Is that why you started doing drugs?"

"Yes."

"Why did you come back during the snowstorm? To fight me? To… *kill* me?" Walt held his breath, unsure if he was prepared to hear Glen's truth.

A torrent of tears spilled down his cheeks as he shook his head. "No."

It took him a full minute before the unfathomable words came out of his mouth.

"I wanted to kill myself."

The vibrant sunrise over the snow-covered mountains filled the valleys with pastel colors, the explosion of light and the new day a welcome relief after the cold, dark night.

Walt sat with Glen until dawn, consoling him in his grief and vowing things between their families would be different moving forward. Glen finally fell into a fitful sleep, his features sweaty and his skin pale from his drug ordeal.

Ever since Walt took over the Kirby property, he often looked out over the lush orchard, mulling over the idea of incorporating apples into a new wine with varietals from the vineyard. He was sure he could come up with a wine with an extra-unique flavor—a delicious blend of fruits aged in oak barrels until ready to be bottled. His idea was more than a good glass of North Georgia wine. It was a true blending of families and an opportunity for Glen to buy back what was rightfully his.

A soft knocking on the door lulled Walt out of his sleep-deprived state. He stood and cracked the door open, revealing his father and Sheriff Jenkins on the other side. The look on the sheriff's face was comical as he craned his neck and looked back and forth between a sleeping Glen and Walt.

"What in the world are you thinking not pressing charges?" the sheriff asked in a hushed whisper.

Walt placed a finger over his mouth and exited the bedroom, shutting the door behind him. Inhaling a deep breath, he steeled himself for a possible debate. "It's my prerogative not to press charges, Sheriff. I want Glen taken to a rehab facility. The man needs help."

Walt had mulled over his decision all night long. He wanted to get Glen into drug rehab where he'd be safe and comfortable going through a medical detox and medication-assisted treatment. Walt could tell by his father's expression that Roy was flabbergasted by Walt's change of heart, unsure if this was the best idea.

"What makes you think he's gonna get clean and let bygones be bygones after everything that's happened?" he asked.

"I just… know. Especially when I make him an offer he can't refuse. Believe me, Dad. Glen wants his life in Langston Falls back."

Sheriff Jenkins scowled. "You know, rehab doesn't mean Glen's gonna change his mind about you or your family."

Walt knew the sheriff was only looking out for his best interest, but he had a plan—a plan that included total forgiveness and reconciliation. It was time to break the violent cycle that started on the night long ago when Glen's brother was accidentally killed. It was time to bury the hatchet and forget past offenses. It was time for a cease-fire and for two grieving families to finally band together in love.

Walt patted the sheriff on the shoulder. "I know what I'm doing. Now, why don't you go into the kitchen and grab a cup of coffee while we wait for Glen to wake up? I'm sure Becky's in there baking up some of her famous monkey bread or a breakfast casserole."

The sheriff's face lit up with pleasure at the thought of delicious food. "All right. I'll wait in the kitchen."

Walt and his father watched Sheriff Jenkins disappear around the corner. When he was out of sight, Roy looked at

Walt with raised eyebrows. He knew that look well—worried and exasperated daddy.

"Please don't worry, Dad. I told you, I know what I'm doing."

"Said the shameless man who named a cat after a country music star," Roy scoffed.

His dad's comment made Walt laugh out loud, the release of feel-good endorphins spreading warmth throughout his body. After everything they'd been through, it felt good to finally let go—and laugh.

Chapter Twenty-Six

ELYSE

Elyse stood next to Becky and watched Walt and James assist Glen into the back of the squad car. Sheriff Jenkins asked her earlier if she wanted to press charges, the thought of Glen behind bars tempting. But after Walt told her the entire story and what his family had been through, she had a change of heart. For Walt to ultimately forgive Glen and offer him a second chance was a game-changer. She knew deep down Walt was a good man, and she was witnessing his change of heart in real-time.

"I feel better knowing he's not in our home anymore," Becky admitted.

Elyse eyed the pretty Bennett sister, knowing this had also been hard on her over the years. Resting her arm across her shoulders, she pulled her close in a side hug. "Let's hope this is a new beginning for all of you."

The remainder of the morning was a blur as they packed up Garth and their things and headed back to Walt's house in Glen's truck. She only knew this place to be Walt's, but now she was starting to understand it wasn't his after all.

The homestead should rightfully be given back to the Kirby family.

The roads had been plowed, and the snow accumulated across the fields and mountains was bright and pristine—unspoiled and pure. The drive only took a few minutes, Garth meowing the entire time from within his kitty carrier.

"I think he's hungry," Walt chuckled.

"Or he knows you're taking him home."

Walt eyed her in the passenger seat, his expression holding disappointment. "I suppose Glen will want his cat back too."

"Maybe? But you don't know how long this will take, when Glen will be released from rehab, or when he'd be strong enough to handle caring for a cat, let alone an entire farm. It could be weeks or even months. You and Garth still have some quality time left together."

"You make it sound like Garth and I are going on an adventure or something before we have to say goodbye."

"Life is an adventure. You should enjoy every second of it."

Walt parked in an area with less snow accumulation closer to the house and shifted his entire body to look at her. "I enjoy every second with you."

Elyse nodded, averting his loving gaze. She knew they needed to talk about what was next for them as a couple. After witnessing the entire Glen fiasco, Walt clearly expressed where he belonged—at his family home at Bennett Farms. And where did that leave her? She'd made her own home in Atlanta, her job as an assistant producer for a television show one she'd worked hard for. She was proud of her career. It wasn't something she was ready to give up.

But then Walt Bennett entered the picture, and she was

a changed woman. She knew she was in love with him, their chemistry and connection one she coveted her entire life. Could a long-distance relationship work for them? She couldn't imagine her day-to-day life in Atlanta without coming home to him, anticipating the slightest touch of his hand. Eating dinner together at the same table. Taking a walk together. Laughing, cuddling, and making love. Perhaps she could view it as a learning journey, the old Chinese proverb "Real gold is not afraid of the test of fire" coming to mind. And besides, Atlanta wasn't that far away. They could take turns visiting each other on the weekends.

"I hope you know I want to be exclusive with you. I do," she said matter-of-factly.

"I'm sensing a 'but,'" he replied.

Elyse finally looked at him—really looked at him. Dark circles appeared under his gentle brown eyes, the weight and stress of the last twenty-four hours taking a toll. His hair was tousled in that sexy boyfriend way, and a smattering of scruff peppered his jaw. The man was drop-dead gorgeous, and she wasn't about to let him get away.

"Love is a force beyond our control. Love just happens, and it happened to us."

His lips came alive with a beaming smile. "So, you admit it? You love me?"

"Yes, Walt. I love you."

"Then what's the problem?" He reached across the truck interior and held one of her gloved hands.

"Neither one of us expected to be in a long-distance relationship. We'll just have to make the most of our situation and stay strong and cheerful when we're apart. I mean, thank God for modern technology with instant messaging and FaceTime, right?"

"We can send each other pictures and short video clips," he added with a boost of energy.

Elyse nodded. Now they were getting somewhere. "Don't forget, I'll be coming to Langston Falls fairly often to help your sister with her brand too. And when I'm not here, we'll try to talk to each other daily."

"Sex-ting with dirty talk and erotic puns."

She laughed. "Erotic puns?"

"I don't know," he laughed. "I'm making it up as I go. I'll come and visit you too. I want to make this work, Elyse. I'm willing if you are."

The way he looked at her with those chocolate eyes and earnest grin filled her with intention.

"I am." And she meant it.

"See what I mean? You take time off, and all hell breaks loose." Elyse's assistant, Geneva, eyed her with concern.

The two women stood in the shadows of the television studio and watched a taping of *Sally's Southern Kitchen* for the first time since the set had been updated. Sally was having difficulty navigating her TV kitchen, bumbling for a measuring cup here and a grater there.

"Did you walk her through where everything is located? Have you rehearsed with the new formation while I was away?" Elyse couldn't believe the director yelled, "cut" yet again. This was the third time in fifteen minutes.

"You know how Sally can be," Geneva said, rolling her eyes. "She said she knows her way around a kitchen like the back of her hand."

"Yeah, her *old* kitchen." Elyse uncrossed her arms against her black turtleneck and started toward the brightly lit set, her high heels clipping against the tiled floor. As she got closer to the woman, she could tell she was stressed.

"Hey, Sal. How're you doing?" Elyse smiled warmly at the woman whose show got her on the map in food network television.

"Lordy, Elyse. For the life of me, I can't figure out why these A-holes put things where they did. I mean, who puts a grater in with the measuring cups and spoons? A grater belongs with the spatulas and the tater masher." Her thick southern accent was peaked in menopausal fury.

Elyse gently held her by the elbow and excused them from the set, telling the director to take five. "Let's you and me have a little break, shall we? Hospitality put out some of those gluten-free donuts you love."

"*Ooo*," she squealed with delight.

Elyse made sure to follow Sally's contract rider to a T, making sure the popular show hostess had healthy food choices per her doctor's request. Being at the helm of a popular southern cooking show had its ups and downs, including overindulging in butter-laden, bacon-infused, sugary recipes that did a number on Sally's waistline.

When it was just the two of them in the Green Room, Elyse watched Sally take her time and pick out the perfect donut. Biting into the doughy ring, she closed her eyes and moaned. "Thank God for Da Vinci's Donuts. They make the best gluten-free option on the planet." She took another large bite, all the stress of the earlier taping seemingly vanished. "Aren't you going to have one, Sugar?"

Elyse loved it when Sally called everyone on set by terms of endearment, her southern mannerisms, big hair, and accent making her more of a caricature than a middle-aged woman hosting her own cooking show. She was loved by so many fans, including Elyse. Unbeknownst to Sally, she was a mother figure in Elyse's eyes, her warm hugs, and cheerful aura something she looked forward to during filming days. That Sally was out of sorts made her mad, her protective nature regarding her successful client rearing its ugly head.

"No thanks. I had one earlier." Filling a mug with black coffee, Elyse took a sip. "Sally? Did anyone give you time to acquaint yourself with the new set while I was gone?"

Sally wiped crumbs from her mouth with a paper napkin, smearing her perfect red lips. "No, honey. They threw me out there like a duck."

"I'm sorry?" She wasn't tracking with her.

"You know, if it looks like a duck, swims like a duck, and quacks like a duck, then it's probably a duck." She snort-laughed. "Don't you worry about me, Sweetie-pie. I'll find my way eventually. It just takes me a little longer these days. I'm not getting any younger."

"Well, you take all the time you need, Miss Sally. If anyone gives you any trouble, you send them over to me. I'll take care of them."

"I'm sure you will." She popped the last bite of donut into her mouth and spoke with her mouth full. "I better find Shira and have her fix my lips."

"You do that. I'll let the director know we're about ready to start again."

"Toodles!" Sally waved and exited the room leaving a waft of sweet, syrupy essence in her wake.

Elyse took another sip of coffee and checked her phone for the umpteenth time. Sure enough, there was a text waiting for her from Walt.

You are unique and perfect in every way. Damn, autocorrect. I meant, good morning.

Elyse giggled, imagining Walt fumbling with his phone, using his large thumbs to type out the message. And then she imagined one of those thumbs sliding down her lower lip, dragging across her chin and down her neck…

"*Elyse!*" Geneva hollered, imploding her daydream.

"What?" Thank God for her turtleneck covering the hot skin underneath. She was sure it'd turned red and blotchy from her naughty Walter thoughts. Quickly, she tucked her phone into her pocket.

Geneva gave her the side-eye as if trying to figure her out. "You okay?"

"Yes, I'm fine." She tilted her chin into the air. "What's up?"

"They're about to start."

"Great. I'll be out in a minute."

"Oh-kay." Geneva turned on her heels and left Elyse alone.

Pulling her phone out again, she quickly typed Walt a reply, her lips pressed into a girlish smile.

Even over text, you're adorable. Miss me yet?

She held her breath, hoping he was in a position where he could reply immediately. She stared at the three dots on her screen, indicating he was typing on the other end.

You have no ducking idea.

She giggled again.

Damn auto correct. You know what I mean.

Her sigh was heavy and lovesick, her response a natural one, like breathing in and out.

I miss you too.

Three little dots appeared again before his words filled her heart with intense longing.

I love you.

Chapter Twenty-Seven

WALT

Walt leaned against the kitchen island at Bennett Farms, his eyes focused on the phone in his hands. He didn't realize his mouth was jacked up in a goofy, lovesick grin until his father spoke.

"I like seeing the happy back in your eyes."

"What?" He startled and ran his free hand through his hair, acting as if his dad hadn't caught him in the act.

"The happy—it's back in your eyes. You're always smiling and a little more laid back these days. It suits you, son."

Walt shrugged and shoved his phone into his back pocket, Elyse's text message saved for later. "It's no big deal."

"No big deal? I beg to differ."

"What do you mean, Dad?"

"You like Miss Farrell, don't you?"

Walt inhaled sharply through his nose, averting his father's gaze. "Love is more like it," he mumbled.

"You love her?" His tone wasn't insinuating, more... surprised.

Walt stood tall and nodded, locking eyes with his dad. "Yes, Dad. I love her. I knew the minute I laid eyes on her the first time she visited the farm."

Roy pressed his lips together to thwart off a smile. "Come here. I want to show you something."

Walt followed his father through the house to his office, where he shut them inside.

"Have a seat."

Was Walt about to be lectured about true love? Or maybe his father thought it was time for him to have the birds and the bees chat with him, although it was a little late in the game with him being in his late twenties. And he'd been well aware of sex since his early teens after a private talk with his mom. What was so important that his dad had them sequestered inside his office?

Roy sat behind the desk and pulled open a bottom drawer. He lifted a thick stack of what appeared to be envelopes and cards in various shapes and sizes tied together with a gossamer ribbon. He plunked the pile smack dab in the middle of his workspace, making Walt frown.

"What are those?"

"Love letters between your mother and me," he said matter-of-factly.

Walt stared at the stack, overcome with a familiar melancholy whenever his mother was mentioned. God, he missed her so. As much as he pined for his mother's love and advice, he couldn't imagine how his father felt. That his old man kept her letters and cards nearby filled him with empathy.

"Back in our day, we didn't have fancy phones we could type on and send messages and photos to each other.

Nope." His dad remained upbeat, as if proud of what he was sharing.

"We had to take pen to paper and write letters. Then we had to put them in an envelope, make a trip to the post office, buy a stamp, and send them off. Long-distance phone calls were costly back then, so the only way to keep in touch was through letters. Sometimes it took days, even weeks before we heard back. But it was all worth it when I'd discover your mother's handwriting on an envelope in the daily mail." He grinned from ear to ear at the memory.

"Why, I'd rip open the envelope and pull out those stationary sheets in a hurry. Her penmanship was girlish, and I swear, I could sometimes smell the faint traces of her perfume on the paper. You have no idea how much patience I learned waiting for just one of these precious love letters." His father gently caressed the top envelope in the stack.

Walt swallowed hard, unsure what his dad was getting at. His heart hurt, knowing how much he profoundly missed his wife. "I'm glad you have your letters, Daddy."

"Me too, son. Me too." He nodded, and then he pushed the stack toward him.

Walt frowned. "You… want me to read them? Aren't they—private?"

"It's our love story, Walter. I'd be honored if you read each and every one. And don't worry, nothing is embarrassing in the words—only love." He stood and nodded one last time. "Well? What are you waiting for?"

Walt stood and picked up the stack, holding it gently against his stomach. "Now? You want me to read them all right now?"

"Now's as good a time as any. You can read them here where it's quiet. Take your time." He shut the door, leaving Walt alone inside.

Two hours later, Walt wiped a rogue tear from the corner of his eye, the final letter in his hands, putting the pieces of his parent's love puzzle into place. Throughout his life, his father and mother often reminisced with him and his siblings the story of how they met.

They were seniors in the local high school and met after Lillian moved to Langston Falls from the Midwest the summer before school started. She was the new girl in town, and they hit it off during lunchtime when she sat at his table, his dad claiming he instantaneously fell madly in love with her right then and there. But after dating for the entire year and after graduation, they had to put their relationship in the long-distance category when Lillian went off to study art at a private college outside of Asheville, North Carolina. Roy was left behind working on Bennett Farms, lovesick and pining for his woman while she was away at school. But that didn't stop them from communicating and visiting each other; they were devoted to making their relationship work. He always knew he was going to marry her, their plans put on the back burner until she finished college.

Walt read about their visits, Roy often traveling to North Carolina to see her. They spent time exploring the Biltmore Estate, where Walt learned that's where his father first became interested in the vineyards and wine-making process, which segued into his own business years later.

I've fallen more in love with the idea and romance of wine after we visited Biltmore. One letter read in his father's slanted cursive writing. *Perhaps one day, we can enjoy our own creation among the beauty of the North Georgia Mountains.*

Walt's heart swelled with pride, knowing what was once his Pawpaw Bennett's dream had come to fruition thanks to Roy, Bennett Farms hand-crafted and award-winning wines something he was now in charge of. When Walt was a child, he remembered turning the old red barn into a working winery wasn't easy. Still, his father and mother knew it was essential to keep the original structure's integrity, which helped them make each decision along the way. His mom and dad were always a team, working together while building their livelihood and family on the farm.

There were other getaways Walt read about in the letters during his parent's time apart: visits to Pigeon Forge and Gatlinburg, Tennessee, where they spent a long weekend together right after the Christmas holidays during his mother's junior year in college. She made witty jokes in one letter about his father's lack of skiing talent, his clumsy moves on the slopes rendering him to stay on the bunny slope suitable for beginners.

Throughout the letters, there was a consistent thread of love and longing, the two of them making every concerted effort to see each other when they had the opportunity. And when Walt read the words of one particular letter included in a red and white heart-shaped card, his mind was totally blown.

My Love,

Happy Valentine's Day. I hope my card finds you happy and healthy during the winter semester. I told you I'd been under the weather when we talked on the telephone long distance last week. Well, I finally went to the student clinic on campus, and they ran some tests. I wanted to tell you in person, but I'm too chicken, and I have mid-terms coming up. I guess there is no other way to tell you than to spell it out right here in this letter:

I'm pregnant.

Walt sat up straight in his chair, rereading the letter three times. His mother was pregnant in college before she and her dad were married? He did the math in his head, Teddy's birthday curiously aligning with the timeline. They

all knew she never finished college but never really knew
why, only imagining she and their dad grew tired of being
apart, ultimately wanting to get married and start their life
together on the farm.

*I'm pretty sure it happened when we went to Gatlinburg after
Christmas. It's a trip I won't ever forget. Please don't be mad at me.
And please, call me as soon as you get this letter. I've tucked my Ma
Bell calling card into the envelope to make it easy. I'll be waiting.*

I love you madly and forever,

Lillian

"Well, I'll be," he mumbled, enlightened by the truth.

There were no other letters in this stack which meant no
reply from his father. He knew without a doubt his dad was
thrilled with the news. He imagined Roy calling his mom,
laughing and crying, thrilled with the joyful news that he
would be a father.

Standing, Walt gently placed the last card and letter on
the stack, intent on perusing the old scrapbooks and photo
albums on the sagging bookshelves of the office walls. A
wedding album caught his attention, the paper pages
yellowed over the years. Holding the book in his hands, he
flipped through the album, his eyes tracing the professional
pictures of his parents captured on their wedding day.

His mother's dress was white and frilly, the early nineties
fashion of her headband veil encrusted with pearls and
sequins across her forehead making him smile. But the
colorful bouquet she held in her hands in every photo in
front of her belly had him nodding. The bride didn't appear
pregnant—she looked joyful, her flower bouquet hiding the
evidence.

Closing the book, Walt wondered what lesson his father
was trying to convey through the love letters during his
mom and dad's time apart? Walt could only chalk it up to

one thing—true love. They were meant to be together, and the universe made sure that happened sooner rather than later, his older brother Ted the caveat expediting their change of plans.

Walt tucked the wedding album back in its rightful spot among the other memories lining the shelves. For the first time in his life, he took in the timeline of knick-knacks and framed photos of his heritage. There were blurry, silver-toned images of his ancestors posed by the barn and farm-house. Numerous awards and plaques, various educational diplomas, and many pictures of his family posed in the fashion of the day showed a timeline of love throughout the years. Walt had to laugh at one particular photo of himself in middle school, his Justin Bieber haircut making him smile. But a loose, unframed photo made him pause—a moment captured and lying alone on the shelf nearest his father's desk.

Bringing the photo near the lamplight to get a better look, Walt realized it was an image of his father's wrinkled hand holding his mother's hand, their wedding rings prominent against the white sheets of her hospital bed. A lump immediately formed in his throat.

Roy Bennett always told his family it was love at first sight when he met Lillian. She was the love of his life.

And he loved her until the very end.

Chapter Twenty-Eight

ELYSE

Elyse sat on a folding chair overseeing the last filmed episode of *Sally's Southern Kitchen*. Sally had finally found her stride on the new set over the past two weeks and cruised through the last eight episodes they taped with very few problems. Elyse's favorite part of filming Sally's show was the creative aspect of using food to tell a story and experiencing all the details that went into the cooking segments the viewers loved on their network. The process was interesting and challenging throughout the different camera angles highlighting the different perspectives of the food. Add the queen of Southern cuisine with her cheery personality, perpetually wide baby blue eyes, and gray bouffant hair, and the new season made the viewers feel like they could conquer any recipe in the kitchen.

Elyse's least favorite part of filming over the last two weeks was not being able to see Walt in the flesh. She didn't have time because of her schedule. Thank goodness for their late-night phone conversations and random texts throughout each day. And now that her crew was wrapping up and going into post-production, she'd have a little more time on her hands—time for a weekend getaway to Langston Falls to reunite with her man.

"How's it going today?" Albert Tompkins, the VP of Programming asked.

"Great," Elyse replied. "We're about ready to wrap this season up."

"Looks that way." He eyed the studio space, his hands parked on his hips in a familiar stance. "Do you have a minute?"

Elyse rose from the uncomfortable folding chair. "Sure."

The two walked out of the studio and down the hall toward a vacant meeting space. When Albert closed them inside, Elyse folded her arms against her chest, wary of his behavior.

"Is everything okay, Al?"

"Everything is fantastic. Have a seat."

The two sat at the long conference table where many a production meeting had taken place over the last year. Elyse sat perfectly erect in her chair, curious about what Al had up his sleeve.

"I have a proposition for you, Elyse. With Sally's show going into post-production and with the recent tension between you and director Phil Lynch, I'd like to suggest something a bit out of the ordinary."

Elyse narrowed her eyes at him, the mere mention of Phil Lynch and his chauvinistic behavior on set making her sigh. "Go on."

"My colleague, Executive Producer Jerry Berg, is looking for an ace for his new project on the horizon. He's looking for someone who has knowledge of the production and film industry and familiarity with lighting and framing —someone with a good eye for scenes."

Elyse's interests perked, hoping the studio was about to secure another blockbuster production. "Great. Who did you have in mind, and I'll get the ball rolling and help set up a meeting for him?"

Albert chuckled, averting her gaze. "Well, I don't need you to set up a meeting with anyone. It's you I had in mind."

"*Me?*"

"Yes. Like I said, he's looking for someone already associated with Live Oak; someone with knowledge, and someone they can trust. I can't say much about the project yet until the official announcement goes to press, but between you and me, this is a huge contract for a new Netflix series. This would be a shift for you going from the reality TV world into scripted television. It's something you've always told me you'd like to explore someday."

Elyse was definitely curious. "Go on."

Albert nodded. "The only problem is, the series takes place in a small town, you know, early nineteen hundred architecture with nearby fields, farms, forests—the whole shebang. Jerry can't do it here on the Atlanta lot. He's got a location scout, and once the area is secured somewhere in North Georgia, I thought you'd be the perfect person to manage it."

Elyse could hardly breathe. Did he just say fields? Farmland? Forests? The small town of Langston Falls immediately popped into her head, the very idea of managing a series in Walt's hometown too good to be true.

"Now, I know you're quite pleased with your role on Sally's show, and that won't go away with everything we've already filmed. But if you and Jerry hit it off, your new title for his show would be location manager. Your new role would also come with a hefty salary increase, although you'd have to be on location for several months while filming."

Elyse stared wide-eyed at Albert, her mind going crazy with possibilities. If she could convince Jerry Berg to set up shop in Langston Falls, she'd take on the new role of location manager in a heartbeat. Location managers were in charge of the cast and crew, negotiating everything from parking and power sources to catering requirements and official permissions with the site's management or owners. She was a whiz at daily logistics and troubleshooting problems during filming. And her knowledge of the film industry, as well as her eye for scenes was a bonus.

When she didn't respond to Al, he seemed disappointed and pursed his lips. "I understand. You've made a home for yourself here in Atlanta and are comfortable in your current role."

"Hold on," she finally muttered, taking a deep, cleansing breath. She could barely contain her smile. "I'm totally interested, Al."

"You are?"

"Yes. But I do have one request."

Al perked up at her excited tone, his eyes glistening with pleasure. "Anything you want, Elyse. Believe me, you've earned it."

She nibbled on her lower lip before the words tumbled out of her mouth. "Put in a good word for me and ask Jerry if he'd allow me to work directly with his location scout up front. From your descriptions, I have an ideal spot already in mind. If the scout feels it could work, and I'm confident he or she will, then I'm all in."

Al nodded and stood as if pleased. "You've got a deal, Elyse."

Driving past the scalloped edges of a white picket fence on the outskirts of Langston Falls, Elyse flashed a grin at her reflection in the rearview mirror, knowing she was about to surprise Walt during the workday at Bennett Farms. Since shooting for Sally's show at Live Oak Studios had wrapped, she was anxious to talk to Walt about Al's proposition in person. They'd planned on reuniting over the weekend, but she couldn't wait and bolted out of Atlanta on Friday morning after rush hour traffic.

Passing under the heavy gauge steel sign of Bennett Farms, Elyse took in her surroundings. The homestead would make an ideal filming location, but she knew that wasn't possible because it was a hard-working farm. Perhaps they could scout some of the open meadows or nearby forests? She was also interested in taking a tour of the Kirby homestead, the apple orchard and small house a viable possibility. And it would mean more income for Glen to repurchase his farm.

Elyse parked her car next to a work truck with the peeling red letters spelling "Bennett Christmas Tree Farm & Winery" on it. Her lips twitched with a smile, and she felt oddly at home. Holding her hand above her eyes to thwart the late morning winter sun, she scanned the rolling vine-yards and evergreen blanket of trees across the land. The setting was perfect.

"Elyse?"

Turning toward the sound of her name, she was happy to see Becky standing on the front porch. Her frilly apron was dusted with what looked like flour, her expression confused.

"Yes! Hey Becky, how are you?"

"I'm good. I'd hug you but I'm covered in flour. Long time no see," she giggled. "Did you finish filming Sally's show? Walt said you've been busier than a beaver building a dam."

Elyse laughed at the euphemism, the southern Bennett family one she missed very much. "Yes. We wrapped this season's production yesterday."

"Oh, wow. I wish I could've seen Sally in action."

"You will. The new season's first episode will be ready to launch in about a month. Once Sally figured out her new set, she was flawless."

"I'll bet." Becky gave Elyse the once-over, settling her hands on her hips. "I like this more casual look you got going on."

Elyse fidgeted with a flannel scarf loosely tied around her neck, the long edges laying against the front of her hooded quilted coat. Her dark blue jeans and flat boots completed her outfit. "Thanks."

"It's a bit chilly out here. Why don't you come on inside? If you're hungry, I've got a few blueberry muffins left over from breakfast and a pot of coffee brewed." The two girls ambled into the house, the aroma of fresh coffee with a hint of cinnamon tempting.

"No, thank you." Elyse noticed a ring light set up on the kitchen island. "Did I interrupt filming for your YouTube channel?"

"I haven't started yet. I'm just plotting everything out for later."

"Well, we need to sit down and discuss a few things since our last meeting. I have a couple of sponsors interested in speaking with you."

Becky's face paled. "Sponsors? Really?"

"Yes. I told you there's money to be made with your

brand on YouTube. Our first goal is to get you to become an affiliate for some product sponsors, using their items in your demonstrations. The products will be available for sale in a link added to your post."

Becky laughed. "I thought you were kidding about all of this."

Elyse's tone turned serious. "I never kid, Becky. I'm quite serious."

"Wow. Okay. Let me know when a good time is, and I'll be sure to be available." She grinned from ear to ear.

Elyse's return smile was genuine. "Sounds perfect."

"I guess you want to see Walter now, huh?"

"Is he available?"

"I don't know. He's been in the vineyard pruning some of the older vines. I can call him in—"

"No. Don't do that," Elyse interrupted. "Can you point me toward the vineyard he's working in? I'd like to surprise him."

Becky nodded as if she understood, the apples of her cheeks flushed with a rosy hue. Taking hold of Elyse by the hand, she led her to the back door of the kitchen and pointed past the red barn toward a field of tidy tilled rows. "He should be out there in the east field with some of the workers. He's wearing a cowboy hat. You can't miss him."

Elyse adjusted the scarf around her neck with pleasure. "Thanks."

Careful in her sensible, flat-heeled boots she decided to wear last minute, Elyse walked down the stone steps leading to the barn and continued along a graveled pathway toward the vineyard. There were remnants of snow in the shade, the blizzard they'd gone through nothing more than a distant, melting memory. In the expansive field, she noticed a familiar cowboy hat bobbing up and down along a row of vines. When she was within earshot, she loudly asked Walt a question.

"Are these vines dead?"

Walt jerked his head up from his focus on the vine and looked over the long trellis, his expression full of shock. He stood tall and gave her the once-over from head to toe with one eyebrow hitched. Clearing his throat, he seemed to thwart off a boyish grin.

"Nope. This vineyard is very much alive. The vines grow below ground, expending their energy into the root system."

"Hmmm. Very interesting." She crossed her arms against her coated chest as if she were an interested somme-lier taking a tour. "And what exactly happens down there under the ground?"

Walt lazily took his gloves off and shoved them into the back pocket of his jeans. "Well, the roots are still growing, soaking up soil nutrients to keep the vine strong during winter while preparing for spring and the emergence of new shoots."

They started to stroll parallel to each other, the vine trel-lises standing between them. When they came to an alleyway amid the vineyard blocks, they paused.

"So basically, the upper half of the vine is asleep."

"Something like that," he chuckled. "Everything in nature falls asleep, the recent snow a sort of white blanket keeping it all cozy and tucked in. It might look like death among the branches now, but after I separate the damaged wood from the healthy wood by cutting it off, I use the dead branches for compost, allowing the natural materials to be put back into the earth."

Elyse stared at him, his handsome face peppered with a smattering of whiskers, his dark eyes piercing her with a look she knew well—one part longing, the other part genuinely happy to see her. She took a few steps closer to him in the alleyway and watched him take his hat off, his hair a tousled mess underneath. Standing before her in his well-worn jeans and untucked flannel over a thermal shirt, her gaze ran the length of his bulging arms down to his strong hands—hands she desperately wanted touching her body.

God bless America.

"So, what was frozen will be newly purposed and turn green again in the spring, right?" she asked, her voice husky with desire. Her shoes touched the tips of his cowboy boots, and she arched her neck to look up at him, her bosom rising and falling in even breaths.

"Yes. Spring is my favorite time of the year."

"Why is that?" Her body trembled being in such close proximity to him, and the urge to reach out and touch him was almost painful.

"Spring is when nature is revived after the cold winter months and when dormant plants begin to grow again. It's an awakening."

"An awakening," she repeated, mesmerized by the low, sexy timbre of his voice.

Finally, he cupped his warm hand against her cheek, his breath an exhale of desire before he closed the gap between them and melded his lips with hers.

Chapter Twenty-Nine

WALT

Walt could barely contain himself, the ride back to the Kirby homestead taking way too long, even though it was less than a two-mile drive on the country back roads. He was still living there for the time being while Glen was in a recommended rehab facility in South Georgia getting treatment. He'd heard from Samantha that Glen was doing well, his former enemy often asking about him. Glen was anxious to do the hard work to get better so he could get back to living his life in Langston Falls. The two had unfinished business to discuss when he was released; Walt's first priority getting Glen and back in the home he shamelessly stole from them.

"What's with all the boxes? I thought you said you weren't moving out until you had Glen's release date?" Elyse eyed a stack of flattened moving boxes leaned against the wall as she gripped his hand through the foyer.

"I'm not moving anytime soon. Just collecting boxes for when the time comes." Walt picked up his pace, pulling her toward the bedroom with purpose. Only one thing was on his mind, and it wasn't moving back to Bennett Farms.

Garth hopped up on the back end of the sofa and meowed a welcome.

"Don't you need to feed him?" Elyse giggled as he completely ignored his pet and dragged her through the house.

"It's not suppertime yet. It's time for something else."

Entering the bedroom, he was quick with his actions, shutting them inside so his cat wouldn't follow them in and interrupt. Peeling off his coat, he threw it toward a corner chair and missed, focusing solely on Elyse's beautiful face. He unbuttoned his flannel shirt and watched as she took off her coat and peeled her scarf from around her neck, her blue flame eyes burning with certain desire. He frowned when he noticed the turtleneck she wore from underneath her casual coat.

"Don't be getting any ideas involving scissors, mister." She laughed and pulled at the edges of the sweater, lifting it effortlessly up and over her head in one fell swoop, tossing it to the side.

Walt mimicked her, lifting his thermal shirt up and over his head and came toward her, his solid chest bare and giving off substantial heat. "I thought I told you, no more turtlenecks," he growled.

Elyse tilted her head with moxie, her lacy black bra driving him wild. She reached around her back and unclasped the garment, allowing it to fall forward into her hands. "But I love them so, and they're warm this time of the year. Besides, it's my signature look." The way she looked at him with her pouty mouth and shimmering baby blues made his dick instantly hard.

"Not in these parts," he insisted. He closed the space

between them and imprisoned her in his arms, backing her against the wall. Caging her in, he devoured her mouth with a searing-hot kiss, every nerve ending in his body catching fire. She reached between them and unzipped his jeans, sliding her hands over his throbbing cock. He was desperate to be inside her again.

"God, I want you," he whispered. "I've never wanted anyone so badly in my entire life." He licked and nipped at the skin of her neck, her stance open to his actions.

"Then take me." Her hot breath seared the shell of his ear.

They were a flurry of hands as they stripped off their boots and pants, Walt's heart galloping like a racehorse. Elyse squealed when he picked her up and slung her cave-man-style over his shoulder, smacking her bare ass with his free hand. Setting her on the bed, her naked body was a vision to touch and behold. He straddled her and ran his finger up her wet seam.

"Did I do this to you?" A gusty sigh escaped him.

"Yes," she panted. Her dark brows drew together. "What are you waiting for?"

Walt held her gaze and admired how breathtakingly gorgeous she looked lying underneath him. Her lovely lips twisted with mischief as she wrapped her hands around his raging boner again, his need to be inside her growing expo-nentially.

"It's you, Elyse. Only you."

"I know. And I'm ready."

"Ready for what?" He wanted her to say it. He *needed* her to say it.

"Everything—as long as it's with you."

Walt was overcome with a primal need and lodged himself deep in her heat, grazing his nose with hers. Warm wisps of her sweet breath hit his flaming cheeks, and he felt the tips of her fingers drag over his buttocks, causing ripples of pleasure to erupt from his core. All the days waiting for her return felt like trudging through heavy snow drifts—slow, cold, and exhausting. But now, being as close as he could get to her, he felt peace and contentment, warmth, and happiness. The positive feelings were a far cry from where he'd once been. And he was grateful.

His eyes trailed up and over her bosom and chin before they found captivating azure pools staring back at him. He was more than ready to dive in with both feet. But the way she looked at him made him pause. He wanted to memorize the moment, his mother and father's love story coming to mind.

Elyse was the one for him. She was his future—a future that showed up out of nowhere and saved him during a time when he thought he was looking for something else.

"So, it's a done deal?" Walt asked, holding a naked Elyse in his arms. They'd made love for hours, slowly and intentionally—without any rules, without anything but adoration between them.

"Almost," she replied. "Jerry Berg and I hit it off, and he's talking to his location scout about hooking up with me."

"Hooking up with you?" Walt teased. He cocked one eyebrow, his menacing frown intentional with predatory focus.

"You know what I mean. We need to get together so I can show him around."

"As long as you're not showing him too good of a time."

"Walter!" She rolled her eyes and swatted at his chest.

"I'm just kidding," he laughed, thankful they could tease each other without getting upset. He loved the feel of her naked body pressed against his as they casually talked about their future together. It's what he so desperately wanted with every fiber of his being. The opportunity for Elyse to live and work in Langston Falls was a thrilling gift from the heavens.

"I know he'll be pleased with Langston Falls as a location for this new series. It's a win-win for the town and the studio."

Walt cleared his throat. "No, Elyse." He tipped her chin to where he could look her right in the eye with purpose. "It's a win-win for you and me."

She nodded. "That too." Rolling off his chest, she flung her arm dramatically across her forehead and stared at the ceiling. "God, Walt. I want this to work out so badly. I want to work here in Langston Falls so we can be together. Can you imagine what that would be like?"

Walt rolled to his side and propped his head in his hand. Staring down at her, he smiled. "Of course I can imagine it. We belong together. Don't you remember when we first met, and I told you how I let the natural ebb and flow of the universe take me where it wants?"

"Yes, I do."

"Well, I think our desire to ultimately be together is manifesting, and the universe switched gears and put this opportunity in your lap. How else can you explain it?" They were silent, the air crackling with hope and strong desire.

"Elyse, I know this is going to work out for us. I have no doubt because our planets and spirits have aligned. We both felt it when it happened. You and I are meant to be together. Why else would Al offer you this opportunity and introduce you to Jerry Berg? Why else would you and Jerry hit it off from the get-go? It's all a domino effect. Can't you see it? All the pieces are falling into place." He continued to stare at her, thankful she seemed to be tracking with him.

"We have nothing but time, Elyse. Everything will work out how it's supposed to. Let's continue to ride this thing out and see where it goes."

Elyse's blue eyes sparkled like jewels as she scooted toward him and used her fingers to push back a lock of hair that had fallen across his forehead. Her brow furrowed for a beat before she stared right into his soul.

"I love you, Walter Bennett."

"And I love you, Elyse Farrell." He wrapped his fingers around the nape of her neck and pulled her forward, kissing her with the skill of an adoring lover.

When she snuggled into his body and pressed her satiny cheek against his chest, he played with the ends of her long dark hair, his body sated and relaxed. He was right where he was meant to be, with Elyse in his arms. He was a better man when they were together. There was no other way to explain it. It was like having one arm out the window and one hand on the wheel while out on a Sunday drive passing the golden meadows of twilight. Her tiny hand fit perfectly right into his like a record player needle into a vinyl groove, the two of them humming in perfect harmony. And the way she said, "I love you," held the gentleness of falling rain on an old tin roof, invoking a sense of melody and calm.

They were a match made in the heavenly universe, better together—and he could not ask for anything more.

Chapter Thirty

ELYSE

With one hand on the steering wheel and the other twirling a strand of hair, Elyse drove along the country road toward downtown Langston Falls, her body relaxed and humming with excitement. She was meeting Jerry Berg's location scout, a woman named Connie Johnston. They'd talked on the phone several times over the last couple of days, Elyse insisting she meet her in the small town so she could give her a tour of possible filming locations. With Walt's help, Elyse made a list of places she carefully considered, ready to provide Connie with her spiel.

"Do you want me to go with you? I've lived here my entire life and know practically everyone in this town," Walt had reminded her.

"I appreciate it, but I'd rather meet with her alone the first time. We'll drive around to get the lay of the land. I promise, if she has any questions I can't answer or wants to dive deeper, I'll call you and have you meet up with us. Sound good?"

"Sounds perfect."

Elyse smiled at the memory of their conversation. They were both excited by the real possibility she could be moving to Langston Falls for an extended period of time. God, to be able to spend quality time with the man she loved for more than a quick weekend or rendezvous was a dream, one she hoped might come true.

Looking back on their time together, she realized he was right about their journey as a couple. From the very beginning, they both felt it—sparks, chemistry, an undeniable connection. It was insta-love. What started out as a mission for her to get handsome Walt to be her beck and call guy transformed into something greater than she could have ever imagined. He wasn't a casual fling or a one-night stand. No, he was someone she could honestly see herself with for the rest of her life.

The gnarled branches of the trees along the roadside were barren, the promise of spring still a few months away. Shrugging her chin into her wooly scarf, she dreamily thought about the spring season—an awakening, as Walt had put it. She was well on her way to an awakening of her own. Becoming acutely aware of her feelings for Walt was a transformative experience. He was right about everything, and the familiar hum of electricity reverberating through her body reminded her of the wish she'd once put out into the universe—the same wish merging with Walt's path, guiding her along the way.

This was her moment to seize, a moment that could potentially change her life forever. Elyse was on a path of spiritual awakening, and it was the grandest adventure she'd ever been on. Being a conscious participant in her growth and evolution was mind-blowing. She recognized the truth and the signs of her journey, ready to embrace the call of her life purpose and destiny, all of it with Walt by her side.

Elyse heard the ping of a text message and looked down at her phone sitting in the cup holder to read it.

Kick some ass today, gorgeous. I love you.

Heat peppered her cheeks, knowing he was her ultimate cheerleader. He wasn't one of those guys intimidated by her career. Quite the opposite. He supported her one-hundred percent, his encouragement to "kick some ass" precisely what she needed as she neared Main Street.

Lifting her eyes back to the road in front of her, she gasped when a deer darted out in front of her. Time seemed to stand still, the animal's large doe eyes locking with hers as a random thought crossed her mind in a millisecond. She once read that when a person saw a deer while driving, it was the universe sending a message to slow down and find inner balance within—to pay attention to everything happening around you...

She swerved to avoid hitting the animal, her sports car skidding across the asphalt into the other lane. The deer galloped through the trees into the forest unscathed.

Elyse held her breath, her grip on the steering wheel tightening as she tried to correct her vehicle's orientation on the road. But when the tires hit the narrow shoulder of gravel and dirt, the car spun violently and careened down an embankment whipping through the underbrush and small saplings. It was all happening so fast, and when she saw the giant tree looming ahead, getting closer and closer by the second, she pressed her eyes shut, bracing for the crash. There was nothing she could do to stop the impact.

The front of her car collided with the tree, the sound of metal and glass breaking filling her ears in a cacophony of noise as the airbag deployed with blunt force. When it was all over, her chest rose and fell in quick breaths, the ensuing quiet after-effect filling her with dread. And then she felt a searing pain in her shoulder. Tears filled her eyes as she looked around the decimation that was once her car, the contents of her purse strewn about the interior. Spotting her cell phone on the passenger seat, she tried to reach for it, but the sting in her shoulder stopped her in her tracks, making her scream in agony.

"*Ahhh!*"

Holding her shoulder with her opposite hand, she waited for the pain to dissipate, the realization of what she'd just been through sobering. Gritting her teeth, she unfastened her seatbelt and gingerly turned her entire body to face the passenger side of the car. She reached for her phone again with her good arm, pressing her lips together to keep from crying. The smell of burnt rubber and gasoline lingered in the interior.

With her hand stretched toward the device, her fingers touched the phone's edges, and she had to dig deep to fight against the excruciating torture her slightest movements caused. Her right shoulder was either broken or dislocated; she was sure of it. Her fingers trembled as she tried scooting the phone closer to where she could finally pick it up. But the pain was too intense, and she gave up.

Taking a deep cleansing breath, she shouted, "Siri, call 9-1-1!" Thank God her blue tooth still worked, the car speaker coming to life with a ringtone before an operator came on the line.

"Hello? Yes, I was... in a car accident. Can you pin my location from where you're at?" She waited for the operator to respond and was relieved when she said she found her location using cell phone technology.

Exhaling a quivering sigh of relief, she nodded. "Thank you. Yes, I'll stay on the line while I wait for the ambulance."

Her eyes filled with hot tears she desperately tried to keep at bay. But it was no use. They spilled down her cheeks, and her body was wracked with uncontrollable sobbing. The operator did her best to give her words of comfort while she waited for help to arrive.

They couldn't get there fast enough.

Elyse glanced at the chair in the corner of the hospital room, her coat and clothes in a neat pile and her boots tucked underneath. Her face was bruised from the impact of the airbag going off, and her right arm was in a sling, her shoulder dislocated from the impact of her car hitting the tree. Good thing she was given medication to take the edge off; her body numbed with relief.

The sweet EMT kept her calm after she was extracted from her totaled vehicle by the Langston Falls fire department. Lying on the stretcher in the ambulance, safely belted in place, she begged the EMT to help her call Becky Bennett so she could tell her what happened. Elyse knew if she called Walt, she might start crying again, and then he'd lose his shit and possibly get into an accident of his own trying to get to her. It was better for his sister to gently and calmly break the news to him so he wouldn't freak out.

"Hey, Elyse. What's up?"

"Hey, Becky. I'm, uh, not doing too good right now. Do you have a minute?"

"Sure. What's wrong?"

Elyse could hear the concerned tone of Becky's voice and explained in short sentences how she was on her way to Langston Hospital after being involved in a car wreck. She also assured her she was alive and kicking.

"Does Walt know? Is he on his way?" Becky fretted.

"No, Becky. I… I didn't think it was wise to call him directly, so I called you. He's going to be so upset—"

"Yes, he is," she interrupted. "I'll break it to him gently. And then I'll get Daddy, and we'll bring him right over so he can be with you. God, Elyse, I'm so happy you're okay."

Elyse closed her eyes with relief. "Me too."

"Can I do anything else for you? Is there anyone else you want me to call before we head your way?"

Elyse thought about calling her parents and sister in Kansas but wanted to wait until a doctor assessed her, knowing they'd barrage her with medical questions and concerns. Calling them could wait. But then she remembered her appointment with Connie Johnston, who was driving from Atlanta to meet her. The location scout was probably already waiting for her in Langston Park, where they agreed to meet.

"Yes, I do have someone I need you to call for me. You see, I was on my way to Langston Park."

"Langston Park? How come?"

Elyse hadn't told anyone in the Bennett family but Walt about her potential opportunity as a location manager for a new film series. "It's a long story, Becky. Can you please just call the lady I was supposed to meet and tell her I've been detained? I'll try to call her later. Her name is Connie Johnston. She's a location scout from the studio." Although it was a half-truth, she hoped the information appeased Becky's curiosity. "I'll have the EMT text her number, okay?"

"Absolutely. I'll call her before I talk to Walt." She paused on the other end, making Elyse think she'd hung up.

"Becky?"

"I'm here. I wanted to say something before we hung up."

"What is it, Becky?"

"Walt's going to take such good care of you."

A lump formed in Elyse's throat. "I know."

The ambulance arrived at Langston Hospital, where Elyse was immediately treated by a team of ER doctors. X-rays were ordered, and an MRI was performed to ensure there wasn't any internal bleeding or broken bones in her body. Unfortunately, the x-rays confirmed her right shoulder was, in fact, dislocated, the unfathomable pain leaving her decimated. Thank goodness the injury wouldn't require surgery, the MRI verifying her ligaments weren't damaged during the accident. Once her shoulder was put back in the normal position, her doctor immobilized it with a sling, telling her she should be good as new after a few weeks of rest.

Battered and bruised, Elyse was placed in a private room where she patiently waited for Walt to arrive. What was taking him so long? When the nurse popped her head into the room a few minutes later and announced she had a visitor, a surge of relief swept through her entire being, like she was finally coming home.

"Please, send him in."

Chapter Thirty-One

WALT

Walt gripped the cellophane wrapper surrounding the red roses he'd picked up from Langston Petals minutes before, his anxious heart thrumming as he approached the hospital room where Elyse recovered.

When Becky had found him in the vineyard, he knew something was wrong by the serious look on her usual smiling face.

"What is it?"

The frosty air chilled him to the bone as he stood tall, ready to accept whatever bad news she had to relay. Had his father taken a fall? The old man wasn't as limber as he used to be, the entire family scolding him numerous times when he'd climb a ladder unsupervised or lift something too heavy. Or maybe one of his brothers needed him, like the time Hank barely missed his femoral artery in an unfortunate chainsaw accident during Christmas tree season.

Becky looked at him with trepidation in her eyes. "It's Elyse."

Walt dropped his pruning shears and took off running,

not even waiting for Becky to tell him exactly what happened. He ran so hard his lungs threatened to split wide open, a painful stitch pinging his side. James stopped him before he could get in his truck and speed off like a bolt of lightning.

"Slow down, Walt!" James demanded. "You're not in your right mind to drive. I'll take you."

All Walt could do was nod and hand off his keys, his mind swirling with worst-case scenarios. As the truck pulled onto the road that would take him to his beloved, he turned in his seat and faced his brother, still panting from his run. "Do you know what happened?"

James nodded. "Elyse called Becky from an ambulance—"

"An ambulance?" he interrupted. He threw off his cowboy hat and gripped his scalp, fearing the worst. "What the fuck happened?"

James' brow furrowed as he concentrated on the blacktop in front of him. "She was in a car accident, Walt, but she's gonna be okay."

Walt's heart fell to his feet, his features twisting with torture.

James reached over and palmed Walt's shoulder with reassurance. "She's gonna be okay, buddy. Do you hear me? She's oh-kay."

Walt numbly nodded as he held on to the truth his trustworthy brother told him.

Elyse was in a car accident.

Elyse was going to be okay.

"Why did she call Becky and not me?" he suddenly realized.

James gave Walt the side-eye. "Come on, Walt. You're

not known for keeping it together in times of undue stress. I mean, look at you right now."

His brother had a point. Still, he was concerned Elyse wasn't comfortable calling him first or even calling him at all. If the tables were turned, she would've been his first call.

"I know what you're thinking, bro," James said.

"What am I thinking, Jimmy?"

"You're stewing over the fact she called our sister and not you."

"And?"

"Buddy, it was for your own safety. Believe me."

Walt had to admit he was simmering in his own feelings. On the one hand, he understood Elyse's actions were intentional, her effort to keep him calm under the circumstances admirable. But hadn't they been through worse? My God, when Glen's gun went off a few weeks ago, Walt had remained calm and cool as a cucumber, right? He'd come a long way.

"Let's pull into the flower shop so you can get Elyse something pretty. You shouldn't go in there empty-handed."

Walt looked at his older brother and nodded. It was a hard reality check to admit his family was right—he would've lost it if she'd called him first. "Okay."

Twenty minutes later, Walt stood outside the hospital room door and collected himself, the red roses clutched in his hand giving off a sweet fragrance. He ran his hands through his disheveled hair, his cowboy hat left on the passenger seat of his truck. Knocking on the door two times, he waited with bated breath.

"Come in," he heard Elyse say.

The sound of her voice was evidence James had told him the truth; she was okay. With the door opened, his gaze landed on her bruised face, her loving smile and glistening eyes telling him everything he needed to know—she was still very much his.

"Are those for me?"

Walt remembered the flowers in his hand and nodded, words catching in his throat. She was dressed in a blue and white hospital gown, and her right arm was held close to her body in a black sling. She reached for him with her good arm.

"Come here, Cowboy."

Walt shuffled across the linoleum toward the bed, never taking his eyes off hers. Gently, he placed the flowers on her lap and slowly lowered himself into the chair next to her, his heart thumping triple time with angst. Even in her bruised state, Elyse was still the most beautiful woman he'd ever seen.

"What happened?" he managed to mumble. Hot tears stung the corners of his eyes, and he had to bite the inside of his cheek to keep his emotions at bay.

"Don't worry, Walt. I'm going to be fine," she started. "And the deer is okay too."

"Deer?"

"Yes. Bambi didn't look both ways while trying to cross the road. I had to swerve my car, so I wouldn't hit him."

Walt knew the Langston Fall mountainous area was populated with tons of deer, and signs along the highway warned drivers to watch out for the animals. He swallowed hard, forcing himself to relax as she explained what had happened.

"But I think you should know there are a few things that aren't so fine because of the accident."

Walt fixated on her face, the urge to stroke her bruises and take away her physical pain very real. "Tell me," he whispered.

"I'm pretty sure my car is totaled. And I dislocated my shoulder." She eyed the sling. "But the doctor was able to put my shoulder back in place, and it doesn't look like I'll need surgery, so that's some good news."

Walt nodded and held his breath, hoping against hope she'd come away from the accident with only minor injuries. A car could be replaced, and a dislocated shoulder and a few bumps and bruises would heal over time. But if she suffered any internal injuries, there was no telling how long she'd be incapacitated.

"But there is one thing that can never be fixed." She nodded toward a pile of clothes folded on a chair in the corner.

Walt frowned, his eyes tracing the stack. "What?"

"Go take a look."

Walt warily stood and went to the pile of clothes to investigate. The top item was neatly folded, looking like nothing out of the ordinary.

"Lift it all the way up," Elyse encouraged.

Walt picked up the fabric and realized it was one of Elyse's turtlenecks, the entire front of the clothing cut in half, the jagged edges alarming.

"Do you see it? They had to cut me out of my turtleneck, Walt because I couldn't move my shoulder. I should've listened to you all along. I should've stopped wearing turtlenecks when you told me to." Elyse was crying and laughing simultaneously, the scared tone of her voice unmistakable. Her professional, turtleneck-wearing persona was fractured, in its place a frightened young woman trembling in the aftermath of a severe accident that could've ended her life.

Walt dropped the shirt and hurried to be by her side. He sat on the hospital bed and clutched her free hand to his lips, his own tears freely dribbling down his cheeks. The feeling was foreign to him—the relief, the angst all rolled up into one and released in a fit of emotion.

"I thought I'd lost you," he uttered between sniffles.

"Never," she replied. Her blue eyes held his captive, the relief emanating from her warm smile filling him with true love.

Walt leaned forward and pressed his lips against her forehead, memorizing every detail—the firm grip of her hand in his. The scent of lingering perfume on her neck. The rise and fall of her warm body as she lay on the bed, very much alive and breathing. He wasn't sure what he'd done in his life to deserve a second chance with this woman. But he was eternally grateful.

"Don't cry, Walter. I can always buy more turtlenecks."

Her comment made him chuckle as he eased back and swiped at his wet face. The only other time he'd ever cried in front of anyone was at his mother's funeral. Looking directly into Elyse's face, he noticed her flirty expression twinkling with amusement. He knew she was pulling his leg, the added injection of humor turning his sorrow into joy.

His voice rumbled in a low timbre. "Darlin', you can buy as many turtlenecks as you like if that's what makes you happy. I won't try to stop you ever again."

Elyse leaned her head against a pillow and sighed. "Promise? After all, it is my signature look."

Walt held her gaze and admired her beauty, even in her battered state—even without her confounded turtleneck.

He kissed the center of her palm. "I promise."

Chapter Thirty-Two

WALT

Walt was thankful when he saw his family camped out in the hospital's waiting room, their concern for Elyse and what she went through heartwarming.

"Hank sends his love and well wishes from Nashville," Becky said. She stood and handed Walt a folded-up flannel in Scotch plaid, the pink, blue, and purple fabric soft to the touch. "I hope this will work. It's a button-up shirt, so she can easily get her arm through it, with some help, of course."

Walt took the item of clothing from her, thankful she'd come through for him again. "Thanks, Becks." He strode to the nurse's station and handed it off to the crew, getting Elyse ready for discharge.

"How's she doing?" Teddy asked. He stood next to his brother James, both still wearing their work clothes.

"She's good. They're getting the papers ready to sign off on so I can take her home."

"I'm glad she won't have to spend the night," James

said. "We can help you get her back to your place if you want."

"I think I can handle it, but thanks. Y'all are the best." His eyes traced each face of his family. "I mean it."

Becky giggled with surprise. "A rare compliment from our brother Walter—what is happening?"

The Bennett boys chuckled in response as Walt pulled his baby sister in for an overdue hug. That's when he realized his father wasn't there among them. "Where's Dad?"

James explained. "He'll be here in a few. He had a meeting with a certain location scout and wanted to give her a personal tour of Langston Falls so Elyse wouldn't fall behind."

Walt inhaled sharply. "Shit! That's right. Elyse was on her way to meet her when the accident happened—"

"Connie," Becky interrupted.

"Excuse me?" Walt replied.

"Her name is Connie Johnston, and she's so cool. Wait till you meet her."

Walt was about to say something else, but the conversation was cut short when he noticed Elyse being pushed in a wheelchair by a nurse toward their group. The soft flannel shirt hung loosely on her frame, and her quilted coat rested on her shoulders. His brothers and sister gathered around the wheelchair and remarked how glad they were to see her, thankful she was okay. The nurse excused herself, saying she'd return with her discharge papers.

"You know, I dislocated my shoulder once. It happened when I was playing football at Langston High School back in the day. Man, it hurt something fierce. I hope you're not in too much pain," Teddy said.

Elyse smiled. "I'm a little achy but not in severe pain like when it first happened." She looked at each one of them with fondness. "Thank you so much for being here for me today. I don't know what I would've done without you."

Becky approached and squeezed Elyse's hand. "You're family, Elyse. And family always helps family."

Walt pressed his lips together, overcome with a sense of deep affection toward his siblings.

"Give me your keys, and I'll get your truck," James offered.

"Thanks, bro." Walt handed off his keys and watched his brother trot off, only to return a few seconds later with his dad and a strange woman by his side.

"Look who I found," James grinned.

Roy pulled his black Stetson off his head and stood directly in front of Elyse. Squatting to be eye level with her, he tenderly held her hand. "Thank God you're all right, darlin'. You had us all worried for a spell."

The apples of Elyse's cheeks turned red, her smile genuine. "Thanks for coming, Mr. Bennett."

He chuckled. "Come on now, it's about time you started calling me Roy, young lady."

"Then Roy it is," she grinned.

Roy stood and swung his hand out to introduce the woman standing nearby. "I know y'all have met over the telephone, but not in person. This here is Connie Johnston in the flesh."

"Connie?" Elyse gasped, stretching her hand out to shake hers. "I'm so sorry I wasn't able to meet with you today—"

"No worries, Elyse," she interrupted, shaking her hand gently. "I'm so glad you're okay. Roy, here, gave me the grand tour."

Elyse's blue eyes widened in surprise as she looked back and forth between Roy and Connie. "He did?"

Walt beamed with pleasure, knowing his dad had come through for Elyse during the emergency, knowing he'd come through for him too.

"Roy drove me around this beautiful town. He showed me all the sights, including Langston Falls and the river, Main Street, Wagoner Farm, the Kirby homestead, and Bennett Farms. I must say, you certainly have an eye for location scouting."

Elyse looked at Walt, and he nodded. "I gave Dad the list we made. I hope you don't mind."

"Mind? Of course I don't mind. What are you Bennett people, guardian angels?"

The entire group laughed as Walt leaned down and kissed Elyse on her temple. She snaked her free hand to his resting on the wheelchair arm and wouldn't let go.

"So, what happens next, Connie? Do you have everything you need to make a final decision?" Elyse asked.

Connie smiled. The middle-aged woman seemed totally at ease. "This is a no-brainer, Elyse. Jerry is going to be thrilled with our new location."

Walt whooped joyfully and high-fived his brothers as if the Atlanta Braves had just won another World Series. The news couldn't have been any better, everything he and Elyse wished for finally coming true. Her new role as a location manager was practically a done deal.

Connie congratulated Elyse and the group and bid them farewell, promising she'd be in touch soon with their next steps.

"You must've pulled out all the stops using your charm to woo Connie into falling in love with Langston Falls," Elyse said to Roy. "I don't know how I can ever repay you. Thank you."

"No, darlin'. Thank you."

"For what?"

Roy slung an arm across Walt's shoulders. "Thank you for bringing the happy back to my boy."

Walt beamed from underneath his father's sturdy arm, his joy and love for his family and Elyse apparent for all the world to see.

Walt carefully drove over the bumpy road and the divots leading to the Kirby home. He helped Elyse out of the truck and offered to carry her inside, but she wasn't having it.

"I can walk, Walt. My legs are just fine," she teased.

"Okay, okay," he laughed. He knew he was being overly cautious. But how could he not be? He could've lost her that morning, the morbid thought making him shiver.

Inside the house, Walt helped her to the sofa in front of the fireplace, where she eased her weary body onto the cushions. Garth hopped into her lap and meowed, rubbing his head against her sling.

"Do you want me to put him in the bathroom so you can rest?"

"No," she said, running her fingers through his sable fur. "He missed me, that's all."

Walt stood there with his hands on his hips and looked around the room. Robyn and his sister had come by earlier with dinner and some flowers from Elyse's family back in Kansas. They'd ordered them from Langston Petals, personally delivered by Robyn herself. The beautiful arrangement was displayed on the mantle, the white hydrangea and rose creation dramatic and fragrant. Walt noticed Robyn and Becky had also straightened up his place before their arrival and prepared the fireplace, so all he had to do was light a match.

Bending low with a wick touching the tip of a newspaper under a few logs, Walt heard Elyse ask, "Who are the beautiful flowers from?" He tossed the remnants of the match into the flames, already licking and devouring the fat wood starter.

"Let's find out," he said, plucking the tiny card from the arrangement. He handed it off to Elyse, knowing she'd be surprised.

"Can you please take it out of the envelope? It's too hard with only one hand."

Walt nodded and sat next to her, pulling the card out from the tiny envelope, and offering it to her.

Her eyes scanned the words as her chest rose and fell in deep breaths.

"Are you all right?" he asked.

Elyse nodded and palmed the card to her chest. "The flowers are from my family." She handed him the card so he could read the words.

Sending our love as you recover.
We miss you,
Dad, Mom, Ava, Rick, and Jagger

"How lucky are we to have such awesome families?" Walt admitted, handing the card back. Elyse turned quiet as she reread the words. Walt kept his mouth shut, knowing she was emotionally drained from the long, painful day.

"It's remarkable how you and your family are always there for each other time and time again. I can't say that about myself. I haven't seen my family in years." Elyse hung her head in shame.

"Hey," Walt turned his body so he faced her and tilted her chin with his fingers to look her directly in the eye. "You have the power to change that, you know. When you're feeling better and out of this sling, let's take a trip and see your family together."

"You'd go with me?" She seemed astonished by the idea.

"Of course I'll go with you; we're a team. You and I... we're family."

Her eyes filled with tears, and he used the pad of his thumb to wipe a wet trail trickling down her cheek.

"I love you, Elyse. And I want to meet your family because..." He paused, knowing he was about to rock her world. "Because I want to ask your father for his blessing."

Her eyes grew wide as she gripped his hand.

"Don't move to Langston Falls because you're working with my sister and her brand. Don't come here to work as a location manager for your studio for an extended period of time."

Walt took a deep breath and shifted to one knee directly in front of her, the following few words out of his mouth ones he'd been mulling over since the day he met her. He loved her—it was as simple as that. Even though he didn't have a ring, he didn't want to hesitate, and he wasn't about to wait for a special occasion, especially after the accident.

"Move to Langston Falls to be with *me*, Elyse. Marry me and make me the happiest guy on the planet." He held his breath, anxious for her reply. When her lips unfurled into a dreamy smile, his heart raced.

"Are you asking me, or are you telling me?"

Her blue flame eyes flickered with amusement, and he knew right then her answer was undoubtedly, yes.

Chapter Thirty-Three

ELYSE

Three Months Later

Elyse eyed the beautiful reflection in the large oval mirror. The long gauzy material of the wedding veil floated in the air like an angel's wing, the lacy edges landing softly on the floor. Robyn adjusted the crystal-embellished headband over her hair and turned to look at Elyse, Becky, and Samantha, exhaling a huge breath.

"Well? What do y'all think?"

The three women started talking all at once.

"You're gorgeous," Elyse said.

"Absolutely stunning," Samantha added.

"My mama's veil is the icing on the cake!" Becky gushed.

Elyse picked up the wedding bouquet of wildflowers on a nearby chair and handed it to Robyn. "Are you ready?"

"I was born ready." Her face flushed with love on her feminine features.

Elyse, Becky, and Samantha wore jewel-toned bridesmaid's dresses. The sapphire blue, citrine yellow, and emerald green matched the bridal bouquet's rich colors and circle of flowers in each of their hair. Becky held the train of Robyn's dress as they escorted the bride to Roy's heavily decorated pick-up truck parked in front of the Bennett farmhouse, her white cowboy boots peeking out from under her dress with each step.

Roy stood chivalrously stoic with his signature hat off and pressed against his chest, his immediate smile at the sight of the bride indicating he was ready to take his future daughter-in-law to the meadow where the nuptials were about to begin. Robyn's father was already there waiting for her, prepared to walk her down the makeshift aisle. When Robyn and Ted planned their small wedding ceremony, Teddy was adamant he wanted to be close to his mother, the giant oak tree anchoring them as a family.

Walt met Elyse out front, his wide eyes raking her figure up and down. "Damn, girl. You look incredible. That shade of blue really makes your eyes pop." He reached for her free hand and squeezed. "And how in the world did Robyn talk you into wearing cowboy boots?"

Elyse turned from side to side, mocking the boots on her feet. "I'm a bridesmaid. I have to do whatever the bride says." She giggled. "Besides, I wanted to match my handsome cowboy on this special day." His dark jeans accentuated his athletic body, and his pale blue shirt and gray vest went well with her dress color. A black cowboy hat was perched on his head, the entire country-themed wedding falling into place.

His lazy grin was immediate. "Come on."

The bridal party drove the short distance to the meadow in separate cars, Walt helping Elyse out of his truck. Charlotte Ross, the owner of Langston Petals, where Robyn worked part-time while she studied for the Georgia bar exam, was the official coordinator of the ceremony. The hem of her short powder blue dress above her tan cowboy boots fluttered in the breeze as she instructed everyone where to line up.

The entire setup was like something from a movie set. Hank was home from Nashville, the strumming sounds from his guitar magical from under the canopy of bright green oak leaves. The blooming meadow was naturally decorated with seasonal wildflowers blowing in the spring breeze. Several dressed-up guests were seated on white folding chairs, many of them wearing hats and boots.

Elyse immediately spotted Glen Kirby and his mother among the crowd. Both families had called a truce, Walt working with Glen since he left rehab on potential business ventures so he could legally buy his farm back. He'd lost a ton of weight and looked nothing like the angry, drug-addicted man who almost took his own life. Glen turned out to be a reasonably handsome, humbled man, ready to work hard to win back respect from his hometown and the entire Bennett family. Teddy was the one who suggested they invite Glen, the noble act proving to everyone how strong and forgiving Ted really was after everything he'd been through. There was still a long road ahead for all of them, but the end goal was worth it with mended fences and genuine mercy.

"He made it," Elyse whispered toward Walt's ear.

"Good. This is good."

Walt and Elyse had moved out of the Kirby house and into Robyn's grandmother's home, the previous renters deciding not to renew their lease. The old farmhouse was close to the pretty cottage where Robyn and Teddy lived, the couple hosting Walt and Elyse's engagement party the month before on the property near the pond with the magnificent view of the North Georgia mountains in the background.

Jerry Berg had signed off on the location of Langston Falls for his new series, the home Elyse and Walt were now living in one of the properties the production company would use to bring fiction magically to life. The Kirby house and land were also determined usable for the production, Elyse and Walt helping Glen negotiate a shooting fee for permission to use his space. Elyse knew full well they could get him two to three grand a day while shooting; the money earned used to start buying back his homestead free and clear from Walt. Crews would be arriving in the next week, her job as a location manager ramping up. Thank God this was all happening after Robyn and Ted's wedding.

Charlotte motioned for them to walk through the gate in the rusted fence line as Hank started strumming and singing *Somewhere Over the Rainbow*. The familiar arrangement by Hawaiian musician Israel Kamakawiwo'ole was fitting among the rainbow of colors in the wedding party and in nature.

"It's show time," she grinned.

Elyse hooked her arm through Walt's, his sexy smile driving her wild. He pressed his lips to hers in a wet kiss before the two strolled toward Teddy, Hank, and the local preacher. The song echoed romantically through the meadow and over the family plot of headstones covered in lichen and moss. Walt's mother's white marble marker was decorated with a lush wreath of happy daisies and yellow roses. Hank winked at them as they disengaged and went to their separate spots under the tree branches opposite each other.

Tendrils of Elyse's hair blew back from her face in the

breeze, her eyes misting witnessing James and Samantha walk together, Becky and her father, Roy, and then Robyn on the arm of her dapper father. As the bride came toward them, the guests stood, and Hank changed his tune to the haunting melody of Elvis' *Can't Help Falling in Love*.

Elyse watched Ted's reaction seeing his beautiful bride for the first time, his lips trembling as he tried to keep it together. Tears streamed down his face and into his well-groomed beard, and when Robyn's father handed her off after a gentle kiss on her cheek, she gently pressed a linen handkerchief to Ted's face with grace and love.

A lump formed in Elyse's throat watching the ceremony unfold, the handwritten vows the couple read poignant and tender. Her eyes found Walt's, his loving gaze filling her with excitement for their own wedding day in the future. Running her thumb against her engagement ring from underneath her wildflower bouquet, she thought about Walt and how it felt like she'd known him her entire life, not for only six months.

Thinking back on how they first met had her all worked up. She was the kind of person who remembered things vividly, using all her senses. She remembered the first night she met him, right before Christmas—the feel of his bicep when she steadied herself after a stumble on the uneven path at the farm. His hard body surrounding her during their first hug goodnight, and the way his warm breath floated across the exposed skin of her blushing cheek. How he smelled like Christmas, the pine trees he worked with infiltrating his clothes with holiday cheer. And how could she ever forget when Walt grabbed her by the hand on New Year's Eve and pulled her into the ladies' room, where he pinned her against the door and ravished her chest before giving her a midnight orgasm?

Before Walt, she'd been careful to keep her heart locked up inside, intent on concentrating on her career. But today, all her memories pushed at the seams, her heart threatening to burst with joy. The sound of the music, the smell of the flowers and the meadow grasses, the taste of his kiss before they walked down the aisle, all with the presence of friends and a loving family there to witness it all. Walt shined a light into her world, and she welcomed the joy he gave her through the love they manifested and believed in—a love she accepted whole-heartedly.

Robyn and Teddy kissed, the preacher announcing them husband and wife. The crowd whooped with excitement, the wedding party following the couple back down the aisle toward the trucks. The lift gates were down, displaying light refreshments, including Bennett Farms wine for the guests to enjoy while the photographer took pictures in the meadow before the reception at the red barn.

They reached the edge of the meadow where it bordered the road. Walt stopped walking and hugged Elyse in his arms. She filled her lungs with a verdant scent she would remember always. She was exhilarated, ruminating in the powerful feeling of being alive and in love.

"Congratulations," she said to Ted and Robyn, kissing them both on the cheek.

"You're next," Ted remarked, playfully punching Walt in the arm. "Unless Jimmy and Samantha beat you to it."

Walt slipped his arm across Elyse's shoulders, his hard body giving off warmth and protection. "I can't wait."

Charlotte offered the couples a short glass of Chardonnay off a tray. "Make it quick. Y'all have pictures under the oak tree before we head to the reception at Bennett Farms."

"Cheers," James proclaimed, holding his glass in the air

with Samantha by his side. Roy and Becky joined them, and the group gathered in a circle. "To my big brother, Teddy, and my new sister, Robyn—the luckiest couple in town."

The wedding party whole-heartedly agreed, the group raising their glasses into the air, the orbs of sunlight dazzling all around them. As Elyse took a sip of wine made from grapes grown on the hillside right down the road at Bennett Farms, she savored the cool sweetness. Gazing at Walt over the rim of her glass, she realized all the wishes she'd put out into the universe had manifested right in front of her.

The promise of the future blazed before them like the golden sun over the land—and they were happy.

Next in The Bennetts of Langston Falls Series

The Bennetts of Langston Falls Series

vinci-books.com/breathlesslove

**She's Nashville's finest. He's a nobody with a dream.
One journey might rewrite their fate.**

His band broke up. Her life is on tour. One road trip, one unforgettable night, and a love that could change everything. But when the music stops, will they still have a song to sing? *Breathless Love* is a steamy country romance where passion and ambition collide.

Turn the page for a free preview…

Breathless Love: Chapter One

HANK BENNETT

Hank Bennett was in an inebriated funk.

Slurping the foamy top of yet another cold beer, he staggered away from the concession stand before the liquid overflowed down the sides of his opaque plastic cup. The outdoor concert was in full swing as he perused the sparse crowd milling about the refreshment area, most fans in their seats watching the live show. A wave of applause surged through the air as one song segued into another. This familiar tune was one of Hank's favorites, the country music upbeat and catchy.

Closing his eyes, he hummed along for a few stanzas before his shoulders sagged, and a wave of disappointment washed over him again. Too bad none of his songs would ever receive the kind of accolades and ovation Travis Miller's demanded. The two-time CMA award winner was one of Hank's idols who inspired him to pursue his own dreams of recording and performing country music. Since he was a young boy, he focused on bending his guitar strings and creating original songs for anyone who would listen.

But no one was listening to his songs—not anymore. He was reduced to nothing more than a fan now, his dreams dashed and destroyed before they even had a chance to get off the ground.

The long-time group he fronted, known as The Bonafide Band, broke up last spring, his buddies he'd played with since high school going their separate ways after an extended trip to Nashville. They'd spent a few weeks in the music city recording some of Hank's original songs at a legit sound studio. Hank spent an exorbitant amount of money just to hear his music professionally recorded, his goal of having his own album finally within reach, or so he thought. Producing music was tedious, time-consuming, and expensive, but he loved every second of the experience. His band, not so much. Sure, they thought it was cool to hear themselves on the tracks, and they even got up on a few Nashville honky-tonk stages at open-mic nights and played for the live crowds while they were in town for their extended stay.

But when it was all said and done, his bass player decided he wanted to settle down and get married to his long-time girlfriend. His lead guitarist headed back to college to finish his degree. And his drummer opted to get out of the south altogether and backpack across Europe. Hank was a lone musician for the first time in his life, and the thought of trying to put together a new band was daunting.

"Hey, cowboy. You wanna buy a t-shirt?"

Hank jerked his head in the direction of the southern female voice, his stumbled movements causing the beer in his cup to slosh onto the front of his black tee.

"Ahh, fuck," he lamented, raising his arms out from his sides.

"Sorry about that. I didn't mean to startle you," the

woman giggled. She came from around the counter of a souvenir shack. The pop-up business was conveniently located near the venue's exit, where concertgoers could grab an official keepsake on their way out to the parking lot after the show. Travis Miller's handsome face was everywhere, on shirts and posters, koozies and key chains, the crooner looking like a model out of a *GQ Magazine* with his chiseled face and signature smile.

Hank flicked his free hand before palming the front of his soaked shirt. "I'm the one who's sorry, ma'am," he slurred.

"Sorry about what?" Her hands were planted on her hips as she grinned back at him.

He noticed her toned and tanned bare legs, her daisy dukes frayed around the edges of her ample bootie. She wore flip-flops, and her toenails were painted a bright aqua-blue. As his eyes roamed upward over the rest of her body, his nostrils flared when his tipsy gaze landed on her face. Damn, she was pretty. Dark brown eyes stared, her long lashes flirty and blinking with humor. She had her brunette hair fashioned into two long braids trailing over her shoulders to the middle of her buxom chest, her crop top revealing more tanned skin around her middle.

"What are you sorry for?" she repeated.

"I beg your pardon?" He swayed uneasily, shifting in his cowboy boots on the hard ground. What had they been talking about?

"You said, 'Sorry about that.' Tell me what you're sorry for."

Hank furrowed his brow and took a quick gulp of what was left of his beer, the country music in the air thrumming through his being. "I have no fucking idea," he mumbled, swiping his wet lips with the back of his free hand. And then it suddenly dawned on him.

"Ah-ha!" he exclaimed, raising his index finger into the air. He gallantly took off his cowboy hat and pressed it against his chest. "I remember now. I'm sorry for using profanity in your presence. My daddy always taught me not to curse in front of a lady."

Awkwardly, he dipped his body in an attempt at a chivalrous bow. But his boots slid right out from under him on the hard-packed dirt, and he dropped his hat, falling in slow motion to his denim-covered knees. The plastic cup tumbled from his fingers and spilled.

"Oh, no!" The woman squealed. She raised her hands to cover her mouth as if squelching another giggle as he made a complete fool of himself in front of her.

Sitting back on his haunches, Hank disappointedly watched the last of his beverage seep into the parched ground. Scratching the stubble on his chin, he shrugged. "No use crying over spilled beer." He ran his hands through his sweaty curls before picking up his cowboy hat and settling it back on his head. The humidity in the middle of summer was oppressive in the mountain town, this week in particular one of the hottest on record. Looking up at the pretty woman, sweat trickled down the sides of his face, and his eyelids felt heavy from overindulging.

"You look a little lonely," she commented.

"Nah." He waved her off. "In limbo, maybe. Butt-faced, definitely. Lonely? Never." Hank harrumphed, carefully easing his tired body up off the ground. "You wanna join me for a fresh one?"

Her smile was immediate, the color of her eyes reminding him of melted chocolate. "I'm working right now. But I've got a cooler full of water bottles. Why don't you drink one of those and keep me company while you... cool off a little?"

Sweat trickled down his cheeks, the thought of a cold sip of water tempting. Perhaps she was right? He needed a break from the booze and a moment to cool off. And besides, he was downright parched.

"Thanks. I think I will take you up on that water." He slapped the dirt off his jeans.

"Good." She smiled.

Hank watched her enter the souvenir hut and disappear behind the counter for a second. When she reappeared, she offered him an icy bottle of water over the ledge. "Here you go."

"Thanks." He took the bottle, twisted the top off, and guzzled half the contents before coming up for air. The woman in front of him stared, her eyebrows hitched with curiosity. "What?" he panted, sliding the chilled plastic across his sweaty brow. God, it felt so damn good.

"You're cute, and I'm Ella Mae." She thrust her hand over the counter to shake his.

Hank licked his lips and carefully set the water bottle next to a stack of neatly folded t-shirts for sale. He did a double-take imagining Travis Miller frowning in the image. Goodness, was he that drunk? Reaching for her hand, he awkwardly leaned forward and pressed his cool lips against her skin, his eyes never leaving hers.

"My name is Hank Bennett. And I'm pleased to meet you, Ella Mae."

Her pink mouth lifted into another one of her dazzling smiles. "Did your daddy teach you that trick, too?"

"Nope. That's all me, Ella Mae. It's a Hank Bennett Special." He gave her one of his signature smirks, hoping she was impressed.

"Easy, fella. I think you need to finish your water." She broke their connection and handed off the half-drunk bottle.

Hank winked and took a sip. "So where'd you get the name Ella Mae from? It's... pretty." He watched her demurely tilt her head as if pleased.

"My daddy was a musician and a huge fan of Ella Fitzgerald, and my grandmother's name was Mae. Put the two together, and you get—"

"Ella Mae," Hank spoke with exuberance. "I love it."

"So... you like Travis Miller's music?" She rested her forearms on the counter and leaned forward as the wail of a steel guitar floated through the air.

Hank noticed the front of her crop top gape, where he caught a glimpse of her lacy bra underneath. A rush of heat surged across his cheeks, and he took a hefty gulp of cold water to cool his surging libido. Damn, she was easy on his eyes.

"I do. Travis is the reason I got into music."

"Oh, so you're a musician, too?" She perked up with interest.

"I thought I was." Hank crushed the empty plastic bottle in his hand, the dejected tone of his voice noticeable.

They were interrupted by a pair of concertgoers who eagerly pointed out t-shirts they wanted to buy, Ella Mae going into sales mode. "Hold that thought." She winked.

Hank watched as she convinced the pair to buy more than just tees. By the end of their five-minute shopping spree, they'd bought matching koozies, baseball hats, and a keychain. As Ella Mae rang them up, he strolled around the side of the stand to an area overlooking the amphitheater audience with a fantastic view of the stage. Travis Miller was smack dab in the middle, lit up in the giant orb of a spotlight, his vocals smooth in a rare ballad among another weeping swell of a steel guitar. Sighing, Hank shoved his hands into his jeans pockets and listened.

From the first moment he held a guitar at the tender age of eight, he knew he wanted to play music for a living. For the most part, his large family encouraged him. His three older brothers and baby sister on the family farm showered him with positive reactions to the silly tunes he'd written and played for anyone who would listen over the years. Those immature songs turned into better songs the older he got, and when he put together his band, he was confident he had what it took to make it in the world of country music. Yeah, like every other dumbass with stars in their eyes.

His hometown of Langston Falls, Georgia, welcomed him and his bandmates with open arms into every bar, restaurant, charity event, and festival that came through town, proud to support one of their own. His family's Christmas tree farm and winery also held annual events, and he'd become the main attraction over the last couple of years thanks to his event-planning sister, Becky. But performing for the local fans he grew up with was one thing —going on the road and playing for strangers was quite another altogether.

Sure, he and his band had fun on the road playing all the popular dive bars in and around his home state of Georgia. But the money could have been better, and the cheap hotels and long hours on the road quickly began to wear on everyone. Folks outside of Langston Falls didn't want to hear his original music. They wanted to listen to covers, the popular music, so they could dance. Hank thought if they could get some original music recorded, they might be able to find a good agent who could find them better gigs. But the competition was fierce, and Hank and his buddies were novices compared to some of the more seasoned bands out on the road. During their brief stint in Nashville, Hank quickly found out his friends weren't as committed as he was, and now he was faced with a decision: should he continue to pursue his dream without them? Or should he give up and work full-time on the family farm?

"Hey, Travis is winding down, and the show will be over soon." Ella Mae came up beside him, twirling one of her braids in her hand. "Are you here with people? With a group of friends, or maybe... a date?"

Hank looked at her and noticed a few freckles smattered across the bridge of her nose. Her large doe eyes did funny things to his insides. "Uh... no. I'm here by myself tonight."

"Great!" She smiled. "I mean..." She laughed and shrugged, not finishing her sentence. The deafening crowd roared as Travis finished his last song, the audience chanting, "one more song" over and over.

"Listen, Hank. I'm gonna be slammed with customers after Travis performs his encore. But when I'm finished, you want to join me for that beer?"

Hank nodded, the thought of spending more time with the cute t-shirt-selling country girl tempting. "Sure. I know of a few bars in Langston Falls."

"We don't have to go anywhere. We can go backstage to the Green Room. They always have a ton of food and drinks for everyone after the performance while the tech crew breaks down the equipment." She made it sound so easy, as if she casually hung out with the famous Travis Miller entourage daily.

"Wow. That's so cool they let you do that."

"Why? Because I'm a lowly t-shirt girl?" There was a definitive challenge in her tone underneath her smile.

Hank shook his head with embarrassment. "No, I didn't mean it that way—"

"I know," she interrupted. "I was just teasing you. I'm not usually the one selling t-shirts. I'm helping out Martina and her husband tonight. They're usually the ones promoting Travis's merchandise, but they had a family wedding in Biloxi. Believe it or not, I'm a musician, too."

Hank's mouth gaped. "You are?" Things were getting interesting. "Do you write? Do you play or sing?"

"Yes, yes, and... yes," she laughed. The happy sound was music to his ears.

"That's amazing. I'd love to hear some of your stuff sometime. Hey, maybe we could collaborate on something, too." He didn't mean to come across so desperate, the exorbitant amount of beers he'd consumed definitely messing with his filters. He cleared his throat to get a grip.

"But you're probably leaving tonight, driving to the next venue for another show, huh?"

"Not necessarily," she said.

"What do you mean?"

Ella Mae turned to see a few customers perusing the shack. "I gotta go tend to business." She tucked a stray hair over her ear and looked right at him, her provocative chocolate gaze causing his toes to curl in his boots. "But after that, I want to introduce you to my brother, Travis."

Before her words registered in his brain, she skipped away as if she'd ding-dong-ditched him. "Wait... *what*?"

"You heard me," she yelled over her shoulder. More patrons filed out of the amphitheater, a line starting to form in front of the shack.

Hank didn't know what to do at that moment. His earlier beer buzz vanished in a flash as a new sensation took over his body. The air was heavy with music and the smell of summer, thick with dreams and possibility. It was sensory overload between the crowd's roaring applause and the pretty smile on Ella Mae's face. Country music superstar Travis Miller was *her brother*?

His mother's voice echoed in his mind, her words often reminding him of the life he'd only dreamt about:

Opportunity is not a lengthy visitor.

Maybe the universe was throwing him a bone, the weird coincidence giving him the nudge he desperately needed. Perhaps his desire to be a musician wasn't over after all? Meeting Travis was a thrilling thought, the country music artist his idol.

But meeting Ella Mae was special, too. Meeting the beautiful female musician was an unexpected twist of fate.

Breathless Love: Chapter Two

ELLA MAE

Ella Mae was excited for the first time in over two months since they boarded the tour bus in Nashville and headed out on the road for the three-month tour. She loved the gypsy lifestyle, going to sleep every night to the hum of the bus wheels on asphalt and waking up in a new town the following day.

But after a few weeks, traveling took a toll on her and her brother. She missed her giant bed back home on her quiet farm in Franklin, Tennessee. She missed her scrappy dog, Lucky, and her brood of chickens. Her travel routine had turned monotonous, lately setting up shop at each venue and dealing with excited, often drunk fans every night while Martina and her husband were in Biloxi. Her favorite time of day was sound check when she filled in for her brother, Travis, and strummed his guitars and sang in his microphone until the sound was dialed in. She also looked forward to hanging out with him on their tour bus, collaborating on new music but only if he was in the mood.

Travis.

Her big brother was her only family and legal guardian after their parents died in a car crash when she was seventeen. He took care of her, working odd jobs until she graduated high school, the two of them often writing music together to cope with their grief.

Within weeks of receiving her diploma, she challenged Travis to take a chance. They drove all the way to California, where he auditioned and landed a spot competing on a popular television singing show. Even though he was eliminated in the playoffs that season, Nashville came calling. They ended up moving full-time to the music city where Travis signed his first record deal, releasing his debut EP to rave reviews. It didn't take long for his career to skyrocket, Ella Mae right beside him and cheering him on every step of the way.

The brother and sister became a writing duo, collaborating on Travis's signature music. One of Ella's most significant achievements was writing the lyrics to his first hit song, which won him a CMA award. Ella could sing and play guitar too, but she preferred to stay out of the spotlight, being there for her brother whenever he needed her. She would never forget his first extensive tour with an entire entourage playing to sold-out venues and festivals, glad she could still be a part of the music world through their joint creations without facing the fans. She'd much rather stay behind the scenes writing and crafting hit songs, leaving her brother to navigate the fame and notoriety.

Now, Ella Mae was used to the spectacle of Travis's stardom, their roles reversed as she ensured *he* was taken care of while they were on the road. The entertainment business was shady at times, some of the folks they met or worked with luring her brother into unsavory after hours. The excessive drinking, drugs, and strippers had taken a toll on their bond over the years, and at one point, she almost left him and the music biz altogether.

But Travis being Travis, convinced her to stay because he needed someone to help keep him accountable and stay on the right track. It also helped that she received legit songwriting credits on his albums, the royalties alone helping her purchase her little piece of land and refurbish her house in Tennessee free and clear. So far, so good this tour go-around, the three months of shows in the Southeast going well without any mishaps.

Enter Hank Bennett. He was a game-changer in Ella Mae's eyes. The lanky, handsome musician was just what the doctor ordered. She needed a friend, and a friend who also happened to be a musician was a bonus. Sure, she hung out with Travis's bandmates, their wives or girlfriends, and crew all day long. But these talented players and workers were part of Travis' world, not hers. Meeting a new friend on tour to call her own was a nice change.

Boxing up the last of the shirts, she secured the mobile credit card reader and the cash she'd collected during the show in her bag looped over her head and flicked off the lights. One of the crew would be by soon to haul the boxes to the bus and store them underneath in the cargo hold until the next show.

"Hey," she said to Hank. He was in a daze watching the tech team break down the stage from afar. When he turned to greet her, she inhaled sharply, thrilled he'd waited for her. Damn, he was good-looking. "You ready?"

"Ready to meet Travis Miller? You better believe it."

Ella's heart sank. Maybe Hank was like all the others she'd tried to befriend while on tour, solely focused on meeting her famous brother. She couldn't blame him. Travis was a celebrity, and when most folks found out she was his sister, they turned star-struck and practically begged for an introduction. Silent, she walked ahead of Hank down a long aisle through the empty amphitheater toward the stage, the sound of his boots closely behind.

"Hold on, Ella Mae."

She ignored his plea to slow down and kept a fast pace, suddenly very tired from the long day. A cool shower, soft pajamas, and reading her latest romance book in her hotel room sounded like a nice consolation prize.

"I said, hold on." Hank gripped her by the arm and pulled her to a stop, his gaze tracing her features. "Was it something I said?"

Ella exhaled an exasperated puff of air through her nose. "I know you're more interested in meeting my brother than having a beer with me. I get it, and it's okay."

Hank rubbed his chin and furrowed his brow. "Of course, I'd love to meet your brother. I mean, any musician in his right mind would. But my first priority is hanging out with you. If Travis is too tired or too busy, it's no big deal. I can meet him another time. I want to hang out with *you*."

Ella's demeanor softened. "You sure about that? You sure you want to hang out with a simple t-shirt gal?" She batted her lashes at him with playfulness.

Hank's smile rivaled the full moon hanging above their heads as he looped his strong arm through hers. "Positive."

Crossing the expansive stage littered with cables among the roadies hard at work disassembling the sound equipment and gear, Ella grabbed Hank by the hand and pulled him through a narrow hallway toward the Green Room. The backstage hubbub was in full throttle, the crowd of lively people sipping cocktails and nibbling on snacks hard not to notice. Ella pulled two cold beers out of a galvanized tub full of ice and handed one to Hank.

"Thanks," he grinned.

The two twisted off the caps and clinked their bottles together before taking a swig, the icy beer hitting the spot. Ella noticed her friend and comrade, Willie Branson, and caught his attention. He was the road manager for Travis's tour.

"Willie!" She waved.

The man was a beast, his long flowing beard and matching hair beneath his tattered cowboy hat reminding her of country music sensation Chris Stapleton. Willie was a big 'ole teddy bear, his calm and easy-going nature a bonus on the road when it came to uptight venue personnel and crusty agents. Willie had a way with Travis, too. Ella touted him, the "Travis-Whisperer," because sometimes, when her brother got out of control, Willie was the only one who could bring him down a notch.

"Hey, darlin'! How'd it go tonight?" He gave her one of his signature bear hugs.

"Great. Willie, I'd like to introduce you to my new friend, Hank Bennett."

Hank's eyes went wide, looking up at Willie who towered over him. He shoved his hand out for a shake. "It's nice to meet you, Willie." The man's hand dwarfed Hank's by three sizes.

"Nice to meet you too, Hank. Where ya from?"

"Down the road in Langston Falls. My family owns a Christmas tree farm and winery on the outskirts of town called Bennett Farms."

This was the first time Ella had heard anything about Hank's family, and she was intrigued.

"You know, last time we played here, I took my wife on a tour of the Bennett Farms winery. Y'all sell a red wine called Big Red, right?"

Hank grinned with obvious pride. "We sure do. It's a staple in these parts. Did you like it?"

"Like it? I loved it! I even ordered a case and had it sent back home to Nashville."

Ella eyed Willie with chagrin. "I didn't know you were a connoisseur of wine."

Willie laughed in his throat, the sound heartfelt and guttural. He leaned in and whispered huskily, "Let's keep this information between the three of us, okay?"

"That's awesome." Hank was all at ease, donning a handsome smile during their exchange. Ella liked the way it made her feel.

"Hey, Willie, where's Travis?"

Willie tipped his head toward the hallway. "He's still in his dressing room, probably showering off. This damn humidity is gonna be the death of me. I don't know how Travis does it at these outdoor events. He looked like a drowned rat when he came offstage."

"I'll bet. I want to introduce him to Hank."

Hank immediately waved her off as if embarrassed. "No, that's okay. Let's give the man a break and finish our beers."

"It's fine, Hank. See ya later, Willie."

"See ya, darlin'."

She grabbed Hank's hand again and pulled him through the hallway.

"Seriously, Ella Mae, I don't want to disturb him while he's bathing."

Ella giggled. "You want to meet him or not?"

"I do, but—"

Ella stopped at the end of the hall in front of a closed dressing room door and banged her knuckles on the wood.

"Travis? You decent?" She turned the knob and opened the door wide, her eyes landing on her brother.

He sat naked in a chair in front of a large makeup mirror with his back toward them. His eyes met hers in the reflection, and he wickedly grinned as an unfamiliar female face popped up from between his knees. She looked like a deer caught in the headlights.

Ella growled and marched toward the woman in a rage. "*Get out!*" she screamed.

"I'm going, I'm going," she hollered. Her southern accent was thick, and her lipstick was smeared across her mouth. She shoved her exposed tit back into her bra and pulled her lacey shirt into place.

Hank stood rigid against the doorframe, giving the female fan enough room to exit in an aggravated huff.

"See ya around, sweetheart!" Travis waved humorously. He shoved a damp towel over his exposed family jewels and leaned back in his seat without a care in the world.

"Seriously, Travis. How'd she end up in here? Where's security? Where the hell is Mario?"

"Oh, come on Ella-Bo-Bella. A little oral sex never hurt anyone. It relaxes me." His grin was wide, and his pearly whites glinted in the light from the bulbs surrounding the long mirror above a built-in ledge. "I see you made a friend, too." His tone held curiosity as his tired brown eyes ran the length of Hank Bennett's reflection in the doorway.

"As a matter of fact, I did. Travis, this is Hank. Hank, this is my shameful brother, Travis Miller. Please excuse his, uh, lack of clothing and good manners." She wrinkled her nose.

Hank didn't seem to mind Travis's naked disposition and slowly entered the room with wide-eyed wonderment.

"It's a real pleasure to meet you, sir." He came up to his chair, stuck his hand out, and waited.

Travis's eyebrows arose, and he looked from Ella to Hank and back again. "Is this guy for real?"

Ella planted one hand on her hip and took a quick sip of beer. "Be cool, Travis," she admonished.

Travis waited for a beat before he stood from his chair, the towel falling from his crotch and exposing his thick cock for all to see.

Ella squealed and shielded her eyes as her brother smiled salaciously and pumped Hank's hand with vigor.

"It's nice to meet you, Romeo."

Grab your copy…
vinci-books.com/breathlesslove

Playlist

The Bennetts of Langston Falls

23 - Sam Hunt
Home Sweet - Russell Dickerson
Freedom Was a Highway - Jimmie Allen
Chasing After You - Ryan Hurd & Maren Morris
Till You Can't - Cody Johnson
Can't Help Falling in Love - Elvis
Slow Down Summer - Thomas Rhett
American Honey - Lady A
Half of my Hometown – Kelsea Ballerini
We Were Us - Keith Urban & Miranda Lambert
Back to Life - Rascal Flats
Leave Before You Love Me - Jonas Brothers
Just a Kiss - Lady A
Never Till Now - Ashley Cooke & Brett Young
The Furthest Thing - Maren Morris
Forever For a Little While - Russell Dickerson
I Believe - Jonas Brothers

Want it Again - Thomas Rhett
Your Body is a Wonderland - John Mayer
I'll Never Love Again - Lady GaGa
Doin This - Luke Combs
What My World Spins Around - Jordan Davis
Somebody - Justin Bieber
XO – John Mayer

About the Author

"The Singing Author," KG Fletcher, lives in her very own frat house in Atlanta, GA, with her husband Ladd and three sons. As a singer/songwriter, she became a recipient of the "Airplay International Award" for "Best New Artist," showcasing original songs at The Bluebird Café in Nashville, TN. She earned her BFA in theater at Valdosta State University and has traveled the world professionally as a singer/actress. She is a two-time Georgia Maggie Award Nominee and currently gets to play rock star as a backup singer in the "Remember When Rock Was Young – the Elton John Experience."

KG is a hopeless romantic. When she's not on the road singing, she's probably at home daydreaming about her swoony book boyfriends or arranging a yummy charcuterie board while sipping red wine and listening to Frank Sinatra. She's also a conference speaker and loves to interact with readers on social media and share about her writing and singing journey.

Acknowledgments

Huge thanks to my fantastic husband and boys, who are my biggest supporters and put up with this Mama constantly working and stressing about deadlines. To all the fantastic readers I met at the Shameless Book Conference in Orlando – you have my heart! Best conference EV-AH! To my Insta-author friends for sharing the love and letting me know I'm not alone in this journey as an indie author. To the best beta readers on the planet, Ladd, Blair, and Craig, thank you for pointing out my strengths and weaknesses and listening to me talk nonstop about the Bennett Family and how much I love them. To my Atlanta bestie, Anne, for introducing me to Linville Falls (the inspiration for Langston Falls) and accompanying me on that EPIC book research trip where we met ninety-one-year-old Jack Wiseman, the patriarch of the Linville Falls Winery. I'm ready to go again!

Special thanks to Vicky Burkholder, my long-time editor and friend, for making this story shine. And to Gigi Blume, you are and always will be my author bestie. Mmwah!

For my incredible team of ARC readers and all the bloggers who came on board with this series - THANK YOU for loving romance books as much as I do. Your gorgeous posts and teasers make my heart sing!

For my critique partner, Carrie, who always has my back, and to all of my readers, thank you for your support. I love your enthusiasm for this series, as well as your kind comments on social media and your private messages urging me to write faster. HA! I'm so glad we can all escape into the wonderful world of books! The consistent reviews you have posted on Goodreads, BookBub, and Amazon are virtual hugs I will cherish forever.

I hope you will continue the Bennett Family's journey in Book Three of the series, *Breathless Love*. Get ready for charming Hank and his country music story!

xoxo
Kelly